Sweet Hart Inn at Harbor Falls

MADDIE JAMES

SAND DUNE BOOKS

All of My Heart

All of My Heart

Maddie James
A Sweet Hart Inn Romance
Book 1

About Sweet Hart Inn

Welcome to Sweet Hart Inn... Where the kitchen is always warm and love is always on the menu.

Nestled on the peaceful edge of Falls Lake in the heart of the Blue Ridge Mountains, Sweet Hart Inn is more than a cozy bed and breakfast—it's a place where hearts heal, friendships form, and romance is served with a side of sass.

At the center of it all is Suzie Hart, a chef-turned-innkeeper whose recipes have a way of bringing people together (and finding their way into her books) —and sometimes, sparking unexpected love. Along with her (soon-to-be, maybe?) husband Brad, Suzie welcomes a delightful cast of characters through the inn's front doors, such as runaway brides, brooding bachelors, holiday guests, disgruntled daters, and more.

Whether you're looking for a heartwarming holiday escape, a second-chance romance, or a cozy story filled with culinary charm, the Sweet Hart Inn series delivers all the feel-good vibes you crave.

Bon Appetit! And enjoy.

All of My Heart

When small-town chef Suzie Hart inherits her aunt's Victorian home in Harbor Falls, North Carolina, she finally gets the chance to pursue her dream—running Sweet Hart Inn and writing a cookbook full of cherished recipes. After a humiliating betrayal by her fiancé and her sister, she is focused on healing—not romance.

Until Brad Matthews roars back into her life on a Harley and books a room at her inn under a fake name.

Once her head chef and secret fling in Asheville, Brad has his own plans—ones that involve renovating the old Falls Lake Lodge and winning Suzie back. But when his business ideas threaten the charm of their quaint mountain town, and stir up the gossip mill, Suzie must decide if risking her heart again is worth the price.

All of My Heart is a heartwarming, food-infused, second chance romance filled with small town charm, mouthwatering moments, and a dash of southern sass. Perfect for readers who love:

- A strong, independent heroine starting over,
- A sexy chef with a plan—and a past,
- Cozy bed and breakfasts in charming mountain towns,

- Found family, food, forgiveness... and flirty banter over fondue.

All of My Heart is the perfect escape, where every chapter serves up a sweet surprise.

From the Kitchen of Suzie Hart, Sweet Hart Inn

Blog Post, May 14: *The view is all good from here.*

Summer is almost here! The front lawn is shaping up beautifully after our unusually cold winter. I've been busy planting everything from perennials to petunias. I love to see the color popping out everywhere! So much to do to keep things in shape and it's not only landscaping and gardening. Let's see....

We've finished the kitchen (more on that soon!) and cooking classes are back. Catering is picking up, too. We're doing BBQ tomorrow at the American Legion Hall in Harbor Falls—remember that North Carolina style, vinegar-based sauce recipe I shared a few weeks ago? Yes, that one. I'll be trying it out on the guys. Last week, I hosted Sara Fischer's wedding reception, cake and all. In two weeks, I'll take part in the Donuts & Dads breakfast event over at Harbor Falls Elementary. Yes, the donuts will be homemade, and I'm enlisting the help of my cousin Sydney Hart, who owns *Sugar High Bakery*, to make this happen. We are expecting *lots* of dads.

And later on this week? What we've all been waiting for—the Taste of Harbor Falls Festival. I'll be sharing lots of info about that in my next post. Plus, you can check out the Chamber of Commerce website for all the details.

But today, I am most excited about my cookbook. I've been in contact with an agent and I'm literally on pins and needles. Me?! Suzie Hart. A cookbook author. *Ohmygoodness!* I have to say that all of my blog readers have helped with that. The agent was impressed with my subscribers. Thank you!

Sweet Hart Inn has officially been open six months now and I can't be more pleased with how business is taking off. Last week all the rooms were full and this weekend I'm expecting a mystery guest who has booked a room indefinitely. Wow! I wonder what *that* is all about?

So yes, life is good. I'm recovering from that rough patch I had last year, before I made lemonade out of lemons and chased my dreams. Sweet Hart Inn is mine and I'm not looking back.

Remember—the sweet tea is always cold, blueberry muffins are on the buffet, and the porch is perfect for sitting. The Blue Ridge Mountains are calling. Come escape for a while! Whether you choose a front porch rocker or an Adirondack chair looking out over the lake—the view is all good from here.

Until next time,
  Suzie

Chapter One

Brad Matthews stood in front of the old lodge, gave it a quick once-over, then turned to the real estate agent standing beside him. "I'll take it."

"You understand the deal is as is."

Brad nodded. "I understand." He looked up at the neglected structure and wondered what it was like in its heyday. Hell, he knew the answer to that—he'd done a good bit of research on the old place before he'd approached the agent with an offer. "The land alone is worth the asking price."

"What will you do with it?" James Martin, the agent, studied him from the side.

"I have a plan."

James scoffed. "Others have had plans, too. I assume you have the financing for renovation. You know it's on the historic register and there are federal guidelines to follow."

"I understand that too—and your assumption is correct." Brad suddenly had financing for just about anything he wished.

"I see."

"I want to move forward as quickly as possible."

"You're in town for a few days?"

"Yes. Indefinitely if need be."

"Then I can make it happen."

"Good." Brad knew his answers were vague. That was intentional. He'd always been wary of small-town types—it was difficult to know what they'd keep confidential or announce in the coffee shop the next morning. That was the last thing he wanted, or needed—the whole town of Harbor Falls, all seven-thousand-plus of them, chewing on his business. Not until he was good and ready.

Raised an Army brat, he didn't fully understand the connections of people who lived in one place for their entire lives—for generations even—and he had difficulty understanding how people could pin themselves down to a world so small. Settling in for a few years in Asheville, for the last chef gig he'd had, was the longest time he'd lived in one place since he was a kid. Back then, he and his parents, and little brother Scott, lived in Atlanta until he was five. To him, small towns were often close-minded, lacking in diversity, and distrustful of strangers.

Well, that was something he was going to have to deal with soon. If all went as planned, and he moved to Harbor Falls, adjusting to small town living and all it entailed would be the utmost priority on his agenda.

Right after—

James interrupted Brad's rambling thoughts. "Falls Lake Lodge is pretty special to folks around here."

He shook himself back to the present. "I figured as much." Figured he'd also have a fight on his hands when they learned what he wanted to do with the old lodge. They'd come around though, eventually, when they realized how the community would benefit. After all, he intended to settle here. Why would he do anything detrimental?

"Pretty special to me." Brad left it at that and turned to James. "I'd like to move on this today."

James rubbed his chin with his forefinger. "Well. Your loan is secure, and the bank is motivated. We can get the paperwork started this afternoon. I'll get it to their agent right after."

Brad felt a lazy grin stretch across his face. "What else to do?"

James studied him. "Well, for starters, I'd check with zoning, a local contractor or two, temporary utilities, and so on."

Good idea. Those were the kinds of tasks that would keep him busy while waiting to take possession—get the details out of the way so he could get right to work. Brad smiled. "I like the way you think." Perhaps he and James could be good friends.

James thrust out a hand to shake Brad's. "Good dealing with you, Mr. Matthews. Got a place to stay while you are in town? I can recommend the Sweet Hart Inn if there are vacancies."

The Sweet Hart Inn.

For the first time since his arrival in Harbor Falls, trepidation skipped down Brad's spine. Slowly, he angled his gaze behind the lodge and looked off toward the lake. The view was the same one featured in an old Falls Lake Lodge brochure he'd dug up at the Harbor Falls Public Library. The view that forty years ago drew tourists to the mountains and the lake in droves—like bees to honey.

If he had anything to do with it, they would again.

His gaze drifted and then rested across the lake on a moderate-sized, two-story Victorian home that sat nestled in a grove of trees bordering the water's edge.

His heart warmed. "Yes. I have a place to stay." He turned to James and shook his hand. "Thank you, Mr. Martin. Let's head down to your office."

James waved and turned toward his older-model Jeep.

Brad watched him stroll across the broken asphalt parking lot. The guy would enjoy the commission from the sale. Well, good for him. He imagined he could use the money. Might as well let Brad's inheritance contribute to the local economy.

Especially since he was taking over a local, legendary property.

Turning away from the lodge, he eyed his newest toy—a brand

spanking new Harley Davidson street bike—and swung a leg over the warm leather seat. Felt good to be in the saddle. In control. Two dreams coming true, two pieces of his plan falling together—a hog of his own and becoming his own boss real, real soon.

He was a man with a plan, and he knew exactly what he wanted.

He kicked the bike into gear, and the rumble broke the mountain calm. Now, to execute the biggest and most important piece of his plan.

SUZIE HART PULLED ONTO THE RAMBLING LANE, followed the drive around the house, and parked beside the yellow clapboard Victorian. Sweet Hart Inn was her home and her business—not to mention her salvation. And right now, she was extremely happy to be home.

Killing the car engine, she stared straight ahead, her gaze landing on the tranquil scene of Falls Lake behind her house. Smiling, she paused for a moment, savoring a brief but welcome break from her frenzied day.

Of course, in her world, the frenzy was normal. She enjoyed keeping busy, but in an orderly, predictable way. Today, a day-long catering event at the American Legion Hall—a fundraiser for the local Wounded Warriors project—kept her hopping. There was corn on the grill to keep moving, pulled pork BBQ that forever needed replenishing, and coleslaw bowls that emptied way too quickly. It was busy and satisfying and worth it all at the same time.

But she wouldn't change anything, even if she could. She loved her life in Harbor Falls. Every. Single. Day. She was busy, of course, but busyness was a blessing.

Busy made her temporarily forget.

And that was good. Right? To forget?

She didn't answer herself.

Blinking away the lake scene until later, when she could unwind with a glass of wine on her deck overlooking the lake, Suzie grabbed her keys and exited her Mazda SUV. At the rear of the vehicle, she lifted the hatch and reached inside to unload. She carried in empty pans and tubs, bags of plastic wear and paper plates, a couple of empty coolers, and more. Earlier, she'd dropped off the soiled tablecloths at the dry cleaner, and before she left town, had delivered the leftover food to the Harbor Falls Youth Center.

The kids there always appreciated an unexpected spread.

Plus, she loved giving back to her community, and this was one way she helped. There were too many people in town who could benefit from the leftovers. She never wasted food and always found someone in need.

Finally, she grabbed a couple of bags of groceries and slammed the hatch.

She'd stopped at Ralph's Food Mart—affectionately called *The Mart,* or just *Ralph's* by the locals—before leaving town. She'd needed a few things—the inn only had one guest booked for the night. But it didn't matter whether she was expecting one guest or ten. She still had breakfast to cook in the morning.

Sweet Hart Inn was, after all, a bed-and-breakfast. No matter what else she put on her plate.

She navigated the back entrance, set her groceries on the oversized kitchen island, and sighed.

"Whew. What a day!"

Allowing herself only a few seconds' pause, she sighed again, then started unpacking. One by one, she lifted the items out of her cotton grocery bags and placed them on the butcher-block countertop. A sinking feeling that she had forgotten something abruptly hit her.

She bit her lip. *What in the world did I forget?* She clicked through the list in her head, touching each item as she called out.

"Flour."

"Eggs."

"Cinnamon. Nutmeg."

"Sugar."

"Blueberries."

"Butter."

She glanced at the refrigerator. Something was missing. Why hadn't she made a list? She *always* made a list.

Chefs make lists. And *she* was a chef. Why didn't she make a list *today?*

Get over this bad habit of second-guessing yourself, Suzie.

She opened the refrigerator and immediately realized her mistake. Milk. She'd forgotten the stupid milk.

And she was bone-dry out.

"Well." Hands on hips, she stared into the refrigerator, as if the milk would magically appear. "There goes my blueberry muffin baking plan for tonight."

She'd wanted to tweak her Falls Mountain Blueberry Muffins recipe for her new cookbook—*At Your Leisure: Recipes of Harbor Falls Sweet Hart Inn.* The plus side of baking tonight was that she'd have muffins ready for morning, and she wouldn't have to get up at the crack of dawn.

Not happening now.

Double drat.

She supposed she could just bite the bullet and go back to Ralph's and get the milk.

Or, she could go to the Piggly-Wiggly in Dalton Springs, but that was a thirty-minute drive over the mountain. Plus, Dalton Springs was where her sister lived.

Not in the mood to run into Shelley today.

No. Ralph's was closer. Not that it would take hours to run the errand. That wasn't the point at all. It was the simple fact that getting back into the car, driving the ten minutes to the store, working her way to the very back corner, securing the milk, and making her way *back* to the checkout aisle would be another exhausting trip down memory lane.

That was one stroll she didn't want to take again today. She'd already been there an hour before.

She could still hear them.

"Suzie, honey, so sorry to hear about, well, you know, Cliff." *Cluck, cluck.* Old Mrs. Wilson. Her dementia had set in about a year earlier, and she recalled everything that had happened exactly one year ago, repeatedly. Whenever she saw Suzie, all the older woman ever thought about was how Cliff, Suzie's fiancé of way too many years, had left her—exactly one year ago.

Poor, poor Suzie.

Pat-pat on her hand.

"You feeling better, dearie? You look a bit off." Mr. Wilson moved his hand up her arm. Suzie knew better than to turn her back on the old man because he'd be pinching her backside before you could say, *Howdy do.*

Then there was Betty Jo, grocery clerk, scowling across the melons. "That sister of yours should have known better. She wasn't raised that way." She shook her head.

Then Geraldine Weissmuller—*tsk tsk*—obviously on her way home from her daycare job as she had baby spit and some sort of green goo on her shoulder. Geraldine sidled up beside her. "Now, tomorrow evening you come over for dinner and we'll have meatloaf and pie and lemonade. You'll forget all about that terrible ordeal and that little b— Um, your little sister."

Best meatloaf in town. At least she thinks so. Suzie begged to differ.

Sympathy ran amok.

She needed no more sympathy running amok, thank you very much. Or any more hand-patting. Or clucking after her ex-fiancé. Or tsk-tsking her sister. Or meatloaf.

She didn't need any of that.

She didn't need a man, either.

No.

She needed milk.

Dammit. Just milk.

And she would not get it today, that was for certain, unless she hauled her butt back to town and braved the gossip mill.

Ralph's, here I come.

Besides, it *had* been over a year since Cliff had run off with Shelley. She was over it. When would they—meaning the entire town of Harbor Falls—give it up, too?

Talk of the town. Yep. Little Suzie Hart. She was that.

But she was tired of the whole sordid affair. *Er,* situation. She and Cliff had stirred up more gossip around these parts since, well... Since Pammy Gruber ran off to Nashville in '68 with the preacher from the Church of Christ to some free love music festival out in California.

Times like these she wished she didn't live in a small town where everybody knew not only your name, but your business, too. Where everybody wanted in on your business in the worst way.

Argh!

There were days she just wanted to run away.

But wait—

She tried that once. Hadn't she?

How'd that turn out for you, Suzie?

BRAD CLICKED OFF HIS CELLPHONE AND DROPPED IT into his shirt pocket. Satisfied, and more certain now than ever of his plan, he stepped from James Martin's office and into the crisp air of downtown Harbor Falls. As he crossed the sidewalk toward his bike parked on the street, he side-stepped a kid speeding by on a skateboard.

"Spud Jones! Come back here and apologize!"

Brad glanced to his right and watched a tall, nicely dressed woman step out of a storefront. She frowned after the preteen boy on the skateboard, who by now was two blocks down the street. "Spud!"

She sighed and looked at him. "I'm so sorry. That child."

Smiling, Brad returned, "No harm done. Yours?"

"Oh, good Heaven's no. I wouldn't know what to do with a child." Her hand went to her hair, and she smoothed back a few stray strands that had escaped from the blond knot atop her head. She bit her lip. "That sounded horrid. It's not that I don't like children, I do. I just don't have any of my own. Not that I wouldn't want one of my own, I would, eventually, but... Goodness, I'm babbling."

Brad laughed. "You're fine, and I understand. Me either. About having a kid, I mean." He pushed out his hand. "I guess I'm babbling too. Kids make me nervous, but I want one or two one day. I'm Brad Matthews."

"Grace Hart. Nice to meet you." She shook his hand, let it go, then ticked her head toward the office next door. "So, if you have business with James, does that mean you're buying in town?"

These small-town Southern types get right to the point, he deduced. "If all goes well. I am looking at some property."

Grace nodded. "I see. Well, new faces are always welcome. New businesses are more than welcome—anything to keep the economy steady around here. Some people worry about it—the economy, that is—but things are good for me. I hope you like it here, Mr. Matthews. Just watch out for flying skateboarders!"

He laughed. "Call me Brad." He glanced up at the sign over the Victorian storefront door. *Romantically Yours.* "Your shop?" He wondered what she sold in there.

Grace glanced behind her. "Oh yes. All mine."

"I see. And you sell...?"

"Oh! Well, a bit of everything if it screams romance—you know, things a woman would like. Candles, aromatherapy products, gift baskets, lingerie…" She eyed him. "Do you have someone special in your life, Mr. Matthews? Er, Brad? If so, just let me know and I can find the perfect gift for her. I specialize in customizing gifts."

Brad's gaze drifted behind her to the store window, where he could make out frilly things and fancy boxes and such. Shifting his weight, he thought for a moment. "Do you have flowers?"

Grace grinned. "Today, I actually do. I do little business in flowers, but one of the local suppliers cuts a few roses for me once a week. Come on in and let's see what we can find."

"Wonderful." He glanced back at his bike. "On second thought, the flowers might pulverize by the time I get to where I am going. Let's see what else you have." She smiled and nodded, then turned for the door.

Brad followed, then stopped up short when he read the proprietor's name on the door. "Wait. Your name is Grace *Hart*?"

She glanced back with a warm smile. "Yes."

He could actually see a resemblance. Small town. Everyone's related. "Any relation to Suzie Hart?"

Her right eyebrow shot up. "Of course. She's my cousin. You know her?"

Nodding, he replied, "I do."

Grace eyed him, then looked him fully up then down. "Hmm. Well, come on in here, then. Let's see what kind of damage we can do."

Chapter Two

She didn't get the milk.

Honestly, she didn't have the bandwidth to wade through the gossipmongers one more time. While Suzie loved her Harbor Falls neighbors—most of them, anyway—there were times they annoyed her. Reason number one why living on the edge of town was ideal. When things were hopping and she was around people all day, she needed her downtime. Time to *unpeople* and let the chatter die down.

Tonight is one of those nights.

She'd work on the muffin recipe next week. The deadline wasn't pressing. This evening, she'd plant the hostas she'd picked up at the nursery yesterday. The evening promised to be perfect for it.

There was something basic and elemental, if not soothing, about digging her fingers into the dirt. It grounded her. The idea of that, and of ridding herself of the lingering voices in her head, was promising.

Suzie knew that no matter how much she disliked the fact that small towns were nosy, she would never leave Harbor Falls.

Again, anyway.

In Harbor Falls, people stayed put.

Mostly.

It was sort of like a rule—one she'd broken once upon a time. But Harbor Falls was her hometown, and she had no plans to leave.

Again.

She was safe here. Secure. Surrounded by family and friends, living in a charming home in a picturesque mountain town, framed by the impressive Blue Ridge Mountains.

Harbor Falls was home.

Plus, there was zero chance of running into unexpected people, or a person here. One who might toss her hormones sideways like he was flipping a pancake on a griddle.

Enough of that.

Suzie shook herself. She was as homegrown and homespun as they come. She couldn't imagine herself living anywhere else, especially in a big city.

She'd tried once—it didn't work out for her.

So be it. No use dwelling on *that.*

Harbor Falls was where she belonged, and Harbor Falls was where she'd stay. And she'd fight to keep this small town, and the lake behind her house, and the mountains they all loved so much the way they were—the way they had always been, no matter the quirks or the characters.

Or the steadily declining local tourist economy.

Sighing, Suzie put that out of her mind, picked up the dozen eggs sitting on the kitchen island, and headed for the refrigerator. Hell's bells. She'd just have to get up earlier than normal in the morning and go get the darn milk. It shouldn't take that long. She had a guest coming in later this evening, so she needed to be here, and she wouldn't need milk before breakfast, anyway. Right?

Right. In her usual professional style, she'd have quite the spread out by seven-thirty, one guest or a whole family in attendance.

After all, she had her reputation to stand on. Well, Sweet Hart Inn's reputation, at the very least. Hers might be questionable.

If one gave any stock to the gossip mill.

She stopped short of the refrigerator and stared at the back door. *Gossip mill indeed.*

The other half of the *talk of the town* story—the question everyone thought, but never asked, was this: *What had Suzie Hart done to make Cliff do what he did?*

Everyone in Harbor Falls knew that Suzie and Cliff would marry since they were in high school. Just why *had* she up and moved to Asheville for those couple of months before Cliff ran off with Shelley Hart and eloped?

Suzie scoffed. Like she'd give them fuel for that conversation.

The groceries. Put away the groceries, Suzie. Quit reliving the past. You're as bad as Mrs. Wilson.

She reached for the refrigerator door handle, juggling the eggs to her other hand, and simultaneously glanced at her landline phone sitting on the counter. A missed call and a message. While her cell phone was her usual device, she kept the house phone basically for business reasons.

Pausing, she punched the voicemail button, still holding the eggs.

The recording crackled. "Um, Suzette?"

She froze. Only one person in the world called her Suzette. And that one person was not anyone she wanted to talk to, or see, or get messages from. She smashed the stop button and cut off any pending dialog. Panic raced through her. No.

He couldn't have found her.

Could he?

Her brain raced with just how he *might* have. She'd changed addresses since living in Asheville. The inn had a new telephone number. But heck, it's a small town, right? Crap.

Suzie held her breath and pushed the voicemail button again and then turned to put the eggs on the top refrigerator shelf.

"Um, Suzette? It's Brad. I'm..." *Mumble, mumble, mumble.* "...in for a... Here's my number. I, uh...proposition...you."

Her fingers went slack. The full carton of eggs smashed to the floor. Startled, Suzie jumped back and swatted at the phone, sending the thing skidding backward against the backsplash.

Dammit. Milk *and* eggs.

Please, God, no. "This can't be happening."

***

Brad stepped out of *Romantically Yours* and into the late afternoon golden light, the sun making its trek across the mountains in the west, and the sweet scent of flowers drifting up from the containers in front of Grace's shop. Harbor Falls was charming in a picture-postcard kind of way. Red brick sidewalks. Wrought iron benches. Hanging baskets brimming with petunias. He could practically hear the town whispering around him.

Not that he minded. Let them whisper. Let them wonder.

He took a moment to glance around him at the cluster of storefronts—*Sassy's Café, Sugar High Bakery, The Artisan Mall,* and a bookstore called *Turn the Page Books.* Most of the signs were hand-painted. That kind of detail didn't happen by accident. It came from pride. From tradition. From people who didn't like surprises.

Which meant they really would not like him.

"Mr. Matthews, is it?"

The voice stopped him mid-stride. He turned to find a tall, broad-shouldered man in a Harbor Falls High Bobcats ball cap approaching from the direction of the town square. Mid-fifties, maybe older, with the easy gait of someone used to being listened to.

"I'm Harold Cunningham," the man said, extending a hand. "Mayor here in Harbor Falls."

Brad clasped his hand firmly. "Nice to meet you, Mayor."

"Heard you've made an offer on the old Falls Lake Lodge." The mayor didn't beat around the bush. "James Martin said you were moving quick on it."

"News travels fast," Brad said.

Mayor Cunningham chuckled. "You must be new to small towns."

Brad gave a tight smile. "You could say that."

The mayor's gaze narrowed slightly, though his smile never wavered. "So what brings a man like you to Harbor Falls? That lodge has been sitting empty for years. A few buyers sniffed around, but they all walked away."

Brad shrugged. "Maybe I don't scare as easy."

"Hmm." The mayor rocked back on his heels, hands resting lightly on his hips. "People around here have fond memories of that place. Weddings, retreats, summer camps back in the day. A lot of history in those walls."

"I respect history," Brad said carefully. "And I understand the significance of the property. I have plans, yes. But they're not fully baked yet."

"You a developer?"

"I'm a chef." Brad let that sit for a beat. "Or I was. These days I'm more interested in long-term investments."

"Interesting," the mayor murmured. "You looking to turn the lodge into a restaurant, or...?"

Brad didn't answer right away. Let the question hang. He let his eyes sweep over the town again—its manicured edges, its pride, its small-town pulse that could either embrace him or chew him up.

"I guess we'll see," Brad said finally. "I'm still getting the lay of the land."

Mayor Cunningham studied him a moment longer. "Well, we

take care of our own around here. We like things the way they are. Just something to keep in mind."

Brad nodded. "Appreciate the advice."

The mayor tipped his cap. "If you've got questions about zoning, permits, or the historical board—you come to me. My office is just on the other side of the town square." He nodded that way. "I like to stay involved in what's happening in my town."

His town. Worth remembering. "Thank you, sir. I'll do that."

The mayor gave him one last look, then turned and strode off, leaving Brad standing alone in the middle of Main Street, the breeze tugging lightly at his jacket.

He exhaled slowly.

Let them wonder.

He wasn't here to fit into Harbor Falls. He was here to fit into something else first—and Falls Lake Lodge was the avenue to do that. Fitting into the community would come in time.

And he would succeed. One way or another.

SUZIE HOISTED THE SECOND TWENTY-FIVE-POUND BAG of mulch from her wheelbarrow to the ground with a grunt, dropping it next to the stone foundation of her house. There. Ready to spread in the morning. The hostas in the ground finally, the weeds could wait until tomorrow. They wouldn't grow much overnight. Time to call it a day.

Her bubble-bath and that glass of wine were waiting.

Straightening, she rubbed her lower back and swiped her gloved hand over her forehead, steadying herself. Dizzy and a little queasy. "Should have eaten earlier," she muttered, then shook it off.

She'd been too busy with the plants and other outside tasks. The feeling passed. She'd eat something with that wine later. Pretty sure she had some nice cheese in the fridge.

Turning, she shaded her eyes with a hand and watched the sun settle over the mountain, shadowing downtown Harbor Falls a half mile or so in the distance. She loved being *just so far* removed from the Harbor Falls daily hustle and bustle. If you could call it that.

But Harbor Falls was definitely small-town at its best. No big-box stores. No strip malls. Just a busy little downtown. And they liked it that way.

Life, business, and living at the inn, were good. Her aunt's passing had been unexpected, and leaving her home to Suzie was even more of a surprise.

Her father's oldest sister was the maiden aunt everyone adored, and Suzie missed her every day. She would never take owning the home for granted and would honor her aunt in the highest regard by keeping the home full of people and laughter.

Aunt Donna loved children. Since Suzie was the oldest of all the cousins, her aunt doted on her more than the others and encouraged her to chase her dreams. And when Suzie did—when she left Harbor Falls to hone her chef skills—Aunt Donna had cheered her on.

She never expected that when she passed, her aunt would leave the beautiful storybook Victorian home to her. Or, that when Suzie returned home—broken and quite a bit lost—the old house would be her salvation.

That's why she did her best, every single day, to take care of the gift entrusted to her.

Sweet Hart Inn was hers.

She spent months converting Aunt Donna's home into a working bed-and-breakfast and had renovated the kitchen for her cooking classes and catering business. It was also the perfect place to work on her cookbook and write her blog.

Cliff had dumped her, yes. Humiliated her and the family. And Shelley had done something unthinkable, too. But secretly she thanked them both and held no grudges, because their decisions had forced her hand.

That's when she left the past behind and started making plans for her future.

Sweet Hart Inn was the rest of her life.

She intended to live there, run the B&B, and do her cooking and writing gig for years to come.

Alone. Blessedly alone.

Chapter Three

Brad leaned into the turn as his Harley purred along the winding lake road, the trees arching overhead like a cathedral of green. Sunlight broke through the canopy in gold-tipped shards, dappling the pavement and flickering across his leather jacket.

The lake came into view around a bend. He slowed, letting the breeze hit his face and the pine-laced air fill his lungs. The evening smelled like woodsmoke and honeysuckle. And something else—something warm and sweet that curled at the edge of remembrance.

Vanilla. Sugar. Cinnamon.

Suzie.

Damn it.

He hadn't expected the air itself to carry her. Or was it the memory?

Breakfast in bed. Hot kisses. Tangled sheets.

He downshifted and eased off the throttle, letting the bike coast. He could almost pretend nothing had changed. That she still made French Toast for breakfast, and tucked her hair behind her ear while concentrating on a new recipe. That she'd smile when she saw him. That she'd forgive him for not chasing her sooner.

But he knew better.

Whatever was waiting for him at Sweet Hart Inn, it wasn't forgiveness.

Still, he wasn't turning back.

SUZIE SPANNED THE HORIZON, HER GAZE SETTLING ON the lake. Smiling, she rubbed her hands together to rid them of some dirt and then wiped them on the thighs of her jeans. As dusk settled in, all she wanted was a quiet walk to the water for a few minutes of silence. Then, that long, hot soak in the tub.

But the rumble of a surly engine down the road grew louder, forcing her to turn back. A large motorcycle—one of those bad-boy types—and its rider leaned into the turn and then made their way up the curvy drive to her home.

For some odd reason, she liked how the bike thundered into her peaceful existence. It was unexpected, but also welcome, and that made no sense at all. Perhaps it provided an edge to the end of her day, a hint of excitement she normally didn't experience.

The rider stopped the bike and abruptly cut off the engine.

Suzie stood spellbound, staring at the man and bike. He wore black from head to toe—helmet, leather jacket, hip-hugging tight jeans, and boots. Yes. Bad boy. The man stood silent and unmoving, staring back at her.

She'd expected a guest this evening, a Mr. Logan, and this man could be him. She hadn't expected a Harley, but again, the unexpected was welcome.

Stepping forward, again wiping her dirty hands on her pants, she silently wished she'd ended her planting early and showered. She kept moving forward, ready to shake his hand and welcome him to the B&B, when—

He dismounted, stood straight up, and slipped off his helmet.

Her breath caught in her throat. The steady gaze that met hers and held while he shifted the helmet to his left hip and ran fingers through his curly brown hair, sent her libido into a lurch, and her heart into panic.

Icy dread shot up Suzie's back, and she sucked in a breath. *No. Not him. Not today.*

Buzzing filled her ears, like a thousand people talking all at once. She'd know that finger-rake mannerism anywhere.

Brad Matthews.

She went a little lightheaded.

Had her temporary escape from reality caught up with her?

"Suzie!"

Brad made brief eye contact, then watched her eyelids flutter, and her body fold into itself and topple to the ground. He rushed forward but was too late—her temple sharply connected with a rock at the edge of the flower bed.

"Dammit!"

His chest pounding, he pulled her onto his lap, fear shaking his arms. "Suzie, darling. I'm sorry. I didn't mean to startle you. Wake up, sweetheart." He caressed her face and cooed soothing words.

He was mortified. Damn. Surprising her was not his best idea. Apparently.

She moaned and shifted, pressing her palms against his chest. "Wha... What the hell are you...?"

"Shhh, darling. Don't talk. Oh, Suzette." Brad glanced about. Where to take her? Inside? To the hospital? He noticed a small SUV parked in the back. He supposed it was hers. Were the keys inside? Obviously, he couldn't take her to the hospital on his bike.

Should he call 9-1-1?

"We need to get you somewhere. Have that bump looked at."

Suzie shifted and huffed out a quick breath, pushing him away. Hard.

"No, Brad. No..." Then she slumped into his arms again.

Chapter Four

Someone was talking to her. Which was, frankly, rude—given that she'd just taken an unscheduled nap in the flowerbed.

The thousand voices parted, and one voice came to the forefront. His words drifted across her face on a whispery breath, edged with a familiar rasp and threading through the noise—low and gravelly, like warm whiskey over rocks. It ghosted across her face, brushing her cheek. Was he...petting her?

No, he wouldn't.

Would he?

She felt warm, tucked in, held tight like a fresh-baked biscuit in a dish towel. His arm was solid under her shoulders. His other hand... Was he actually stroking her hair?

Well, that was new.

Who?

"I didn't mean to scare you," he whispered.

Suzie blinked several times. Her brain slowly surfaced from its fog, squinting toward clarity. That voice. That cologne. That smug, Southern-tinged rasp.

Brad.

He *was* holding her.

Her eyes fluttered open. And there he was. Brad Matthews, in the flesh. And not just in the flesh but *cradling* her like she was some kind of swoony heroine from a southern soap opera.

Shit! She bolted upright with a sharp gasp.

Or tried to.

Brad's arm caught her like a net. He tugged her back down onto his lap. "Suzette! Sit still. You passed out and hit your head."

Suzette. God help me.

"What... What are you doing here? Oh..."

Dizzy again. Dammit. Of course, she was dizzy. She hadn't eaten since lunch and had spent the last two hours gardening like she was auditioning for a reality show called *Extreme Landscaping for the Emotionally Unwell.*

And she knew better than to let her blood sugar get out of whack.

"Would you quit squirming? I will not hurt you."

Please. Brad Matthews might not hurt her body, but her heart? That man had her emotional number programmed into his phone under *Devastation, Speed Dial 1.*

No, Brad Matthews would never hurt her—*physically.*

Emotionally? Without a doubt.

She squinted up at him through her not-quite-focused vision. It had been eighteen months since she'd seen him. She didn't want to acknowledge how much she had missed that face. But no, there he was—dimples and all—like some rugged biker-chef version of regret wrapped in leather and poor decisions.

"Brad, I... I don't know what you're doing here but—"

"Later," he said, his voice gentle but firm. "Let's get an ice pack for your head. And a painkiller. You're going to have a nasty bump. We might need to get you checked out."

Oh, hell no.

She was not—repeat, *not*—going to let this man cart her off to the Harbor Falls Hospital like some damn damsel in distress. Brad

Matthews carrying Suzie Hart into the ER? That story would make it to Ralph's *and* the pastor's inbox by breakfast. She'd be the lead topic at every hair salon, diner booth, and nail table within thirty miles.

Bad-boy type motorcycle dude carrying poor Suzie in his arms. What is that all about?

Too close. Too intimate. Too many memories. Abort mission.

"Come on, sweetheart. Let's get you inside."

"I'm fine," she snapped, wriggling upright and batting away his helping hands. "You can go. Really."

She stood, a little wobbly, but determined, brushing dirt from her jeans and indignity from her pride.

He didn't move. Just stood there with that face and that smirk and those damn warm eyes that made her feel... Ugh. Stuff. Too much stuff.

He reached out again, trying to steady her.

She swatted his hand away without ceremony. "No puppy dog heroics. I'm good."

But of course, he fell into step beside her anyway, trailing her like a determined golden retriever, all quiet concern and respectful distance.

She didn't say it out loud—but fine, okay, maybe it was nice. Maybe.

Still. This was not how the evening was supposed to go.

She was supposed to finish planting the hostas, pour a glass of wine, sink into a warm bubble bath, and feel smugly accomplished.

Instead, she'd been ambushed by her past, fainted into a petunia patch, and was now being escorted inside by the one man in the state of North Carolina who could unravel her with a look.

And not for one second could she pretend it was the lack of dinner that had her knees weak.

Brad took a deep breath as he entered Suzie's home, glanced about, and settled her on the sofa in the living room.

"You sit tight," he ordered. "I'm going for ice. Which way is the kitchen?"

Slinking back into the sofa cushions, Suzie's glazed eyes worried him. She pointed down the hall, and he moved in that direction. The last thing he wanted to do was frighten her. Or hurt her. That was certainly not his plan.

He'd contemplated how she'd react when she saw him, when she realized the Mr. Logan who made the reservation last week was really him. She might even get mad. He'd walked himself through every scenario a hundred times and knew exactly how he would react to any of a dozen things she might toss at him.

But he hadn't planned to scare the hell out of her. Hurt her. *Dammit!*

He bolted into her kitchen, looking right and left. Ice. Yes, that's what he needed.

The kitchen, however, momentarily took him off guard, and for a split second, he admired the bright and cheery room painted sunshine yellow with white accents. A large center island balanced a trellis of polished pots hanging above. The stainless restaurant-style gas stove sat on the spit-shined hardwood floors. Bright white cabinets, some open shelving and some with glass doors, plus a host of professional-grade appliances, cutlery, and cookery items completed the upscale kitchen design.

With a glance, he knew it was easily the best home kitchen layout he'd ever seen.

He could get lost there. *Never mind, Matthews. Salivate over her kitchen later.*

His gaze shot to the side-by-side stainless refrigerator. He located ice, a large zipper bag, and a hand towel. In a few quick steps, he was back by her side in the living room.

Her eyes were closed, her breathing slow.

For a moment, all he wanted to do was look at her. A flash of memory seared his brain. Watching her wake each morning was a gift, and one of his fondest memories. Strawberry blond hair slinked lazily over her brow, honey-brown freckles sprinkled over a pert nose and peaches-and-cream complexion—heaven, pure heaven. Those small chili-pepper lips could both tempt and beckon.

Not now, Matthews. Not now.

"Suzette. Wake up, sweetheart. You shouldn't sleep."

He roused her. A few quick eyeblinks batted back at him.

"Hm?"

Moving closer, he shook her shoulder, then lifted her head to place the ice on her growing head bump. "I'm going to put the ice—"

When the ice bag made contact with her temple, Suzie bolted, hands flailing, knocking a clenched fist into his arm. His hand holding the ice bag shot back and knocked him square in the right eye.

"Ow!" he shouted.

Suzie stared at him, wide-eyed. "You're *bleeding!*"

Brad swiped a finger across his eyebrow. Yep. Blood. Running down his face. A sharp corner of an ice cube must have sliced his eyelid. Suzie raced for the kitchen.

Brad grabbed at her. "Wait! You shouldn't run like that."

"You're bleeding. My new sofa. Get *up!*"

He did. Warm trickles ran down the side of his face now. Brad followed her into the kitchen. She stood at the sink, rinsing out another towel, her hands frantically wringing and twisting the wet terry fabric. Abruptly she stopped, braced herself against the sink, and closed her eyes. Her body weaved a little.

Brad stepped closer. "Here," he mumbled. "Give me that."

He took the soaked towel, wrung it out until it was barely damp, and then pressed it against his bleeding eye. Simultaneously, she swayed, and he pulled her closer to him.

"Ah, honey," he whispered. "Slow down and stop running away from me, okay?"

Finally, Suzie relaxed against him and Brad exhaled for the first time in what felt like days. Maybe months. Nothing had happened as planned—but finally, his Suzie was back in his arms.

STOP RUNNING FROM ME.

Suzie squeezed her eyes shut and breathed in the musky male scent of the man holding her. Yes, running was what she'd been doing, wasn't it? Running from *him*. Running from love. Running from...herself?

Gah. If she'd be brave enough to admit it, she kind of liked where she was right now. Back in Brad's arms. She'd relish it for the moment. A freakishly small moment. A few drive-by seconds, perhaps. What could it hurt? Later, she could rationalize that her silly minor head injury and queasy stomach was causing her to do things she normally wouldn't do.

Right?

Wrong.

Months ago, before the Cliff debacle, it wasn't a silly head injury that caused her to fall into Brad's arms. It was lust, *pure and simple*, that made her do it. It was chocolate ganache and whipped cream and sugared strawberries and wine that made her do it.

The man knew how to lure and tempt with food, and she was his sucker.

Damned if she'd make that mistake again.

Running was the exact thing she *should* be doing at this moment. And as soon as this darn head thing passed, she'd be running again.

If she could find the strength to push him away.

Grabbing onto the gumption gathering inside her, Suzie

pressed her palms against Brad's chest and backed a good five feet away. She settled her rear against the cooking island and glared.

There he stood, in the middle of her kitchen, all tall and dark and handsome and man-in-black and all. A smear of blood dripped down his cheek, adding to his bad-boy charm and decadent lure.

I will not sway.

Even though her voice may have been softer than she had intended, and quite possibly could have wavered a bit, she mustered up her words with conviction. "What the hell are you doing in my kitchen, Brad Matthews?"

He dabbed at his eyebrow. "At the moment, I'm trying to stop this bleeding."

She crossed her arms. "That's not what I mean, and you know it. What are you doing here, in Harbor Falls?"

He tossed the bloody towel in the sink and peered straight at her. "Suzie, all right. So we need to talk."

"Yes, we do." Her foot began a sudden and erratic tap-tap-tap on the hardwood floor.

He moved a step closer. "But I'm worried about your head."

She slid to the left. "My head is fine. A small bump. No one will be the wiser in the morning."

"I will."

"What?"

"I'll be the wiser. I'll know."

"Know what?"

"About your bump."

Suzie sighed. "Forget about the bump! I want to know why you are here and when you are leaving." She really needed to know what was going on.

Brad cleared his throat and took another hesitant step forward. "I suppose that depends on you."

Suzie narrowed her gaze. "Don't play games with me, Brad."

He shook his head. "No games, Suzie. I'm here for serious business."

Okay, finally we're getting somewhere. "Tell me. What's so serious?"

He moved closer. His gaze never left hers, his eyes all dreamy and misty and full of intent. Suddenly, Suzie felt like the world was turning on her again. Spinning. What *was* that look on his face? Like he was after something. Like he was hell-bent on getting his way.

Like he was going to ask her to marry him, or something.

Oh shit.

One of those looks. *Oh, God. No!*

She put up her hands. "Brad Matthews, stop right where you are. Don't you dare take another step and stop looking at me like that!"

He stopped. "Like how?"

"Like, like… Oh hell." She had to turn the tide. Deflect. Distract him with something, anything, to stop this train wreck that was about to happen. Her gaze skittered and then landed on his face again. It was then she got a good gander at his eyebrows.

"My God. Your eye!"

"What the hell?"

She moved closer and peered at his face. "Good Lord, Brad. That has to hurt."

"What?"

She poked at his wound.

"Ow!"

"See? That's a nice little slice there. Needs fixing." She blubbered on, avoiding his gaze. "You really busted that open good. Probably need stitches. Not that I want to go to the emergency room with you. In fact, it's the last place I want to be seen with—"

She started to say, *with a drop-dead gorgeous male specimen such as yourself,* but didn't.

"—with you this evening, but I think we might need to go. Come here."

Evidently, he didn't need to be told twice. In a blink, he moved right up next to her. Damn, he was tall. She'd forgotten.

No, she hadn't.

She pulled over a bar stool. "Sit."

"Are you still dizzy?"

"Sit!"

"Guess not." He sat.

Yes, she was still dizzy. Crazy dizzy, but it wasn't from the hit on her head. She moved back to the sink and retrieved the towel. The whole mess had left her disoriented and off-balance. She needed to think. Clear her head. Gain a moment or two to get a grip.

What in the world *was* he going to ask her?

She rinsed and wrung out the towel, then returned to Brad. "Let me see that cut a little closer."

Brad put his hands on her rear and pulled her into the cradle of his thighs.

She took a comfortable step backwards. "Stop it!"

"Sorry."

"Let me see that eye."

"Sure, doc."

Suzie glared, then studied the eyebrow. Dabbing with the damp towel, she removed the dried blood around the edges and determined a butterfly bandage or two would do the trick.

"Stay here. I'll be right back."

Chapter Five

Brad couldn't help but watch Suzie's backside as she sashayed away from him.

He stared as she opened a cabinet door and took down a small first aid kit. She rummaged around in it while his gaze lingered over the length of her body. When she moved toward him again, he jerked his head back to stare at the sink.

She narrowed her gaze. "No funny business, Brad Matthews. Keep those hands to yourself while I put this on your cut."

How did she know his hands itched to touch her again? To caress the bump on her forehead and make her pain go away? He wanted to touch a whole lot more than that.

After a while, she'd cleaned the wound, applied antibacterial cream and a couple of bandages, and then stepped back to survey her handiwork. All the while, Brad sat still and let her hands work over him, like a good little boy.

"There. I think that will do." Her gaze fell lower, inspecting his face, then his lips.

Don't look at me like that, Suzette.

Backing up against the sink, she widened the distance between them. Lowering her voice, she asked, "Brad, why are you here?"

Now or never. He had to spill it. "I came to find you. I miss you. And I'm sorry I didn't get here sooner."

She shook her head. "Why? And how did you find me? It's been months. Why now?"

"Because I needed to see you again."

She shook her head again. "Not good enough. There is something else."

He stood. "Yes, you're right. There is something else."

"Then tell me."

"It's simple, really, Suzette. I need you in my life. I want to know what happened."

"Because...?"

"Because I can't get you out of my head, dammit. I want to know why you left and didn't tell me you were leaving. Because you turned my life upside down and around again. Because you walked out of my life right when I realized I was in love with you. Because things in my life have changed, and now I want—"

"Stop." She interrupted. "I get the picture."

More. I want more. "You understand?"

She crossed her arms. "No. Yes. I mean, maybe." Her arms dropped and she paced back and forth in front of him.

She looked so damn cute, all dirt-smudged and homey. And beautiful.

Abruptly, she stopped square in front of him and blurted out. "I was engaged back then."

"I know."

"You *knew*?"

"Not at the time. I found out later."

Her face screwed up. "How?"

"You mentioned it to Sara, one of the servers, and after you left, she made some comment that you probably went back to your fiancé."

"Oh."

"I have to tell you that hurt like hell, and I didn't know what to think. In fact, I was pretty angry with you for a long time because you'd not been honest with me. How could you let me fall for you when you had someone back home? That didn't seem like you."

Her eyes widened. "I'm sorry, Brad. I shouldn't have—done that. It was wrong. Truly, it wasn't like me. I was confused, we— my fiancé and I—were on a break, and you were wonderful. We were great together, and... Oh, hell."

She sighed and glanced away, avoiding his eyes. *Oh, hell is right.*

"Look. I know you, Suzie. So you were on a break. I don't call that cheating. I can understand that you might have felt guilty— but maybe the relationship wasn't right, anyway?"

She looked back at him. "There was a lot wrong with that relationship, Brad. But I shouldn't have let myself fall for you. I went to Asheville to further my education, my career, and gain new skills. Not to have a fling. And definitely not to hurt you."

"I *was* hurt. But I figured there was more to your story than I knew."

She nodded. "Yes."

"Tell me?"

Suzie crossed her arms and glanced away.

"Just tell me."

"Okay. I needed a break from Harbor Falls, and yes, from Cliff, my fiancé. I needed to figure out where my life was going. My dreams weren't coming true, and I wasn't getting any younger. I felt stuck, stalled in my life. I was trying to save enough to buy my own place and open a B&B, so I took the job in Asheville. Cliff wasn't exactly supportive and gave me an ultimatum—him or the job. I was unsatisfied enough in life to let him go.

"But before I left, I made it clear that I needed a break from the relationship. In my head, I'd made the split. Apparently, he hadn't realized that we'd broken up—at least that's what he told everyone on this side of the mountain."

Brad studied her for a moment. "Look, let's face reality here. If you needed to get away, and he wasn't supportive, then things weren't peachy keen between the two of you, right?"

She sighed. "Truth? No, things weren't peachy keen and yes, I needed to think about my pending marriage, and if that was truly what I wanted. After fourteen years together, you think you know someone."

"Fourteen years?"

"Yes. Ridiculous, right? We had been a couple since we were teenagers."

Brad frowned. "I know you, Suzie. And it didn't take me fourteen years."

She exhaled and then glanced at the floor. Wrapping her arms tighter around her chest, she turned away.

"Look. I need to hear what happened, and I think you need to tell me."

She shook her head briskly . "That's not what's important. I shouldn't have jumped into that—" she flipped her hand through the air, "that thing I had with you, whatever it was. So I left."

"And I've missed you every day since."

She turned and looked at him. "I left because it was wrong, Brad. I felt guilty. And as great as it was, I knew I wasn't the woman for you. You talked about goals that obviously didn't include anyone else. Especially not me. I'm just... Well, I am just me, little Suzie Hart from Harbor Falls. We weren't right."

"Now that's a ridiculous statement if I ever heard one. And make no mistake, Suzie Hart from Harbor Falls, whatever we had? It was special, and I want it again."

Her brow arched. "What?"

He pushed the bar stool back toward the kitchen island. That you could never be the woman for me is ridiculous. You *were* the woman for me, Suzie-Q, and I want you to be the woman in my life from this day forward."

"But I... But you...."

"But nothing. Your boyfriend, dumbass that he was, let you

go. Can't say I'm sad about that. You aren't together anymore. It doesn't matter now. Why you didn't come back, I don't know. But I was tired of waiting, so I figured I'd find you myself. So, you listen to me. I'm here. I want you. And I'm not leaving until I get what I want."

He smoothed back a stray lock of hair that had fallen over her eye, smiled and waited.

"You have everything figured out, don't you?"

"Yes, honey, I do."

She cocked her head to the side. "Except for one thing."

He moved closer, his fingers itching again, wanting to haul her against him and run his hands over her body.

"And what is that?"

"There is a reason I didn't come looking for you when Cliff left, Brad."

"Oh?"

"Look, I'm sorry. I didn't want to find you," she mumbled. "I wanted to put that part of my life behind me."

Brad stepped back, his brain reeling. Once again, a scenario he hadn't expected. She didn't want him? *Ridiculous.*

"Suzette, you can't mean that."

"Stop calling me that!"

Puzzled, he peered into her eyes. They were misty. Frightened. Overwrought.

Shit. Too much. It had all been too much. "Look. Let's table this for tonight. We're running close to overkill here."

She agreed and pushed back. "Good idea. I'm sure a nice, long, cool ride on your bike will make you see all of this is an impossible situation and—"

"Stop." This time it was Brad who held up his hand. "I'm not going anywhere. I have a room reserved for tonight, and I intend to stay here."

"Wha—"

That last statement may have been her undoing. He continued. "I'm Mr. Logan. I know you have a room for me. So, okay, I gave you a fake name, but admit it, you wouldn't have given me a room if I'd told you the truth. I'll go get my things from the bike and we'll finish this discussion in the morning."

He turned toward the kitchen door. Suzie's footsteps padded along behind him.

"Okay, fine. Stay."

He walked down the hall, through the living room, and toward the front door. "I intend to."

Suzie followed. "But it means nothing," she went on. "It's late, and with your injury, you shouldn't be riding the bike, but first thing in the morning I'll be expecting you to be on your way and...."

He turned. His stare bore into her eyes. "I believe I reserved my room indefinitely. Did I not?"

She clamped her lips tight, took a deep breath and blew it out. "Your *room* is at the top of the stairs on the right," she uttered. "Lock the front door behind you when you come back in and shut off the downstairs lights. I'm turning in and I really don't want to be disturbed."

The look on her face said she meant business. He would not rock this boat anymore tonight. "Of course," he told her. "Sweet dreams."

She turned on her heel and headed for the kitchen, each step punctuating her last statement. She moved straight through the kitchen—he watched her sashay through, pause at a wine rack and grab a bottle—and into a room beyond. Then he heard the door slam.

Good. He liked to get a lay of the land. So, she'd be downstairs, off the kitchen. Must be her master suite, her personal quarters. He bet there would be a sturdy lock on the door, too.

The sharp snap of a deadbolt echoed throughout the empty kitchen and into the entrance hall.

Thought so. Yes, he knew her. And she'd come around. Eventually.

He grinned and went out to get his things.

BUBBLE THERAPY WAS EVERYTHING IT WAS CRACKED UP to be—and unlike *therapy therapy*, it didn't ask questions or interrupt.

That and a few other amenities were Suzie's guilty pleasures.

Low lights. One flickering candle. A mostly full bottle of Merlot balanced precariously on the edge of the tub. Madeleine Peyroux crooning on her phone like heartbreak was something soft and stylish. The only thing missing was a slab of dark chocolate. And possibly a man.

But no. Scratch that.

Sex was the *last* thing Suzie Hart needed.

Sex was what got her into this mess in the first place. Well... Sex and emotional recklessness. And Brad Matthews in a chef's coat. So, yeah. Basically sex.

She slid lower into the whirlpool tub, neck propped on a rolled towel, bubbles up to her ears, and her hair piled like a meringue on top of her head. The steam carried a hint of lilac—courtesy of the bush blooming outside her bedroom window and a splash of over-priced bath oil she didn't regret buying one bit.

Her stomach growled, and she lamented the fact that she hadn't grabbed some cheese from the fridge on her way through too—but there'd not been time. And she sure as hell wasn't going back into her kitchen tonight.

She flicked the jets on with a toe. The bubbles churned, the water gurgled, and she let herself pretend that maybe—just maybe—the bath could scrub the last few hours off her skin and out of her memory. She might've been on her third cycle of hot water. Maybe fourth. Whatever. She was going full raisin.

The bubbles surged.

"Erase the day," she whispered. "Just... delete it."

But not everything today had been bad, right? Uncomfortable? Yes. Unexpected? Oh, very. But technically, she hadn't been arrested. Or proposed to. Yet.

She sighed. Cliff never made her feel this confused. Cliff barely made her feel anything at all.

Her little sister, Shelley, on the other hand? Oh, Shelley knew how to stir things up.

Funny, when Cliff called everything off, she did not have to think about it. She'd accepted it and told him to go on his merry way. When she realized it was her sister he wanted, well then, that had required some thought.

Wouldn't any woman stop to think about that?

Shelley had cornered the market on cute from an early age. Suzie was always...practical. Average.

Shelley was younger. Thinner. Fertile.

So fertile.

Shelley popped out a baby the moment Cliff slipped a ring on her finger—like her uterus was on standby.

Meanwhile, Suzie had a uterus that waved a white flag sometime around age twenty-three and never looked back. "Defective parts," she muttered. "Can't return 'em. Can't sell 'em on eBay."

And yet, somehow, it was Suzie who'd been expected to produce the first grandchild. Being the oldest came with a timeline. A family legacy. A pressure cooker she never signed up for.

But Shelley? She got the man. The house. The baby. And, thank God, she got the hell out of Harbor Falls.

Yes, little sister Shelley was quite the girl. Landed herself quite the man. Now she had quite the baby too. Along with an ideal picket-fence life in Dalton Springs down the road. Thank God she and Cliff had decided Harbor Falls was too close for comfort.

When Suzie left town, it wasn't to escape. It was to chase something. A sous chef job in Asheville. A future in food. A life where people didn't look at her like she was half-baked just because she'd chosen recipes over rings. Working for Brad, she'd been over-the-moon putting her culinary skills to good use.

Cliff thought cooking was something wives did while wearing mascara and disappointment. He only tolerated her working on her cookbook because he thought it was a great hobby.

Hobby. Bleh.

Brad? Brad saw it. Saw *her*. Her talent. Her spark. Her possibilities.

Which, of course, was exactly why she had to leave him.

Brad Matthews was the top-dog chef at the Mountain View, the Chef de Cuisine for the resort. He was a hotshot chef with six-pack abs and a smirk that could melt steel—and he wanted a family one day. Suzie couldn't give him that. Not in the traditional baby-shower-and-birth-announcements way. She couldn't give him a future with kids, or diaper bags, or messy highchairs. All she could give him was a killer risotto and maybe a kiss that curled his toes.

And that wasn't enough.

Of course, she never told him about her baby-making defect. It wasn't exactly the thing you blurted when a younger guy was steaming your tomatoes. And just as well.

Brad Matthews was a fantasy. He wasn't real life.

He was five years younger and wanted a someday family. Something she could never give him because she couldn't have a someday baby.

So, she'd walked away.

Thirty-four years old. A little pudgy from years of butter and baking. A dash of heartbreak. And a spoonful of secrets.

So, she poured herself out of his life and back into Harbor Falls.

Only to find Cliff shacked up with Shelley. Surprise!

She slapped at a rogue bubble teasing her ear. "I swear, the only consistent relationship I've ever had is with carbs."

The bath was cooling. Her toes had turned to prunes. She took a long drink of Merlot straight from the bottle. Elegant.

"Time to get out, Suzie-Q," she muttered.

The nickname hung in the air, sweet and sharp. Brad's name for her. The one she pretended to hate but secretly missed.

God help her, she missed the whole damn thing.

How in the hell was she going to send him away in the morning?

BRAD TURNED OFF HIS PHONE AND LAY BACK ON THE BED with a flop. He glanced at the top of the dresser where he had set the box of chocolate candy he'd bought for Suzie earlier today at Grace's shop. When he'd bought them, he had envisioned this evening differently. No matter. He'd give the confections to her another day. Might be nice to have something waiting in the wings, just in case.

The day had its ups and downs, for sure, and nothing had gone according to plan—but at least they'd reconnected. He was hopeful for a fresh start. What more could he ask for, anyway?

For her to fall into his arms and profess her undying love to him, after he'd sprung himself on her from out of nowhere? No, he hadn't thought that would happen, but in retrospect he wondered if he had thought things through. Her resistance was worrisome, but he was pretty sure she would warm up, eventually.

Right?

He sure hoped so.

Blowing out a breath, he crossed his feet at the ankles and propped his arms under his head. Earlier he had cracked the window beside the bed. Eyes closed, he listened to the night sounds.

Birds.

Rustling leaves.

Waves lapping.

Tranquil and calm. Comforting. A lot different from Asheville night noises.

A sweet floral smell wafted up from below and he wondered about the scent. Something flowery and sweet drifting on the humid breeze. It smelled like Suzie.

Somehow, he felt at peace after all these months, even though his arrival was a bit rocky. If anything, it felt damn good to be under the same roof again with Ms. Suzie Hart.

From the Kitchen of Suzie Hart, Sweet Hart Inn

Blog Post, May 16: *What We Stir Inn*

Let's talk batter. And baggage.

Some folks say baking is about following instructions. Step-by-step, measurement by measurement, precise and predictable. (And let me tell you, I *love* a good predictable recipe.)

But there's always something else we stir in, isn't there?

This week I found myself elbow-deep in blueberry muffin batter. Again. And not because the rooms were full and guests were asking for more. No, this batch had nothing to do with breakfast service, or testing recipes for the cookbook, but everything to do with nerves, memory, and that knot-in-the-stomach kind of uncertainty I thought I'd baked out of my life a year ago.

It's funny how the right—or wrong—person walking back into your kitchen can toss your whole sense of calm out with the coffee grounds.

So, I stirred.

And while the oven preheated and the batter rested, I thought about what we carry with us, what we bring to the mixing bowl.

Regret, hope, love, fear. Sometimes a little anger, too (I may or may not have slammed a cabinet door—sorry, hinges).

What we stir in flavors the whole batch. And maybe that's okay.

So, to those of you going through it this week—whatever *it* is —may I recommend a little kitchen therapy? Bake something simple. Stir slowly. Let it rest. And when the timer dings, give yourself permission to sit down with a warm muffin, maybe a cup of coffee or a glass of ice-cold sweet tea (whatever your preference) and remember that nothing good happens all at once.

We rise slowly. Together.

Today's recipe: Lavender Honey Muffins
2 cups flour
2 tsp baking powder
½ tsp salt
1 tbsp dried culinary lavender
1/2 cup honey
2/3 cup buttermilk
1/2 cup melted butter
1 egg

Whisk wet + dry separately, fold together, scoop into muffin tins, bake at 375 for 18-20 mins. Sprinkle tops with sugar if desired.

Until next time—
Suzie

Chapter Six

Two days later, Suzie stood in the middle of the Harbor Falls Town Square, clipboard in hand and a determined smile on her face. The Taste of Harbor Falls festival was literally upon them, and half the town seemed to think it would organize itself.

She knew better.

"This is going to be fine," she told herself aloud, marking off the third vendor to arrive on her list. "Famous last words."

Today was set-up day and the vendors were out in full-force—some of them even trying to sneak in a few early sales, it seemed. Whatever worked, she supposed. They were all trying to make a living.

When Cassie Campbell went into labor over the weekend, a whole month earlier than expected, she had to hand over the festival reins to someone else. So, Suzie, ever the eager beaver, volunteered to coordinate the event for one reason: distraction. A big, messy, complicated distraction to keep her from thinking about Brad Matthews and the way he'd turned his arrival in Harbor Falls into a rom-com flashback scene she hadn't asked for.

Meet cute? No.

Second chance romance? Unlikely.

They'd managed to be civil and keep their distance. He was gone most of the past two days, and she'd been busy, too. He cited "business" as the reason he was gone, and she found it seriously curious that he had apparent business in Harbor Falls.

Like, what business could the guy have here?

But his absence during the days weren't what got to her—it was the evenings, with Brad in her house, that were becoming rather trying. Uncomfortable.

Difficult to ignore.

How dare he invade her space? Her life? And act so damn nonchalant about it all?

So, when the call came about Candy, she'd jumped at the opportunity and kept herself busy with the festival.

Besides, the town needed her. And it needed this event. With tourism down and spirits low, Taste of Harbor Falls could be a bright spot—a celebration of everything local, delicious, and southern. And maybe, just maybe, she'd remember how it felt to be the Suzie who didn't trip over her own heartbeat every time a certain man walked into the room.

"Hey, Suze!"

She turned to see Grace weaving her way across the square wearing a pair of wedges no sane woman should wear on cobblestone. But stuff like that didn't faze her—apropos, as her name was Grace.

Her cousin held two large paper bags in one arm and waved with the other.

"I got candles and gift cards for my raffle basket," Grace announced. "My booth is next to yours. Also, you're a lunatic. This is way too much to take on."

Suzie gave her a tight-lipped smile. "Said the woman who once planned a midnight Valentine's lingerie fashion show in six hours."

"Touché. But I wasn't dodging my feelings. This reeks of avoidance, or something."

Suzie made a mark on her clipboard with more force than necessary. "I'm not dodging anything. I'm just trying to pull off a community-wide event with limited volunteers, dwindling funds, and a million moving parts. Totally normal."

Grace arched a perfectly waxed brow. "Mmhmm. And has Brad volunteered for anything yet?"

"I didn't ask him," Suzie said too quickly. "He's been too busy with some sort of business. I haven't a clue what."

"You didn't have to ask him. He asked me."

She looked up sharply. "What?"

Grace smirked. "Well, I am in charge of booth planning. Right? He's manning that booth over there." She pointed. "Number fifteen."

"I don't understand."

"It's the Falls Lake Lodge booth. Didn't you hear? Apparently, he's bought the old place and plans to renovate. I managed to get the scoop from James Martin. You should see Brad's fancy vision board, and the sample menu cards he's handing out. And, he's donating to the pie auction. Apparently, the man makes a mean bourbon pecan pie."

Of course he does. *And where did you bake those pies, Mr. Matthews?*

But wait.

Vision boards? Sample menu cards? *He bought the old lodge?*

"You should go over there and see what he's doing. I'm surprised he hasn't mentioned it."

Suzie sensed a serious conversation with the man upcoming. She faced Grace. "Later."

Talking to Brad right now, at this moment, could be disastrous —for him and for her. How dare he come to her town and buy property, and not tell her?

"No time like the present. He's really rather hot, Suzie."

"I'm busy." Suzie swallowed any additional retort and turned her focus back to the task at hand. "And as long as he doesn't turn this whole lodge thing into the *Brad Matthews Show*, I'm fine with it."

Grace winked. "You keep telling yourself that."

Suzie huffed. "What I'm telling myself is that Harbor Falls needs a win. That's why I'm doing this. For the town. For the businesses. For the community."

Grace looped her arm through Suzie's. "Sure, sweetie. And not at all to prove to yourself that you're fine without a certain Harley-riding, pie-baking, charm-dripping chef making your hormones stage a coup."

Suzie bit back a cynical laugh, unwilling to give Grace the satisfaction.

But her gaze had a mind of its own, darting over to Brad's booth again. *What is the man up to?*

"Come on," she said, instead of lingering on that thought. "Let's check out Bets Martin's real estate booth. She's likely to turn it into an open house with baked cookies and a mortgage quiz."

They walked off together toward the edge of the square, the hum of small-town life buzzing around them. Kids darted between booths, the Ackermans were arguing over flower arrangements, and someone somewhere was playing a banjo slightly off-key.

Harbor Falls at its finest.

And Suzie—heart muddled, clipboard firm in hand, apron strings double-knotted—was going to survive this weekend, and Brad Matthews, with her head held high.

Probably.

Maybe.

She hoped.

Suzie stopped mid-step in front of booth eleven and blinked.

"What in the homemade hell...?"

Bets Martin had, in fact, turned her real estate booth into a full-blown open house—complete with cookies, coffee, and a life-size cardboard cutout of herself holding a SOLD sign.

A child was licking frosting off the cutout's chin.

"I knew it," Suzie muttered.

Grace snorted behind her. "You did say cookies and a mortgage quiz."

"There's literally a QR code taped to the punch bowl."

"I admire the hustle."

Suzie scribbled an aggressive note on her clipboard and moved along, already behind schedule. She still needed to check vendor power hookups, make sure the bakery booth hadn't caught on fire again (thanks to Claire Harper's "experimental caramel torch"), and confirm the pie auction table hadn't been hijacked by the Baptist Women's Circle.

Again.

What she absolutely, positively, did *not* need was to detour near the Falls Lake Lodge booth. Which meant she had to treat it like a sinkhole. A charming, smug, six-foot-two sinkhole with a slow smile and world-class pastry.

Just keep moving.

She took a sharp right turn toward the gazebo and nearly collided with Greg Monroe, a childhood friend, who held a paper plate stacked with three varieties of ribs in one hand, and a beer in a red Solo cup in the other.

"Easy, Suz. You're gonna take someone out with that clipboard."

"I'm on a schedule, Greg."

He looked at her the way gym teachers look at people who try to fake pull-ups. Of course, he was the high school football coach, so close.

"Sure, you are."

"I am."

"You're also sweating like you just ran a 10K through molasses."

"It's eighty degrees and I'm wearing an apron," she snapped. "And for your information, I'm the only thing standing between this festival and total chaos."

Greg raised an eyebrow and took a bite of rib. "I thought Brad was helping with—"

She stared at him. Stunned. "Brad? Brad Matthews?"

He shrugged. "Yeah."

"And how do you know him?"

Greg glanced toward the lodge booth. "Everyone knows Brad. He bought the lodge. And he's had lunch with us guys over at Sassy's the past two days."

"Excuse. Me?"

Greg held her gaze. "What's the big deal? I like him. I hear you two had a thing going in Asheville. Is that why Cliff flew the coop?"

Suddenly, Suzie's cheeks heated up like a five-hundred-degree oven waiting to sear the fat off a juicy rib-eye. "Un-be-lievable!"

Greg appeared unfazed. "So, is he helping you?"

"Nope," she said quickly. "He's not helping me. He has his own booth. For his own lodge, apparently, which everyone knows about. Except for me, of course. A booth where he does his own things. Things that have nothing to do with me, of course. Or this apron."

Greg blinked. "Right. Totally unrelated."

Suzie spun away, nearly taking out Sarah Harper with her clipboard. Sarah squeaked and dropped her tote bag, sending a pack of lavender-scented essential oils skidding across the pavement like tiny wellness grenades.

"Sorry!" Suzie called back, not slowing down. "So sorry! Smells great though!"

She ducked behind the pie auction tent and exhaled hard. Her pulse was doing that gallopy thing again. Like it knew she was heading into enemy territory. Except the enemy had a charming smile and had baked a bourbon pecan pie that had no business smelling that good.

"Focus," she whispered to herself. "You are not here for Brad Matthews. You are here for the people. The town. The fundraiser. The muffins."

Deal with this lodge mess later!

Taking another deep breath, she squared her shoulders, and marched toward the sign-in table.

Which, unfortunately, meant heading straight toward Booth Fifteen.

THE AIR SMELLED LIKE BARBECUE SMOKE, KETTLE CORN, and blooming crepe myrtles—sweet, tangy, and just enough to make a woman believe anything was possible, even a second chance at love.

Not.

Suzie adjusted the "Taste of Harbor Falls" official volunteer badge clipped to her apron and looked directly at him. Might as well face this head-on.

He stood there, under a blue canopy with *Falls Lake Lodge* stenciled across the top, sleeves rolled up, and a bourbon pecan pie in each hand like he was born for the job.

He saw her at the same moment.

Suzie considered turning on her heel and pretending she needed to check the power cords behind the bandstand. But it was too late. Brad was already heading her way, pie in tow, that slow, sure smile tugging at the corners of his mouth like it knew secrets she didn't want uncovered.

"Afternoon, Suzie-Q."

She crossed her arms, forcing a tight-lipped smile. "Don't call me that in public."

"Got it," he said, unbothered. "Only behind closed doors, then?"

She glared. "What do you want, Brad?"

"To contribute to your wildly successful event. Officially."

He held out the pie. She looked at it, mostly smirking at his offering

"It's for the auction," he said, still watching her too closely. "But I have another for you. It's your favorite. I remember."

Damn him. Of course he remembered.

"Thanks," she said, careful to keep her voice neutral. "But I don't accept bribes."

Brad tilted his head. "Who said anything about bribery? I'm just a local business owner trying to be supportive."

"Yeah. About that. You bought the lodge?"

He nodded. "I did."

"News travels fast."

"Yes. Small town, as they say."

She glared and tapped her pen on her clipboard. "What the hell are you doing, Brad? You bought *the lodge?*"

"You say that in reverence, like it's untouchable, or something.

"It's a local landmark and yes, well respected. What are you going to do with it?"

Brad said nothing, just grinned. After a moment, he leaned closer and whispered near her ear. "Let's talk about that later, Suzette, back at the house. I'll tell you everything. For now, we both have work to do."

"Damn straight."

He handed her the bourbon confection on a tin plate. "Relax and have some pie."

Suzie grasped the pie by the edges and took a half-step back. "Good. You're right. Lots to do. Then you'll support me staying focused. This is a community event. Not a reunion."

Brad's eyes softened. "I'm not trying to make this harder on you. I just... I miss talking to you. Really talking. I hope we can find a moment later, like I said."

She looked around quickly. A couple of townspeople were watching. Greg Monroe stood with his arms crossed, clearly eavesdropping. Sarah Harper was fanning herself three booths away and whispering behind her hand to her aunt Claire, who was, as usual, drinking from a mystery tumbler.

Suzie dropped her voice. "Don't do this here."

"You've been avoiding me all week."

"Because I don't know what this is, Brad. You showing up like this. Saying all the right things. Stirring up everything I've worked hard to move past."

"I'm not trying to stir things up," he said, "but maybe it's time to stop pretending nothing's still there. Between us."

She hated how her heart fluttered at that. Hated more that her silence gave him permission to take a step closer.

"You said this event was about community," Brad added. "Well, I want to be part of it. Of this. Of you. If you'll let me."

Suzie swallowed, then forced a laugh that didn't quite land. "You're very smooth, you know that?"

He grinned. "Only with you."

"I need to get this pie to the auction tent," she said, holding it like a shield. "Excuse me."

But as she turned, he said just loud enough for her to hear, "I'll wait, Suzie. I'm not going anywhere."

She didn't respond, didn't look back. But as she walked away, heart thudding, she realized something terrifying and exhilarating all at once.

She didn't want him to leave.

Not really.

From the Kitchen of Suzie Hart, Sweet Hart Inn

Blog Post, May 21: *Taste of Harbor Falls*

It's been two days, and I still smell like kettle corn.

If you've ever worked a town festival, you know what I mean —the blend of funnel cakes, grilled sausage, handmade soaps, hot pavement, and just a hint of fried anxiety. It's a very *specific* scent. And honestly? I kind of love it.

This year's *Taste of Harbor Falls* was the biggest we've ever hosted. We had booths stretching from the library to the lake trail, a pie auction that made three grown men weep, and a temporary tattoo stand that I am *fairly* certain the mayor visited twice. (Don't worry, Harold. Your secret's safe.)

Sweet Hart Inn had a table set up just beside the bandstand, and we passed out over 300 mini muffin samples before noon. (Note to self: triple the next batch.) I also managed to spill sweet tea on my blouse, negotiate with a child over the last lemon bar, and get absolutely roasted by Claire Harper for wearing shoes she deemed "city slicker impractical."

So... business as usual.

But here's what really stuck with me:

A woman I'd never met before came up to our booth, sampled a muffin, and said, "This tastes like something I didn't know I missed."

And it hit me—how often do we move through life not realizing we've left something behind? A flavor. A memory. A person. A part of ourselves?

This festival was never just about food. It was about flavor, and feeling, and finding our way back to what feeds us.

So, whether you were there for the peach preserves or the porch concerts, thank you. Harbor Falls isn't just a place—it's a recipe. And it only works because of *all* the ingredients.

Today's Recipe: Mini Banana Walnut Muffins with Cinnamon Crunch Tops

2 ripe bananas, mashed
1/3 cup oil
1 egg
1/2 cup sugar
1 tsp vanilla
1 1/2 cups flour
1/2 tsp baking soda
1/2 tsp baking powder
1/4 tsp salt
1/2 cup chopped walnuts

Crunch Topping:
2 tbsp brown sugar
1 tbsp flour
1/4 tsp cinnamon
1 tbsp cold butter, cubed

Mix muffin batter. Spoon into lined mini tins. Combine topping and sprinkle over each. Bake at 375 for 15 minutes.

Bake a batch. Share with someone. Maybe even someone you didn't know you missed.

Always grateful,
Suzie

Chapter Seven

"Aunt Claire's drinking the cooking wine again."

Suzie tossed a glance over her shoulder while slowly stirring the fondue pot filled with a mixture of Emmental and Gruyère cheeses, a little kirsch, and some white cooking wine—the latter of which she'd purposely kept clear from Claire Harper. Or so she had thought. "Precisely why, Sarah Harper, that I do not put the good stuff out for my cooking classes. Although it pains me to cook with anything but real alcohol, I will not waste expensive liquor on your aunt's indulgences."

"Nasty stuff!" Claire replaced the bottle on the counter and toddled away.

Suzie watched the older woman move toward her bedroom, supposing that when one was ninety-one and holding, one could do whatever one wished.

"Sarah, honey, perhaps your auntie is ready for her nap. Why don't you take her back to my bed to doze?"

Always the obedient niece, fifty-year-old Sarah Harper did just that. After a few minutes, she returned. "Aunt Claire will sleep like a baby now."

Suzie swiped her brow with the back of her hand. "Good," she whispered under her breath.

This Saturday's cooking class was a disaster waiting to happen. Now that Claire was safely tucked into bed and out of harm's way, Suzie figured they could get down to business.

She had to admit, it was a motley crew that had assembled this morning for culinary instruction—which may turn out to be more like culinary deconstruction....

Suzie sidled a glance toward Greg Monroe, an unlikely candidate for cooking lessons. She and Greg had been two peas in a pod growing up, their parents still good friends. They had even dated at one point in their early teens—before Cliff. Greg had gone off and made a big name for himself playing professional football for a few years after college. Now, he was the head football coach and athletic director at Harbor Falls High. His new wife, Marnie—the reason for his attendance today—sat to his left. Ever since Marnie had moved to Harbor Falls and fell hopelessly in love with Greg, she and Suzie had also become fast friends.

"Ladies and *gentleman*." Suzie gave a nod to Greg, her gaze then sweeping the women in the group. "Today we're going to discuss the fine art of fondue. It's a great way to use old bread, cheese and leftover wine, and a really cool way to impress a date or hubby." She glanced at Greg again. "Or wife. Spouse, I guess I should say. Of course, most hubbies around here wouldn't know what to do with a fondue if it hit them in the face on a Tuesday afternoon since it didn't once stand on all fours, eat grass, and moo. But nevertheless, the more cultured of us in this small town might like to spice up the moment with something new. Hence, fondue."

Suzie had no earthly idea why she was babbling. Likely had nothing to do with Brad Matthews upstairs in her blue room.

Five sets of eyes stared back at her.

"All right!" She shoved the small fondue pots toward her students. "You each have your own pot and can choose the kind of fondue you want to make. You can cook in broth or oil, make cheese fondue like I've demonstrated, or do a chocolate dessert fondue. The recipes and the ingredients are in front of you. Choose your poison."

Her students appeared hesitant.

Suzie studied Sarah Harper. She appeared confused, looking from Suzie to the fondue pot and back to Suzie again. "Do you need some help, Sarah?"

A sigh came from her lips. "Being a true Libra," she began, "I'll need a moment before I can decide, weighing my choices carefully. I'm not eating meat this week so I can't do the broth fondue. Is the chocolate made with any animal biproducts?"

Suzie screwed up her lips. "Sarah, I have no clue but the chocolate labels are in the garbage. You can look. If it's easier for you, then feel free to take the rest of the cooking wine and join Auntie Claire on my bed."

Sarah seemed to ponder that idea too. "But—"

"I don't know," Suzie said quickly, figuring that whatever question Sarah Harper asked, Suzie would not know the answer. She turned toward Greg, praying for safer territory. "How are things coming over here?"

Greg and Marnie were oblivious. They leaned closer together and mumbled over their choices, finally choosing chocolate with lush strawberries for dipping. Suzie should have known. The stuff of love. Her attention then turned to Steph Brown, still home on pregnancy leave from her downtown government job, who had appeared to talk the fondue choices over with her cooking partner, very young and just-wed Winnie Burns. The two of them decided to do cheese.

"Suzie, one question."

She turned and smiled. "Sure Greg, what's up?"

He grinned one of those half-sideways grins that she'd learned long ago meant trouble. Damn. She was not in the mood for his shenanigans today.

"Well, Ms. Cookie. I must know. What the hell happened to your forehead?"

Suzie's hand flew to the ugly yellowing and blue-green bruised bump above her right eye. She'd covered it up nicely for the festival, but just this moment realized she'd forgotten to put on makeup that morning.

Her cheeks heated. The discussion of the origins of her bump was the last thing she needed or wanted.

"Oh! Well, silly me. Um. A few days ago I was doing some planting..." She turned to the rest of the group. "Did you all see my new hostas on the lake side of the house? Well, I got carried away and stepped back on a shovel and clumsy old me, it flew back and hit me upside the head."

They stared like she had *three* heads or something. It wasn't *that* big of a bump.

"Suzie Hart, you don't have a clumsy bone in your body." Greg grinned again. Damn him. Did he *know* something?

"Well, ha! I guess I did then." She waved him off. "You guys get to work. I'll float around and will be here if you need help." She believed in learning by doing and wasn't about to guide these adults step-by-step through the process. Mistakes were lessons learned, in her book. Failures make for better cooks. They would do it right the next time.

And anything to get them off the subject of her head was fine by her.

"Oh, Suzie. Your flame went out under your pot." Suzie looked toward where Sarah pointed.

"Darn. You're right." The little canned flame under the fondue pot had been difficult to light earlier. Maybe it was out of juice. Or perhaps it just needed re-lit. She reached for the fireplace lighter she had used earlier and snap-snap-snapped it but no spark. "Darn it."

"I think that one's done for," Greg remarked.

Scowling, Suzie bent to inspect the non-flame again. With her lip tucked between her teeth, hands on hips, she rose to assess the situation. "Surely I have another lighter," she said under her breath. After rummaging around in a nearby utility drawer, she finally found a small one. Bending again, she pulled the can-o-flame from under the fondue pot and struggled with the snap-snap-snap of the trigger to ignite a flame.

She looked up. All eyes were still on her.

"Never mind about me, you all go on with your ingredients. When you're ready, we'll light your fires."

She bent to fiddle once more with the lighter. "Darn thing." She snap-snapped. No luck.

"Mind if I try?"

The voice startled her. She rose to find herself face-to-face with a very nice, black T-shirt covered chest—a chest that she knew all too well—and then gazed up into an intoxicating set of deep brown eyes.

Brad. *Hells bells.* "Huh?" She licked her lips.

"Mind if I try lighting your flame?"

Greg guffawed.

Suzie swallowed. "Um."

Grinning like a Cheshire cat, Brad removed the lighter from her hand. Five pairs of eyes were stuck to her like glue. She could feel them, each and every one, and whipped back to face them.

"Are you all going to make fondue or what?"

Five sets of hands scrambled to grab something, hastily assembling their ingredients.

Brad gave Suzie a wink and then bent to fiddle with the lighter. "Fondue is the greatest foodie invention for decades, in my opinion," he said. "Makes use of leftovers and hell, anything with wine is good right?" Within a few seconds, he lit the flame, carefully moved it back under the fondue pot, and handed the lighter back to Suzie. "There, that should do it."

She managed a half-smile. "Um, thanks."

Brad peered into the pot of cheese and then picked up a whisk off the counter. "May I?"

Suzie waved toward the fondue pot. "Of course, Chef."

He grinned. "One of the keys to a good fondue," he began, glancing at the group, "is in the whisking of the cheese and wine mixture." With several rapid flicks of his wrist, he managed to whip the cheese and wine into a batter-like consistency. Suzie couldn't help but notice the sinews of his forearm and wrist and the firm grasp of his long fingers on the whisk. Her gaze traveled up from his wrist, to his forearm, past his elbow to rock-hard biceps—which then led to strong shoulders and his also-muscled and quite sexy chest.

She swallowed. Sighed. And dropped her gaze to his hands again.

Smoothing. Whisking. Kneading her....

Whoa.

A flush of heat snaked up the sides of her neck and settled on her cheeks. Great.

"Suzette?"

She glanced up.

Brad grinned and handed her the whisk. "I'll leave you to your class now."

"Um. Oh. Thank you." She turned to her students, each of whom were staring back at her with blank expressions. "Um, so, Mr. Matthews is a guest here at Sweet Hart Inn this weekend and well, as you can probably tell, he knows his way around a kitchen and other things... I mean, he's a chef, so..." She turned back to Brad, hopefully pleading with her eyes to get the hell out of her kitchen! Why could she not speak coherently around him?

She continued, "We appreciate your time, Chef. I'm sure my students will all benefit from your hands, uh, whisking demonstration, uh, motions, whatever... And, the lighting of the flame thing." *Holy cow. What is wrong with me?*

Brad dipped his head with a devilish grin, leaning slightly toward her, and whispered. "Always ready to light your flame, ma'am." With another wink, he edged out of the room.

Suzie's jaw dropped.

For a moment, no one moved. Then collectively, every woman in the room sighed.

On the heels of that collective exhale, Greg released a loud cackle. "Looks like our Suzie's got herself a boyfriend."

She spun toward Greg. "I most certainly do not!"

"Methinks one protests too loudly and too quickly."

"That's ridiculous. He's a guest. And he just happens to be a chef. That's all."

Greg cleared his throat and gave Marnie a side-eye glance. "Well then tell me, Ms. Cookie. I'm curious about just one thing. That bump on your head have anything to do with the shiner over his left eye? You guys been touching toes or something?" He belly-laughed as he spat out the words.

Marnie side-armed her husband in the gut.

Suzie picked up a strawberry and threw it. She missed his open mouth by a mile.

BRAD SAT ON HIS HARLEY, THE ENGINE RUMBLING, AND glanced back up the hill to the inn, where he'd just left Suzie—a slightly flabbergasted Suzie, he might add. Smiling at that, liking that she obviously cared enough to get flustered, he backed around and headed his bike out her drive and toward Harbor Falls. Mentally, he ticked off the day's to-do list—busy day.

He had another appointment with James at his office downtown. The bank holding the note on the lodge had apparently accepted his offer but James had written a couple of contingencies into the contract regarding the inspection and appraisal, so they had some work to do there. Brad also needed to locate an inspector.

Those were the first two things on his list.

He had an initial appointment with a contractor set up for one o'clock, a stop down at city hall to check on permits and the like— he had to do that before they closed at noon—and after that, a meeting the town planner James had mentioned to him yesterday. He'd been busy making calls all morning.

After all, if he planned to live and work in Harbor Falls, he wanted to contribute to the community, and he wanted to know what kind of future this community was looking at. If this new business of his could play a role in boosting the small town's economy, he wanted to do it right.

All good things, in his book. A thrill of excitement about his pending future zipped through him as he sped along Lake Road heading toward town. Things might not have ended on the best note with Suzie last night, but this morning he could see the confusion, and the desire, in her eyes. All he needed was to convince her that he was the right man for her, and that she was exactly the right woman for him.

Things were looking up.

SUZIE MADE ONE LAST SWIPE AT THE COOKING ISLAND and glanced about. The kitchen was back in order. Finally. Breadcrumbs swept away. Cheese and chocolate drips wiped clean. Every one of her students was sent home with a plastic container of their fondue-of-choice and dippers du jour.

She'd even taken an hour this afternoon late to write her next blog post.

What a day.

Even her bones ached.

She was ready for more bubble therapy but that was not happening yet.

She glanced at her kitchen wall clock, a retro-version of a black cat with a swinging tail, silhouetted against her yellow walls, ticking off the seconds.

Four-forty-three.

"Hell's bells."

The town meeting was at five. She needed to get moving.

No time to change, or upload the post—no worries, she can do that later. But she did manage a quick look in the bathroom mirror and frowned at the face staring back—the face that had started out that morning sans make-up and was worse for the wear now because of it. And no time to slather makeup over the bump. She pulled her long hair into some semblance of a ponytail, drew a baseball cap over her head—mindful of the bump—and headed for the back door. At the last second she paused at her bedroom full-length mirror and took in her reflection.

Ugh.

She had a little height—that helped. And at thirty-four she supposed she wasn't too pudgy. Her snug jeans fit nicely at her hips and she still had a hint of a waist. At least she wasn't top-heavy and didn't look dowdy. She hated dowdy. She leaned closer. Disregarding the bruise, her complexion was nice. Pale and clear skin, a smattering of freckles, no age blemishes. Hair. Still long and thick and....

She was still five years older than Brad.

Ugh. Ugh!

She turned and studied herself back and front for a moment longer. Could Brad really be interested in her? Did she have what it takes? Him being a younger man and all? It didn't bother her eighteen months ago.

Or him.

Did it?

Forget about it, Suzie.

But—*was* she interested? She hated to admit it, but she was. Darned hard to forget those blissful two months she spent in his arms. She had to admit the memories of their nights together had warmed her on cold lonely nights this past winter.

And she still got hot every time he was near. Like this morning.

Damn him for interrupting her cooking class and setting her cheeks on fire.

Could she even consider it?

Was she really the reason he came back? To get back together? Permanently?

What other reason could there be?

The chime of her grandfather clock signaled five o'clock. She raced out the bedroom door and stumbled down her back steps. Lucky for her the antique was permanently set ten minutes fast. Although she had tried, there was nothing she could do to set it right. Most days it worked to her advantage.

Like now.

From the Kitchen of Suzie Hart, Sweet Hart Inn

Blog Post, May 27: *Cooking Class Confidential*

There should be a reality show called "When Cheese Goes Rogue."

This morning's fondue class at Sweet Hart Inn took a turn for the dramatic when Aunt Claire mistook the cooking wine for sipping wine (again), Greg Monroe lit his fondue canister with what looked suspiciously like a camping torch, and Sarah Harper had a Libra-induced crisis about whether to choose chocolate or cheese.

For the record, she went with both. As one should.

I started these cooking classes thinking I'd offer helpful culinary tips, maybe a little recipe sharing, and a fun evening out for folks in town. I did *not* expect matchmaking sidebars, impromptu confessions of love (you know who you are), or the great "cheddar incident" of cooking pair number three.

And yet... This is why I love it.

Food brings people together. Sometimes it brings *way* more than we bargained for—burnt edges, bubbly messes, miscommunications—but it also brings laughter, memories, and second chances.

If you've ever needed an excuse to stir something sweet, call up your best friend and say, "Want to melt some chocolate and talk about life?" You're officially invited to join us next class.

Recipe: Dark Chocolate Dipping Sauce (aka The Love Potion)
1 cup heavy cream
8 oz dark chocolate chips or chunks
1/2 tsp vanilla extract
A pinch of sea salt

Heat cream to a simmer. Pour over chocolate. Stir until smooth. Dip strawberries, marshmallows, secrets, and second chances.

Now, I need to run off to a town meeting and solve world problems. More to come.

Stay sweet,
    Suzie

Chapter Eight

Suzie rushed out the backdoor and skipped down the deck steps.

Her Mazda sat pointed toward the road. She slipped inside and pushed the key button to start the engine. Brad's bike was no longer parked on the gravel lane. She'd not seen him since his fondue demonstration, which was fine. She wasn't in the right frame of mind to deal with him. Yet.

Maybe he'd realized that.

Earlier that morning he'd been in and out of the house, making calls from her front porch. Business, he'd said, when she'd laid out coffee and muffins. He'd grabbed a to-go cup, filled it to the brim with her special blend, plucked up two fresh-baked signature muffins, and headed back out to the porch rocker—a spot that he had apparently claimed as his temporary office.

And that was the way it had been since the festival. He dodged her questions and avoided her presence if he were at the inn—and when he went into town, he was silent about his doings there.

So be it.

None of your business, Suzie.

However... She had to wonder about the lodge, why he had

bought it, and what kind of business Brad Matthews had in Harbor Falls because of it.

She'd think about that later. Right now, she was running late for the town meeting. Luckily, Harbor Falls' town hall was only seven and a half minutes away, if one drove the speed limit.

Which she did. Of course. Usually.

The meeting this evening was one in a series to discuss the natural progression of Harbor Falls' growth. Most of the town residents were for development and job security. They wanted the factory to come to town. Others wanted to keep Harbor Falls as it was—a replica of Mayberry R.F.D. Suzie found herself somewhere in the middle. Although, she was all for doing whatever was needed to keep the town's economy stable, she felt the goal could be accomplished by successfully revitalizing Harbor Falls' downtown business district, which was definitely on the upswing the past couple of years. Making good with what was already here, rather than leveling prime woods outside of town to build big box stores or adding an industrial park, made sense to her.

She favored preservation and she valued history. She was a strong proponent for the respectful renewal of their quaint downtown and the surrounding lake and mountain areas, and firmly believed preserving the past would be the key to bringing more visitors and shoppers into their town.

She, like many others, didn't want Harbor Falls to become another strip mall destination shopping site—like in some of the mountain towns in Tennessee. Although she liked to shop at malls as much as anyone, she couldn't imagine living with one down the street. She wanted her little mountain town to stay the same—just be more economically sound.

The Mayor and the Town Council had been meeting with local committee members, town planners, business developers, and consultants over the past year. Tonight, the topic was on the local economy and how to keep Harbor Falls alive and vital for future generations.

Suzie rushed into the room and fell into an empty back row seat. Glancing at the filled and busy room, she searched to see who all was there. Greg and Marnie sat several seats down to her right. James Martin to her left. Her friend Nora Patterson, who owned Nora's Novel Niche, sat in front. Nora was a steadfast proponent of downtown preservation. Her father had owned the bookstore there for years, before Nora took it over.

Suzie's cousins, Grace and Sydney, were positioned near the front of the room. Both small business owners were huge supporters of the downtown area too. Sydney owned the local bakery, and Grace had a boutique shop. Eliza Kelley, who owned The Trading Post, sat several seats down from them. Finally, she spied old Mr. and Mrs. Wilson, whom she needed to avoid like the plague, if possible, across the room.

A warm body sat down next to her.

She glanced at the latecomer as Mayor Harold Cunningham hammered the gavel on a wooden podium, on which a poster was tacked that read, *Support Local Merchants. Save Harbor Falls' Trees and Forests!* Simultaneously, she caught a hint of a familiar men's cologne and turned to an eye toward that warm body and spied a sexy black t-shirt.

Brad leaned close. "Promises to be an interesting evening, huh?"

Taken aback, she nodded. "Could be, I suppose. I'm just here for the info."

Brad cocked his head. "I hear there could be a hot topic on the agenda."

Her interest piqued, she stared. "Oh? And how would you know that? You've been in town all of what...? Five days?"

"Four." He shrugged and smiled. "But I get around."

I bet. Suzie turned toward Harold Cunningham who introduced the council's recently hired town planner consultant. He appeared a slimy fellow and she didn't like the looks of him at all.

Of course, looks could be deceiving. She'd reserve judgement until she heard what he had to say.

The man had a narrow chicken face and his round, wire-rimmed glasses tilted on the end of his nose as he looked down at everyone. She'd seen him around, poking in and out of stores and businesses. Asking questions. He even came to see her once at the inn. He was probably an okay guy but his questions were a little alarming—at least to her. She wasn't quite sure what his role or task was in all of this. Guess she'd find out tonight.

He droned on about local economy and the employment rate. He mentioned the necessity to capitalize on Harbor Falls' natural resources, its people, and their talents. He stressed the needs of the community. He ranted about positive growth, keeping Harbor Falls green, and the strong revitalization of downtown. All things they'd heard before.

Brad leaned closer, his elbows propped on his knees, listening intently. She glanced sideways at him, catching a new-found sparkle in his eye. For a moment, she studied his profile, and then the droning dragged her away.

The chicken-beaked consultant continued, this time with dire news. New threats to the economy. The drop-out rate. Unemployment. Loss of population in the town. Young people moving to the cities for jobs. No commerce to support college graduates. No local industry to support entry-level workers.

The bottom line: arts and crafts, mom and pop, home-spun and home-grown, and Mother Nature just wouldn't cut it anymore, on their own. Harbor Falls needed more.

Huh?

Suzie screwed up her face and glanced around her. She was *mom and pop*, well, *mom* and was doing okay. Right? What was this man saying? By the looks on the faces around her, she wasn't the only one concerned.

Greg cleared his throat and stood. With a confidence gained from his years playing football, he commanded quite a presence and demanded attention when he wanted it. Harold acknowledged him.

"So let me make sure I understand," he nodded toward the consultant, "you're saying that Harbor Falls needs to make changes? That the downtown isn't going to make it? That we need more? More of what?"

The older man nodded. "Your economy is gradually dwindling. To be honest, it needs a swift kick in the butt. Your young people need to work and there are no jobs. If jobs don't come here within the next five years, your beautiful little town could become a ghost town."

Small gasps went up in the crowd.

Greg countered. "But our downtown is booming. My wife recently opened a store that outdid itself this past month. Business is getting better all the time. She just hired a new part-time worker yesterday."

The consultant stepped around the podium and looked toward Marnie. "Yes, I understand. I've spoken at length with your wife, Mr. Monroe. The fact of the matter is, as successful as her new baby boutique business appears to be today, she'll likely close shop within two years. I predict she won't make it."

Marnie stood up. "Wait a minute. Babies are always a good business. If there is one thing we can count on in life people keep having babies and people need affordable clothing for those children. I defy you to rubber stamp the demise of my business. I seriously question your ability to..."

Suzie watched Greg lay a hand on his wife's forearm. She stopped talking and looked to her husband, then back toward the mayor. "I just want to say—for the record—that I disagree with the assessment of your so-called, narrow-minded, seriously off-target, and quite a bit rude, consultant."

She planted herself back in her chair seat and tugged her husband's sleeve to join her.

The consultant paused to glance about. "If babies are such a hot commodity, Mrs. Monroe, then why is the school board considering closing the elementary school due to lack of students?" He paused for a moment, then said, "If I could continue..."

Suzie registered the scowl on Marnie's face. Uh-oh. Not a happy face.

"As I look out on this crowd, I see a number of small business owners here," he spanned the crowd. "In addition to the lovely and persistent Ms. Monroe, I've interviewed most. Each of you will be hard-pressed to make a profit in the next three-to-five years." The consultant's gaze landed on Suzie and stuck.

Suzie swallowed and glared back.

"For example, the Sweet Hart Inn."

Swallowing harder and biting her tongue, Suzie countered his gape. "Go on," she urged. *I can't wait to hear this.*

He nodded. "Like most of the businesses in Harbor Falls, the focus is too broad. You need targeted marketing and branding. You need a business plan with gumption, focusing your efforts on the parts of the business that are providing you a proven return on your investment, instead of dallying with efforts such as cooking classes. You should, perhaps, focus on wedding and honeymoon packages and do away with the bed and breakfast and cooking themes altogether. You should be—"

Themes? She'd heard enough. "Ridiculous!" Suzie jumped up and shouted the word before she realized it. She didn't care. It was about time someone truly spoke up defending their little community. "The sheer fact that you are recommending my inn as a honeymoon destination location shows how little you know about me, my business, or this town. You just lost all credibility with me, sir. How dare you come here and tell us we are doomed! Or tell me what my heart-and-soul business should be made up of."

"Successful businesses are not run by the heart-and-soul, Ms. Hart."

She bristled. "The hell they aren't! Small business is all about heart-and-soul, Mr. Consultant. That's who we are here. The residents of Harbor Falls aren't about to give up, or to change, on your advice. We persevere. We work hard. We live our dreams. We don't give up. And we don't change our business models on the advice of some outside town planner consultant who has no earthly idea who we are or what we are about!"

Silence fell over the crowd, then a slow and sporadic applause erupted throughout the town hall. Suzie jerked her shoulders back and stood a little taller. It felt darn good to stand up for something she believed in.

A lone voice came from the back of the room. "That may be well and good, however, perseverance doesn't pay the bills, Suzie."

"Wait a minute." She glanced behind her. Who was that? "Most of us are small business owners. We're not struggling, are we?"

Another blanket of silence fell over the crowd as a slow realization seemed to set in.

"My daughter went off to college and never came back." The response edged up from someone to her right.

"Tired of living from check-to-check, wondering each month which bill I might have to wait to pay," squeaked out another.

"The kids say there is nothing here for them," came one more.

Suzie crossed her arms. "I don't get it." She set her gaze on several faces. "Harbor Falls is beautiful! We have so much to offer. Nothing for the kids? We have a mountain and a lake and...."

"That's great for recreation, Suzie," Harold interjected. "The kids want real jobs. They go away to college and get their degrees, see the world, and don't want to come back and work in a craft shop, stock shelves at Ralph's, wait tables at the diner, or work at the marina."

A cacophony of voices burst forth. Heads bobbed back and forth discussing the situation with their neighbors.

"But we sure as hell don't need a damn factory to ruin our beautiful landscape!"

"My kid wants a job at Valu-Mart. Why can't we have a Valu-Mart?"

Nora Patterson shot to her feet. "Because those of us who love downtown Harbor Falls will lose our businesses. That is why we don't need a Valu-Mart! My bookstore would be doomed with a Valu-Mart on the outskirts of town. So would Sydney's bakery, and Eliza's Trading Post, and Grace's gift shop, just to name a few."

Nora continued, "And we've worked so hard to rebuild our downtown. We got that grant money. And people shop here. It's on the tourist route. Why, didn't we have a bus load of senior citizens here last week from Ohio?"

Oh, hell, Suzie thought. What is happening? She searched the room. Where was...? "Eliza!" She pointed to the owner of the Trading Post, who had been actively strategizing to increase marketing tactics to lure more consumers to Harbor Falls. "Tell them about the Harbor Falls Market Square project and what a success that was this past fall. The website. The marketing strategy. The entrepreneurship project and the plans for this coming fall. We are not doomed. We are actively taking steps to bring tourists and buyers to the downtown area. Eliza, please tell them!"

Eliza stood halfway up when Harold Cunningham cracked his gavel on the podium. She sat back down with a frown.

"Another time." He pounded the gavel again with a rat-a-tat-tat. "If I could have your attention. Attention *please!*"

The rampant discord in the crowd abruptly stopped and everyone turned the mayor's way. How was old Harold going to handle this one? Elections were around the corner and if he stepped too much one way or the other, he could either lose his job or be set for another term.

"Folks let's be reasonable here," he said slowly. "There may be a solution, so let's hear some alternatives. We're not finished yet. James?"

The crowd turned to James Martin. Suzie noticed Brad shift in his seat. She had been so caught up in all of the action she'd almost forgotten he was there. No. How could she forget the smell of his after-shave wafting toward her and the heat of his thigh searing against hers? Suddenly she was drawn to him like flies on honey. Leaning his way, and resisting the urge to lay her hand on his thigh, she whispered, "Wonder what this is all about?"

Brad angled toward her. What was it about him that turned her on so much? Despite the fact that he spilled over with decadent sex appeal?

James cleared his throat and rose. Reluctantly, Suzie skidded her gaze away from Brad and focused on the Realtor.

"I know all of this is a touchy subject," James said, "but I think there are alternatives. I've been working with our consultant and others, and perhaps we can come to an agreement about the kind of development that could benefit Harbor Falls' economy. Suzie is right, our natural resources are a draw, despite what we've heard here tonight. The lake. The mountains. Tourists do come for recreation, to buy local crafts, and the like."

An angry male voice bubbled up from the back of the room. "Ah, hell, James. You just want to sell land. You don't care about the economy."

James's face turned all but purple. "I want what is good for our town and the people who live in it. I think we can invest in projects that can do just that. We have to be picky and plan for the kind of growth we want. For example, we've done a great job revitalizing downtown and I differ slightly in opinion from what our consultant says." He glanced to his right at Eliza Kelley.

Suzie smiled. She'd known when Eliza had stayed at the inn a few months ago while she was finding a home in Harbor Falls that something was up between her and James. The way he looked at her just now confirmed that. Eliza's Trading Post was taking off. Business was good. And Suzie would bet nickels that Eliza would be hard-pressed to admit her new business wasn't a good thing.

"So, I'd like to elevate this conversation and introduce someone who can explain a new project. I think you will like this. It will bring jobs and support the local economy, as well as revitalize a bit of our past. Mr. Matthews has a plan. Folks, meet Brad Matthews."

Suzie's breath caught in her throat. *What the serious hell?*

Brad rose. "Thanks, James." Suzie watched him shove his hands into his jean pockets, then toss a nervous glance her way. He looked...uncertain. And that was an anomaly for Brad Matthews, who was the most self-assured man she'd ever met. He faced the crowd.

"I'll be brief. One solution, it appears to me, is to capitalize on what you already have. The downtown is great. Tourists ride in here every week on buses. They stay for a couple of hours, buy lunch, a few souvenirs, and then leave. I think one way to boost the economy is to provide quality lodging services so tourists will stay longer."

Suzie sat straighter in her chair, her back ramrod stiff. Her attention was definitely at high pique with this particular statement. Harbor Falls *had* quality lodging services. *The Sweet Hart Inn!*

He didn't look at her. Coward.

"Old Falls Lodge was a boon in its heyday. People came in droves to experience the mountains, stay the week, and unwind. They would plan their entire vacations around the availability at the lodge. Since the bankruptcy more than thirty-five years ago, the lodge has sat abandoned, empty and virtually unused."

Suzie scooted to the edge of her seat, her face growing warm. What in the hell was he proposing? The room was silent.

He measured the crowd. "Look, I know I am an outsider. The residents of Harbor Falls don't know me from Adam but I've been studying your town for a while and I've decided to move here."

Abruptly, Suzie broke into a choking fit. Someone behind her reached over to pat her hard on the back. She glanced to her rear through watery eyes and nodded her thanks to Geraldine and then swung her gaze around to Brad.

"Sorry, please go on. I find this information extremely interesting." She glared, not entirely certain she understood the look he shot back.

Brad returned to the crowd. "I've purchased the old lodge." A twitter of conversation broke in the room. "And the surrounding sixty-two acres. I've been meeting with local contractors, zoning, utilities, and the town council. I am prepared to put a lot of money into the local economy in two ways. One, by providing jobs for locals in the construction of a new mega-hotel, restaurant and spa on the old Falls Lake Lodge site. Two, once it is finished, providing a hefty number of jobs required to run the business, in the areas of hotel management, culinary arts, recreation and relaxation, housekeeping, maintenance and such. I believe, and your town council agrees, that this is a viable compromise to the situation. The 'kick in the butt' as the consultant so eloquently put it."

A palpable pause settled about the still room. Suzie didn't know what to think or say. An ache landed in the pit of her gut—the kind of ache she usually only got when she knew something was off-kilter. She wanted to stand but wasn't sure her legs worked.

"You're tearing down old Falls Lodge?" Mr. Wilson feebly raised his hand and uttered the words. "My wife and I were married there sixty years ago last month."

Suzie's heart fell. The lodge was old and abandoned but it was a part of their history. Mr. and Mrs. Wilson were old, too. Did that mean you just got rid of them? No.

"Unfortunately, the lodge will have to go." Brad took a deep breath, his face as hard as stone. "And part of the mountain. Not much, because we want to preserve what we can but we need more level land."

Finally, Suzie found her legs and rose. Her jaw tight and her fists clenched, she directed to Brad, "Surely you are not serious, Brad. You're going to level our lodge and blow up our mountain? Do you want to suck the lake dry, too?"

Brad fixed his gaze on her and she fixed hers right back.

Yes, I am angry. Damn angry. Not only was Brad ruining part of Harbor Falls' history, but he was single-handedly, albeit perhaps unknowingly, destroying her business as well. How in the hell would Sweet Hart Inn size up against the likes of a mega-hotel and spa?

It wouldn't. In the matter of a few minutes, her *fling* had managed to kill everything she'd worked so hard for the past year and longer. She wasn't about to sit around and let that happen. Not for one moment. She had to set him straight.

Now.

Chapter Nine

To say he was taken aback at Suzie's declaration was an understatement. Brad took in her wide-eyed gaze, her stiff-armed stance, and was suddenly gut-punched. He had some explaining to do, and quick.

But Suzi was not about to give up. "So, I'll ask again," she said. "Are you planning to blow up our mountain?"

He turned toward her and lowered his voice. "What I said was that we needed to level more land. Can we talk about this later? Right now, I need to get on with this meeting. You and I can hash this out back at your place."

Voices flitted through the crowd.

Suzie ignored the chatter.

"Brad, you can't raze the lodge and blow up the mountain!"

He shook his head and his voice raised again. "Most likely we'll clear off a few acres of trees and yes, we will need to dynamite to make way for...."

Suzie stepped forward, shaking her head. "So, you *are* going to blow up the mountain, kill several hundred trees, level a piece of local history, and ruin the view from my home and business? A small "mom and pop" business, I might add, that according to Mr.

Consultant here—" she swept her arm toward the front of the room, "—is doomed in a couple of years, anyway? Is that what you are thinking?"

"Suzette...."

By now the argument was largely between the two of them. She put up her hand. "No. Stop, Brad. Stop right where you are. It's time for you to go. Time for you to cut your losses and get out of town. You are not wanted here. We don't need your super, mega-hotel slash five-star-restaurant slash spa. We've survived on what we have for many, many years and we'll do quite nicely after you and your ideas are gone. So *leave*, Mr. Matthews. Please."

Suddenly it felt like his world was spinning out of control and taking his gut with it. That *please* did him in more than anything, particularly when he registered the ache in her eyes as she said it. Brad watched the woman who lambasted him—the same woman who held the key to his heart, unfortunately—and knew he needed to back pedal and fast.

"Suzie...."

A male voice boomed up from across the room and Brad angled his gaze that way. The man in the cooking class yesterday. Greg Monroe. Local football jock, he'd learned from his lunch outings downtown.

"Suzie," Monroe continued, "this man's idea is not a bad one."

Surprised, Brad watched Suzie swivel toward him. "You can't be serious, Greg. What good would this idea do for Harbor Falls?"

"Think about it," he urged. "There are a lot of jobs connected to a project like this and it sounds as though he has considered what is important to our town. It's not a discount department store or a factory. If we have to invest in something, to keep our downtown the way it is, this could be the better option."

"For whom?" Her nostrils flared when she glanced from face to expectant face. "What about keeping all of our businesses the same? I'm not downtown but I'm still Harbor Falls and I still count!"

She turned, leveling her gaze firmly on Brad. "Mr. Matthews is only considering one thing, himself. And I can't believe all of you have fallen for it." Her words cut like ice.

Mr. Matthews? "Suzie, please. Let me explain."

But she jerked her gaze away and yanked at his heart at the same time. Her eyes looked a little misty and that notion tore at his heartstrings. Dammit. He'd screwed up royally here. He had totally thought he was doing the right thing, for her, for the town, for everyone, but—

"Go back to Asheville, Brad. That's where you belong. Go back before we all regret it." Suzie stumbled away. His heart as heavy as it had ever been, he helplessly watched her head for the door, making an ungraceful getaway by shuffling over empty, metal folding chairs as well as a few Harbor Falls citizens' feet.

She was one pissed off woman.

No. That wasn't a pissed-off look. That was hurt. Pure and simple.

Brad released a loud, long pent-up breath and glanced back to the crowd, all of whom had witnessed the entire exchange between them.

Dammit.

Yet, he couldn't do anything about that at this moment. He perused the crowd watching him, and knew he had some more talking to do. "I understand she is upset," he said to the townsfolk, "but I would sure like to continue this conversation, if we could."

The mayor nodded. "Let's get down to business."

Tucked into an Adirondack chair facing the lake, Suzie sniffled and swiped a tear from the corner of her eye, then hugged her knees a little tighter under her chin. *I am not going to lose everything I have worked so hard for.* She stared at the shadow of old Lake Lodge across the way and sighed.

Dusk was falling and a full moon sat low over the water, casting a mellow glow on the scene before her. Quiet. Peaceful. Waves rocked against the old dock pilings where she tied her small motorboat, soothing both her soul and her demeanor. Her trolling motor was great for tooling around and doing a little fishing and she loved early mornings on the lake in her little cove. A few miles down the lakeshore at the park, paddleboats were the thing. Everybody loved those, kids and oldsters alike. Fishing and speedboats generally stayed on the deeper end of the lake near the marina—there was a low speed limit for boats in this residential area—far removed from where she sat right now.

This was another reason why she loved this place of hers, this town. There was a lot to offer. Another reason why she disliked what Brad had proposed to the community tonight.

She hated crying and didn't do it often. She felt damn proud of herself that she'd held her tears in all the way home from town and for at least a full five minutes while sitting there.

Then little by little they started falling, and she had started unraveling.

How long *had* she been sitting there, anyway?

It didn't matter. What mattered was that yet again she had made a damn fool out of herself in front of the entire town, and she was confused as hell about the real reason Brad was here.

His coming back wasn't really for her, was it? It was for the lodge. It was so he could create his own business and make inroads in the community. His coming to Harbor Falls was in no way connected to making her his—maybe even she was a way in for him, a means to his end.

What a damn fool she had been.

She thought about that for a minute, still staring at the image of the lodge in the distance. It all made sense. Eighteen months had gone by—why did he wait so long to come after her? He was getting his plan together, that's why. The man she just described in her head was not the Brad she knew eighteen months ago. He wouldn't have used her like then then, and he wouldn't now.

Would he?

Sniffling, she pushed her hair away from her forehead and lifted her gaze to watch the mountain opposite the lake. If she searched real hard, she could see silhouettes of some of the smaller cabins, too, tucked in the trees around the lodge. She supposed Brad bought those as well—he said so, right? They were part of the original property. All had been deserted for years. She'd heard so many stories from the locals about the past, about how Falls Lake Lodge was a sought-after summer destination place in the fifties and sixties, kind of like a southern Catskills. She chuckled, imagining the setting to be like the 80s movie *Dirty Dancing*.

Would it have been like that?

Could it be again?

Nonsense.

Times were different now.

You had to have money to stay back then, she was certain. Maybe that's why it all went away. The late sixties and seventies were different times. Priorities changed. Families didn't, couldn't, take off a whole summer to play golf or take Merengue and Mambo lessons. It all when went away before she was born but she'd heard the stories from her parents and older family members.

When she was a teenager, she and some friends had camped on the site, braving ghost stories and mountain folklore. They even broke into the old lodge one evening—her parents would have killed her had they found out or had she gotten caught for trespassing. They spent the night on the ballroom floor in their sleeping bags, actually sleeping very little, while daring ghosts and goblins to roll down the winding stairway to haunt them.

That didn't happen, of course. The only heebie-jeebies they got were the ones they brought on themselves. That and a few bottles of gawd-awful strawberry wine.

The lodge was magnificent, however, and made a lasting

impression on her. To this day she would sit, right where she sat at this moment, to look and wonder. She could only imagine what it had been like in its heyday. Back then she saw through the dust and cobwebs. She marveled at the rich pine plank floors, huge log beams, the incredible stairway and landing, chandeliers made from curvy wood branches and deer antlers, and a stained-glass window to die for on the second-floor landing. Often, she had daydreamed of what it could someday be again.

Gone.

If Brad had his way, it would all be gone. And she might as well say Sweet Hart Inn would be gone, too.

"Damn him," her whispered curse floated on a breeze. She swiped her nose. "And I was just beginning to get used to the possibility of having him around."

The drone of an engine came closer, moving steadily toward her home. The Harley. Unmistakable. *Shit.*

She didn't want to see him.

The house was dark. She couldn't remember whether she'd locked up or not. Had she given Brad a front door key? Honestly, she didn't care. He was a big boy and could fend for himself. He could sleep on the porch glider for all she cared. And she'd gladly charge him a nightly rate for doing so.

She slinked down in the Adirondack and remained perfectly still. She wasn't in the mood for company or conversation with anyone, least of all him. Her brain and her heart were confused and working overtime trying to figure out her next steps. She needed to be alone. It wouldn't be the first time she'd spent the night in this chair overlooking the lake. She might as well enjoy the view while she had it.

No lights illuminated the windows or the porch of Sweet Hart Inn. Brad glanced around while tucking his helmet onto the bike seat. Suzie's Mazda was parked further up the drive, near the back of the house. He moved toward the front porch, listening for any sound that indicated she was home.

Perhaps she'd gone to the meeting with a friend, and they weren't home yet. No, it couldn't be, he reasoned. Her Mazda was parked on the street in front of the town hall earlier. But maybe she'd come home and left again. Wouldn't she leave a porch light on or something?

Was she already asleep? Had she barricaded herself in her owner's suite for the night?

He took the steps to the wrap-around porch, his boot heels echoed against the night. He reached for the screen door, opened it, and jiggled the door's brass handle. It swung open. Would she go somewhere and leave her house unlocked? He couldn't imagine anyone doing that. Not in this day. Not even in Harbor Falls.

He locked the front door behind him and took a quick walk through the foyer, the dining room, and then the kitchen, and finally toward her private quarters. The door there was left ajar and the room was dark.

The house was empty.

Where was she? He really needed to talk with her. She had misunderstood. He had to set things right.

He glanced out the back door. The large upper windowpane expertly framed a serene picture of a lake, moon and mountain.

Breathtaking.

He'd bet his inheritance that Suzie thought so, too.

Chapter Ten

Suzie sensed Brad's presence before she heard his footsteps shuffling in the damp grass. She knew it was him. Who else would it be? She silenced her sniffles and sucked in a steadying breath and willed herself not to look his way. If she didn't give him the time of day, perhaps he would give up and go away.

Not likely. She was pretty much a captive audience here.

Just don't look his way. Don't give in. Stand your ground, Suzie.

"Suzie-Q?"

He stood beside her chair as he spoke his nickname for her. His low voice rippled over her like the waves lapping at the dock. The sound was a little unsettling since it came to her with an edge of concern and perhaps empathy. She stared straight ahead.

Don't. Look. At. Him.

But that was impossible. Brad moved around the chair and crouched directly in front of her, blocking her view of the lake. He gazed into her face. She glared passed his right shoulder.

"Suzette. You have to talk to me."

She opened her mouth. *No. Don't. Talk.* Then snapped it shut again.

He fidgeted but remained steadfast.

"I know you are mad."

"Ha!" *Shit.*

"But let me explain," he continued. "And it is okay if you are mad because, well, hey, let's face it, a lot of things have happened in the last few days and I'm sure you're pretty confused and upset and...."

She glared. "You have a lot of nerve, Brad Matthews, coming back here and talking to me like this. You have a *helluva* lot of nerve. I do not want to talk to you. Now. Later. Ever. Go away."

Suzie watched his face fall and his head lower. His dark hair shimmered against the moonlight. Was he staring at her bright red toenails? That felt way too sexy for her liking at the moment. She curled her toes up under her feet.

Might as well get this over with. She cleared her throat and punched his shoulder. Brad jerked his head up.

"Do you realize what you did tonight? You nailed the coffin on my business, Brad. My blood-sweat-and-tears, my hard fought and won existence, the rest of my life." She straightened in the chair. "My only life. Do you understand that? This...." she slapped a hand on the wooden chair, "is my life. All I have. Did you not think about what your super-mega-freaking honker of a hotel is going to do to me? What in the hell were you thinking?" Her voice rose. "And, you said you came back here because you wanted me. Because you wanted us to get back together. What was I thinking? I was even starting to consider the possibilities, but now... I hope you realize that you've killed any chance of that, Mister."

He took in a deep breath while still looking at her toes—which caused heat to rise in her cheeks and was rather unnerving—then he reached for her ankles, clasped his long and strong fingers around them, and jerked. In a flash, he pulled her completely off the Adirondack chair and toppled backwards.

She fell on top of him.

They rolled.

He laughed.

She spewed a number of obscenities.

Finally, they landed in a heap against the hull of an old dry-docked boat. Suzie, unfortunately, was firmly pinned beneath Brad —a position she didn't want to be in at the moment. "Ouch! Get off me."

"Hold still," he told her.

"Get *off* me, Brad." She pushed.

"Give me a second your leg is wrapped around mine."

"I've lost my flip-flop, dammit!" She twisted and batted at his chest.

"Stop pushing."

"What the hell do you think you were doing? I think you broke my neck."

"Hell. I did not break your neck. Would you quit squirming?" Brad groaned but didn't move one iota.

"I want up now!"

Damn him. She could tell by the way the moonlight backlit the smirk on his face that he had no intention of moving.

Damn. Him.

She whacked at his bicep. "I'm not kidding, Brad. This isn't one bit funny. Let me up!"

Brad grasped her wrists and pinned her hands back to the ground, at ear level. "Not until you listen to me."

Shaking her head, she returned, "I don't need to listen to you. I want up. I want to go into my house. I want you to leave."

He shook his head. "Not a chance, sweetheart. You are going to hear me out."

"Like hell I will."

"Suzette."

"Quit with the Suzette and Suzie-Q, Brad. I don't like it."

He chuckled. "Yes, you do, honey. You always did." He swiped a strand of hair out of her eye. Suzie stifled the tremble that wanted to race up through her chest at his touch.

She sighed and softened her voice. "Quit changing the subject. I mean it. Let me up now."

He didn't. He looked at her. And the way he looked at her, all dreamy-eyed and everything—she wanted to melt. Gosh-darn full moon. Why in the hell was the man so god-awful delicious?

She turned her head to the side.

Brad grasped her chin and gently moved her face back toward his. His warm touch was firm and downright magical. In the next instant, his mouth lowered to capture hers.

"Suzette..." he whispered.

Don't kiss him.

Oh. Hell's bells.

She'd forgotten how soft and firm his lips could be, all at the same time. How they tasted of spice and musk. Strong and smooth. Hot and wet and....

Tantalizing and painful.

Oh....

He nibbled softly at first, his fingers stroking her chin. He relaxed more fully against her and dammit, she felt herself letting go.

Putty. Butter.

Goner. Yup.

He moaned and pressed his lips over the corners of her mouth. His fingers tangled in her hair. Her body arched upward and her hands moved to that thick crown of wild hair on his head.

Damn him. Damn him to hell and back.

IN ONE SWIFT MOVEMENT, BRAD STOOD AND SCOOPED Suzie into his arms and headed for the back door of the house. One thought kept running through his head. *Now or never.* She laced her fingers around his neck and held on tightly and didn't try to deck him. Good sign.

"What do you think you are doing?" she whispered.

He ducked to capture her mouth again. Walking and kissing was definitely not his forte but he managed to shut her up and shuffle along to get her into the house where she couldn't easily escape. Hell, that sounded rather predatory but at the moment, he was feeling a little possessive and well, Alpha. He should rein that back in but while she was not protesting, he was definitely going to take advantage of reducing the space between the lawn chair she'd curled herself into, and her bedroom.

Damn, but she felt good in his arms, his mouth nibbling at hers. He loved the way she sucked and drew his lower lip inside her mouth. Stumbling a little, he broke the kiss with a quick exhale, then righted himself and shifted her firmly in his arms.

"You're going to kill us before we get there."

"Not a chance," he whispered against her mouth, tracing her puffy, sexy and sweet lips with his tongue. "Not a damn chance."

Breathless, he took the steps to the back porch two at a time.

"Put me down. I can walk."

"No sweetheart. I'm not letting you go."

He fumbled with the door handle and bumped it open with his hip, moved swiftly through the doorway and then slammed it shut with a kick. Traveling through the kitchen on a blur, he barely registered rushing through her bedroom, followed by falling solidly, completely, and finally into the middle of her king-sized bed.

With her beneath him.

And she didn't protest, lying there looking up at him. Waiting.

Thank God for small miracles.

Man, she felt good. The heat of her chest seared through his thin t-shirt.

She tugged at that shirt and whispered, "Hurry."

"Hell yes." He straddled her hips, ripped the shirt off his head and tossed it aside. Her hands covered his as he reached for his belt.

Brad drank in every soft feature of her face. Sweet Suzette. His Suzette. Back in his arms. In her bed. Could life get any better?

A thin niggle of doubt tugged at him. Making love with her wouldn't solve anything, would it? Perhaps they should talk first....

She yanked at his buckle.

"You're sure?"

"Yes," she breathed. "Yes, Brad. Now."

Her fingers fumbled with the buckle in hot pursuit. Deft hands played over his belt, his fly, sliding under the waistband of his jeans.

He groaned. In seconds he'd rolled off and pushed his jeans to his ankles. He struggled momentarily with the boots and socks but, with her help, hastily kicked them away. His attention focused on her, he slowly started to unbutton her shirt.

In a flash she switched momentum and pushed him onto his back. She was over him, straddling him, kissing him. Raising up, she stared down and stripped the ponytail holder from her hair, strawberry locks spilling over her shoulders. Her gaze never left his. The moonlight filtered from the lakeside windows of her room, perfectly illuminating her features.

The look on her face was, well, priceless. She really was *his*.

Her fingers moved over the buttons of her knit shirt and within seconds, she had jerked the garment over her head and tossed it aside. She popped the fly on her jeans and leisurely lowered the zipper. He caught a glimpse of silky, lace pink panties and his libido soared. With a flick of her wrist, she snapped at the back of her matching bra and her ample breasts tumbled out.

"My God, you are beautiful," he whispered. "Come here."

She leaned closer and he cupped one of her full breasts. Damn, how he'd missed fondling them. They were the most beautiful and delicate mounds of flesh he'd ever seen in his life. Full. Pink. Firm. Ripe.

His.

Heaving a contented sigh, he smoothed both hands around her

back to hold her, and settled one delectable dusky nipple between his lips. Suzie let out a soft moan and melted into him. Sweet Jesus. She *was* his. She felt so wonderful in his mouth. Like, it was why she had breasts, for him.

He moved from that breast to the other. "Equal time," he rasped.

"Um, yes."

His hands played across her back, relishing in the satin feel of her ivory skin. He dipped under the waistband of her jeans to cup her round buttocks.

"Get rid of these." He broke away and flipped her over onto her back.

"Gladly."

With one whoosh he finished undressing her.

SUZIE SIGHED. GOD, HOW SHE HAD MISSED HIM. HAD missed *this*. How could she have forgotten, and pushed aside, all of the wonderful feelings Brad had stirred within her all those months ago? How he woke her from the dead, mundane sleep she'd been in with Cliff for so long, and held her captive with every touch of his fingers and lips?

Brad's hands skillfully moved over her body. With every stroke she sprang alive. With each groan she wanted more. To hell with everything else. The town, the lodge, the fact that she was confused as hell. This—this intimate moment with Brad—she needed now. The rest she'd just have to sort through later.

For now, all she wanted was to feel.

Besides, people need sex. Right? She'd read that recently in a women's magazine. It had something to do with hormones. Was it testosterone? Sex was important for that. And she'd been deprived lately, so it was okay.

Stop thinking, Suzie. Just feel.

He stripped away the last of her clothing and lay over her. "I need your skin next to mine."

"Yes," she whispered.

She loved how he made her feel. How her body responded to his touch. How her inner vixen retorted to his urgent groans.

"I love..." His voice raspy, he searched her face. "I love how you look. How you feel. How you...look."

"You're driving me crazy," she whispered.

"Good. Be crazy with me. Because I'm crazy about you, Suzie."

Anticipatory spirals of pleasure sprinted through her body. Brad urged her to lie back. Relax. His mouth covered hers.

"I love...you...." he breathed against her lips.

Suzie floated into a haze of never-ending pleasure.

Tension built inside her like an out-of-control freight train. She wrapped her arms and legs around him, imprisoning him against her...her little love slave. What? She giggled to herself. Where did that come from in this dizzy and spiraling out of control brain of hers?

Love slave. Ha!

Her younger man. Her boy toy. Damn, she was turned on! "God, Brad. I want you. Please, Mr. Love Slave, please take me..."

A deep throaty chuckle escaped him. She heard it, but soon dismissed it, because all thought abruptly ceased. Pleasure took its place.

Chapter Eleven

Brad pinned her firmly against the bed. Waves of pleasure racked his body. She was his. They were together. And that was all that mattered. The intense pleasure he got from making her feel wanted and special and protected was more powerful than anything.

Suzie trembled and slumped backward against the bed and he released his lip-hold on her. Sweet Suzette. He never wanted to be rid of the taste of her on his lips. "Suzette, my Suzette...."

They wound together legs and arms. With every stroke that bordered on excruciating pleasure, he reveled in the wicked delight of pleasing her, experiencing again the no-holds-barred passion they'd once had.

She shook and gasped and dug her fingernails into his back.

His explosion was powerful and loud. He growled out her name in a primal shout, then followed with a whisper of passion from his lips to her cheek.

Their sighs mingled. When he rose to look into Suzie's face, he noticed the mist of tears in her eyes. No small thing, those tears. And for some reason, they scared the hell out of him.

SUZIE WOKE TANGLED IN SHEETS, BODY PARTS, AND stray pieces of clothing. A sunbeam slanted into her bedroom and her right eye. Groggily, she stretched and moaned, then snuggled into Brad's warm and naked body.

Holy shit. What in the hell had she done?

Her brain spun. She was too tired to ponder it now. She was feeling too lethargic to move or think about it. All she wanted was to roll over in bed and burrow into Brad's side and sleep some more. It was Sunday morning, right? One deserved the right to sleep in on a Sunday.

Instead, she rolled to her left and glanced at the grandfather clock against the far wall.

Eight-thirty-three. Which meant it was really eight-twenty-three. Which meant she should have had breakfast fixed one hour and twenty-three minutes ago. She never slept this late!

She shot up taking the sheets with her. "Breakfast!"

Brad pulled her back down to the bed and wrapped his arms around her. "Relax, sweetheart. Your only guest is me, remember? And I'd just as soon have breakfast in bed."

Sighing, she relaxed and snuggled close. He was right. There were no other guests. Fortunately, since she was late. "Um, what *do* you want for breakfast?"

"You."

Not ready to go there again, she pushed nervously on his chest. "No, I'm serious. I'll fix us something. What do you want? Omelet? You know I can do a great omelet."

Brad nuzzled her neck and smoothed his hands over her back, down to her buttocks. "No worries. No omelet. Not now, maybe later. The only thing I want for breakfast is you," he said lazily. "And since I'm your guest, I'm assuming you'll accommodate? Bed, breakfast, and you. Perfect."

Why did he have to be so freaking romantic? He had to stop

this or she was going to fall for all of this crap. Hook, line and sinker.

Suzie smirked and sat up. "Smart ass. C'mon, we need to get up. What do you want?" It was a little too cozy, too familiar, too much like old times. She didn't want it to be like old times.

Did she?

He tugged on a lock of her hair and pulled her face closer to his. "I want you for breakfast," he moaned. "My little love slave."

Groan....

Suzie backed away and jumped off the bed. Hell's bells. He could turn her on like a light switch. "We need to talk first, Brad."

He smiled and burrowed further into the pillows, his left leg and hip exposed from under the covers. "Hm."

Suzie smacked him on the butt with the back of her hand.

"Ow!"

"C'mon, Brad. You can't avoid this. We have things to talk about."

With a lengthy exhale, Brad moved to a sitting position and looked at her. "Well, then sit." He patted the mattress. "I'm not going to have you lording over me. At least let's be on equal ground."

Grabbing the tail of the sheet, she wrapped it around her and sat. "You could cut me a little slack," she told him. Brad grinned and lifted himself so she could easily wrap the sheet around her, leaving him uncovered.

She tossed him a pillow. "Here. Lay something over...that."

Brad grinned a lazy, slack-eyed grin and did as she said. "There, you comfy?"

"Yes."

"Then what do we need to talk about?"

Men. Doesn't he know? "Um, well, Brad we have to talk about...um...this." She patted the bed. "Us. You and me. What happened last night. And all that."

He nodded. "Okay."

"And...."

"And what else?"

"The hotel thing. We need to talk about the hotel thing."

He concurred with another nod. "So you start. You pick."

She stared at him. Why was he being so accommodating? She watched his gaze lower to her chest and hers followed. Cleavage. He was looking at her cleavage.

And the fact that he'd gotten laid last night, which contributed to part of his plan, was likely making him...accommodating.

"I think I can talk about both of them at the same time, Brad Matthews, but quit ogling me!"

He jerked his gaze back to her face. "Sorry, sweetheart. It's just that...."

Suzie yanked the sheet beneath her chin. "Brad, this hotel thing. I mean, why?" She fiddled with the corner of the sheet. "Did you not think about what this would do to me? To my business?"

He stared at her with a blank expression, then huffed out a breath and said, "I *was* thinking about you. All the time, every plan I made. With every detail. You, Suzie-Q, are why I came here in the first place. I want to be with you. And I made a lot of changes in my life to do that."

"But I don't understand."

He leaned closer. "Suzie. My grandmother died six months ago."

"Oh no...." She reached for his hand. Large and strong, she loved his hands.

He shook his head. "Yeah, I miss her, but she lived a full life. Thing is, she wanted me to live a full life, too. She left me a good chunk of money with instructions to follow my dream. My dream, Suzie-Q, is right here. With you. In Harbor Falls. And Falls Lodge? That's part of my dream, too. My own business. A wonderful woman by my side. Family."

There it was. *Family.*

Stunned, Suzie sat watching his face. His gaze played over her and he waited. What could she say? He had it all planned out. But what would happen if she couldn't fulfill the rest of his plan? His dreams. Give him that family?

He squeezed her hand. "Sweetheart," he softly said. "You don't have to say anything now. We'll work all of this out. Let's think it through."

How could she think of anything else? Bewildered, she looked away.

"You'll see. It will be great," he added. He leaned closer to kiss her cheek. "Oh, and I nearly forgot! When the hotel is built, it's going to be the two of us again. Chef de Cuisine and his sous chef."

Grasping her face in his hands, he looked longingly into her eyes and whispered, "You and me, baby. Like old times."

She pulled back. "But I don't see why you need to tear down the lodge, Brad. Why can't you fix it the way it is? Renovate it or something?"

Why can't you do something that won't put me out of business? What about me? My dream?

He shook his head. "The structure is too bad, honey. It would take too long, too much money, Suzie. Better off razing the thing and starting from scratch."

He rose then, tossed the pillow aside and walked toward the bathroom.

Better off starting from scratch?

Maybe he'd be better off starting from scratch with a new relationship. Someone more his age who could give him kids. Thing was, he had it all figured out. Did he not realize that sometimes plans don't work and dreams don't come true?

"I am getting a little hungry after all," he called from the bathroom.

"Yeah," she said, not directing her response to him. "I'll go fix some eggs, or something...."

He popped his head out of the doorframe smiled. "No, sweetheart. We cook together, remember? Wait for me."

Shit. Suzie bit her lip. There he goes again, being so damn perfect.

BRAD LEFT SUZIE IN THE BEDROOM AND HEADED FOR THE shower. What he needed was a good long stream of hot water beating on his head to clear his brain and make sure he was thinking straight.

What had he been thinking, anyway?

Of course, he had come off all cocky and self-assured the night before, and he had definitely hauled her butt cave man style into her bed—but was that the right thing to do? At that moment he had felt all predatory and possessive, like he wanted to claim or mark her or something. Too primal. He wasn't normally like that.

But he could feel the moment slipping away and he'd wanted to grab it and hold on with everything he could. He needed that chance, needed that intimacy with her.

And it had been the right thing to do, hadn't it? Making love with Suzie?

It wasn't like she was pushing him away or anything. Quite the opposite, in fact. She was more than into it.

He twisted the shower nozzle and a blast of icy water hit him square in the chest. He jumped back. Perhaps that was the jolt he needed. A jolt of reality—because Suzie had definitely presented him with a huge dose of reality this morning with her immediate questions about the lodge and their relationship. Plus, she had made it quite clear that the two were intertwined.

Why do women always have to complicate things? Ask so many questions?

Perhaps it was a measure to protect themselves from hurt—or to prepare themselves for potential hurt.

He didn't want to hurt Suzie, that was for certain, but it seemed he had unintentionally done that with his disclosure about the lodge and his plans at the town council meeting. Perhaps he should have given her a heads up—but when? There had not been much time for the two of them to discuss much of anything.

It was true, though, that he'd been avoiding the discussion until he was sure the town was on his side.

They would just have to work this through. They could do it, right?

He sure as hell hoped so.

From the Kitchen of Suzie Hart, Sweet Hart Inn

Blog Post, May 28: ***Donuts, Dads, and Drama***

Falls Mountain Elementary never disappoints.

I just rolled in from the annual Donuts & Dads breakfast and let me tell you—those kids can eat! I baked 144 donuts (don't worry, I didn't count the ones I tested), and not a single one made it home. My cousin, Sydney from Sugar High Bakery, pitched in with sprinkles and smiles, and the dads? Let's just say we had a few donut-eating contests break out by accident. Ahem. Coach Monroe, I'm looking at you.

One of my favorite things about these community events is how they blur the line between "business" and "belonging." It's a lesson I hope we all learn in this small town, sooner rather than later. Shall I bring donuts to the next town council meeting?

You decide and let me know, please.

But back to the school event. It's one thing to run a B&B and make your guests feel at home—it's another to see your old third-grade teacher devour a bacon maple-glazed in under twenty seconds. (Yes, Mrs. Vernon, you *are* still a legend.)

Of course, not all the excitement was donut related. Let's just say small-town mornings come with their own flavor of gossip. A few of the mamas cornered me about a certain "handsome stranger" seen lurking around the lake (and possibly Sweet Hart Inn?) on a motorcycle. Apparently, word spreads in this burg faster than hot sugar glaze on an angel food cake.

Of course, I already knew/have had experience with that.

All I can say is this: I serve my muffins with side-eyes and syrup, but secrets? Those are for another time.

Today's Recipe: Baked Maple-Glazed Donuts

    2 cups flour
    3/4 cup brown sugar
    2 tsp baking powder
    1/2 tsp cinnamon
    2 eggs
    1/2 cup milk
    1/4 cup sour cream
    1/4 cup melted butter
    1 tsp vanilla

Maple Glaze:
    1/2 cup powdered sugar
    2 tbsp maple syrup
    Splash of milk

Mix wet with wet, dry with dry, then combine. Bake at 350 for 15 minutes in greased donut pans. Dip in glaze. Try not to inhale three in a row.

Hug a kid. Thank a teacher.

And always eat the extra donut.

Suzie

Chapter Twelve

S uzie fingered a lacey baby bonnet at Marnie Monroe's new baby boutique, The Purple Pelican, wondering why she was even there. A baby store, of all places. As she and Marnie sat in the cozy corner chatting, Suzie realized she was actually glad to have someone to talk to about all of this. Marnie had been full of questions about Brad and finally, Suzie spilled the beans—the entire sordid story. "It's just not going to work," she finally said. "He wants a family, and I can't give him that."

Marnie, her eyes wide and her gaze full of compassion, looked up from a pile of baby clothing she was tagging. "Why not? Don't you want children?"

"Oh, I would love a child." Suzie shrugged. "But I can't get pregnant. I came to grips with that years ago."

"Oh, sugar!" Marnie moved closer to Suzie and put her arm around her shoulders. "I didn't know that. What happened?"

Twice in one week, Suzie fought back tears. Oh hell. Why not let them fall? "Nothing happened, really, it's just that I can't get pregnant. I've known ever since I was a teenager that I might have difficulty. I have a bad case of endometriosis and my gynecologist wonders if my ovaries are really producing eggs."

"Oh sweetie." Marnie cupped her cheek in her palm. "I had no clue. Are you okay?"

Suzie shrugged again and nodded. "Sure. Or I was." She glanced off and stared at the pattern in the carpet at her feet. "At least I thought I was okay with it."

"Doesn't sound that way," Marnie said. "Of course, given the circumstances I would think it would be normal for it to weight heavy on your mind right now. Do you want to talk about it?"

Sighing, Suzie agreed. "All right. It hasn't always been easy, especially with Cliff. He was always pissed about my *inability*, he called it. He said it didn't matter, that he really wasn't into kids anyway, and so I took him at his word, but—" She laughed and shook her head. "But look at him now. Nice young wife, ripe as a plum, spitting babies out like there is no tomorrow. Oh, and Shelley is pregnant again."

Marnie's eyes widened in shock. "Again? I thought they recently had a baby?"

Suzie nodded. "They did. In fact, you should get them on your mailing list. Way she's going, she'll be spending a lot of money in here. She got pregnant again when baby number one was two months old. She's about to deliver again soon."

"That little bitch. How dare she?"

They burst into laughter. Suzie loved Marnie Monroe with all her heart. She was like the sister Shelley never was.

Marnie looked at her. "So what did Brad say when you told him?"

Suzie hesitated, pretending to inspect the lace on a very small dress. "When I told him what?"

"That you couldn't get pregnant."

"I didn't tell him."

Marnie remained silent.

Suzie glanced up. "What?"

"You didn't tell him?"

Tossing the dress aside, Suzie rose and paced a few feet between the store window and where Marnie sat perched on a soft white wicker chair. Stuffing her hands in her back jeans pockets she returned, "What would I say? Oh, one thing about your plan here, Brad, the big dream of your life? You know, business, family, kids.... Oh, well, the kids part, scratch that if you're thinking about my participation. I hope you don't mind if we skip that little piece of your dream." She swiped at her nose. "Besides, he's too young for me."

"Pish. You look younger than you are and you're in great shape."

"I'm pudgy."

Marnie laughed and stood. "You are not. You're beautiful." She placed her hands on Suzie's shoulders and shook her. "Now get yourself out of this funk, you hear me? Go tell him what's going on with you before he turns tail and runs. Because when he's gone, you'll up and change your mind and mourn after him for the next thirty years. And as your official newest best friend, I'm here to tell you I don't need to hear any of that whining for the next three decades. Okay?"

Suzie shrugged and sighed. "I suppose."

Marnie hugged her. "Sweetie? Are you *sure* you can't get pregnant?"

She turned to look at her friend. "I'm sure. Cliff and I never used protection and I never got pregnant." She paused, her mouth screwed into a bow. "Good Lord, I can't even believe we risked that not being married and all but... Well, you see? No babies for me in all these years. I wonder if that was the reason Cliff was in no hurry to get married."

Marnie's eyes flew wide open.

"Oh my God." Suzie blew out a breath.

"You think he was putting you off all these years because he really didn't want to get married because he wanted kids?"

"I do! Well, I'll be spanked! That *is* the reason why he kept dragging the damn engagement out for all of these years! He was holding out for fresher eggs!"

Marnie scowled. "The bastard."

"How could I be so blind?"

Marnie smiled and wrapped her arms around Suzie's shoulder. "Honey. Maybe it's because he's not so great a sperm donor. Or maybe he wasn't doing things right for you."

Suzie laughed. "I love you, Marnie Monroe."

"You better. Now go get things fixed with that man of yours."

Nodding, Suzie replied, "You think?"

"I do think."

Suzie wasn't convinced. It didn't feel like the right time and there was so much else to discuss. The baby thing was one issue. The whole hotel mess was something else entirely. Besides, how in the world, knowing what she did now about Cliff, could she even think about heading into another relationship with a man whose dream is kids, family, and the picket fence?

The only thing she had to contribute was the damn fence.

THE MEETING WITH THE ARCHITECT LASTED A LOT longer than Brad expected. Again. Dinner would probably be waiting, warming in the oven. Suzie had been great that way for the past few days. Breakfast ready every morning. Dinner waiting at the end of his day. She was a gem and he appreciated it. He had told her not to wait for him if he was running late—which he had been for the past several days—but wished she would ignore his request and be waiting for him anyway, tonight. He needed to see her and spend some time with her. They needed to talk.

Of course, if she *were* waiting on him *in bed,* he'd gladly skip the dinner—but that scenario had not happened lately and he doubted if it would tonight.

She needed space, she told him a few days ago. Brad figured that given how she felt about the whole hotel business, and the way he'd bulldogged his way into her life again, she deserved to feel like her apple cart was upset. He knew she wasn't prepared to deal with both the possibility of a relationship *and* the intrusion of the new hotel into her Harbor Falls lifestyle, so he'd backed off for a while. He'd had months to figure things out. She, on the other hand, had not. So he'd give her the time and space she needed, if that was what would make her more comfortable with the entire situation.

His days were busy, though. Good thing. Kept his mind off sex.

Of course, she was always on his mind.

Besides meeting with the architect, a contractor, and the local employment agency, he'd started thinking about marketing. He'd learned that James Martin's girlfriend, Eliza Kelley, had some fantastic ideas about promotion and he'd met with her about the Harbor Falls Market Square campaign. Eliza was a whiz at technology and had made a commitment to help him build his future website, which excited him to no end.

Things were moving along quite nicely.

He'd asked for and borrowed Suzie's Mazda for the day because of the paperwork he was carrying around. She was agreeable, saying most of her work that day was in the house. He drove around to the back and parked, looking for signs of her out by the lake or on the deck. A quick glance at his watch told him it was almost nine o'clock. No light shone from her window at the back of the house.

Hm. Had she gone to bed already? He just wanted to talk with her for a few minutes.

In the kitchen he found a note on the cooking island. *Dinner in the fridge. Hope your day was good. Talk to you in the morning. I'm pooped.*

Frowning, he crumpled the note. He could give her space but

he didn't expect to be ignored. This was the third night in a row she'd holed herself up in her bedroom.

Was she avoiding him?

Hell. Of course she was. And this was as much his fault as anything. Tossing the wad of paper at the garbage can, he turned and took the stairs to his bedroom. To hell with dinner.

SUZIE WINCED WITH EACH STEP BRAD TOOK UP THE stairs and she jerked in her bed when he slammed the door. She figured she'd pushed it too far, might as well have just shown him to the door and told him to leave. She'd been masterful at neglecting him and she sensed his frustration. She had to come to closure with all this soon, figure this thing out, or Marnie would be right. Brad would turn tail and run faster than a frog on a fly, and the choice would no longer be hers.

Thing was, she didn't want to lead him on.

But she didn't want to push him away either.

Her heart and her head were in total conflict and the more she avoided him, the worse the conflict inside her became. On top of that, just having him in her house, under her roof, was nearly too much.

She wanted him. Wanted him like a crazy horny woman and didn't know what to do with that. Her hormones must be working overtime.

She was afraid, too. Afraid to give herself over to him. Afraid if she made love with him more time it would seal the deal on her heart. And his. Then where would they be?

They'd be stuck in another damn dilemma and she'd have to tell him about her faulty eggs.

And then they would be done. Kaput. Finished.

Suzie lay back into her stacked pillows and closed her eyes. At that same moment, her cell phone vibrated on the bedside table. She picked it up.

A text message from Brad. *I miss you.*

Those three words nearly brought her to tears.

I miss you too, she texted back.

Then what are you going to do about it? Came the immediate reply.

Suzie swallowed. She didn't text back. She didn't think. She simply got out of her bed, crossed her bedroom to the door and opened it. There, on the other side, stood Brad, naked as a J-bird and holding his phone. He walked her backward until they tumbled into bed.

Chapter Thirteen

A flurry of last-minute guests the past two weeks had kept Suzie busy than a one-armed paperhanger, and secretly, she'd been glad of it. Eliza was hosting a craft expo at The Trading Post, continuing her search for more juried crafters. They all needed a place to stay, which was very, very good for the Sweet Hart Inn and for Suzie.

For her business and for her sanity.

She made breakfast every morning at seven and a light brunch around ten-thirty for those who lingered late. The continental buffet was set up in the dining room and guests helped themselves.

Then there was cleanup—the kitchen, the guest rooms, the house in general. And yard work. She couldn't neglect her yard, garden, and plants.

Of course, there was always the cookbook. An agent had loved her book proposal and was interested in representing her. She had options. She also had to get the darned thing finished, and fast. She'd been given a deadline.

A deadline!

Work kept her mind off other things. Obvious things. Making love with Brad again probably hadn't been the best idea she'd ever had—but it had happened nevertheless. And even though she probably shouldn't have done it, she loved every second and knew Brad did too.

However, it only served to complicate the matter in her head.

The bacon frying in the pan crackled and hissed, sending that sharp, smoky scent her way. Home. The scent reminded her of home. Wasn't that all she ever wanted? To be happy and content with the perfect life, career, and a home of her own?

Why couldn't she just let her guard down for once and be happy, without trying to analyze things? She was going to have to turn a leaf. Maybe this hotel thing wouldn't be such a bad idea. Maybe she should ask Brad more about it...

She sighed. Maybe later. She had work to do first.

It was Saturday and she had loved this entire, busy week. Yes, it was hectic, but it was her week. This was what she wanted to do with the rest of her life—run Sweet Hart Inn. She had to admit that she didn't want to be a sous chef—not even for Brad—even though she was damn good at doing that job.

And even though she loved Brad—yes, dammit, she did love him—she didn't want to cook beside him anymore. Not at the hotel. That was his dream, not hers.

She was conflicted about things, but she knew she wanted him in her life.

Period.

There. She admitted it.

Suddenly Suzie realized she'd been the one holding the cards all along. She was the one making the choices for both of them. Brad had not been given a chance. Marnie was right. Brad needed to know everything. She'd been holding back, probably because she was afraid, deep down, of losing him.

Afraid she could never measure up. Like with Cliff. That she could never please the man, and worse, that he would reject her because she couldn't have a baby.

But Brad was nothing like Cliff. Not one bit. So why was she so worried?

She'd have to suck it up and deal. She couldn't go on like this any longer and neither, she suspected, could he. He needed to hear from her exactly how she felt about the lodge, about not being his sous chef, about the inn and her business and how she felt about all that hotel situation, and the baby. Or lack thereof. He had to know.

"Bacon sure smells good."

Startled, Suzie looked up from where she was lazily pushing around half-cooked slices of bacon. Brad reached over, plucked a piece draining on a paper towel, smiled at her and placed a quick kiss on her cheek. Then, he put one end of the bacon in his mouth, the other end sticking out toward her. "Here, have a bite," he muttered.

She smiled and rubbed her tummy. She felt a little queasy this morning. She had to start eating better.

"Quit playing around and eat it."

He moved closer, flipped off the burner under the pan, and pointed to the bacon. "Take a bite," he mumbled.

Sighing, Suzie relaxed. "Okay," she smiled and stepped closer. Brad put his hands on her hips and tugged her to him. Her arms fell naturally over his shoulders. She took the bacon into her mouth and bit off a piece, barely grazing his lips, and chewed.

Brad's face was close. Hell's bells, she loved those dark eyes.

"You do good bacon, sweetheart."

"I do good lots of things," she countered, still chewing.

That bad-boy grin returned and he pulled her in tight. "Yes, my love. You do."

Love.

About the time she swallowed the bacon, he captured her lips with his in a gentle caress. Leaning into him, for the first time in days, Suzie let herself enjoy the sensual play of his lips on hers.

They broke the kiss after a moment and she laid her head on his shoulder. His arms came around her and he held her close.

"I've missed you like crazy," he whispered into her hair.

Squeezing her eyes tight, she once more fought back tears. "I've missed you, too. I'm a insanely busy woman and you've entered my insanely busy life...."

Talk to him, Suzie. This is the time. The door is open. Now or never.

Brad pulled back and pointed his thumb toward the dining room. "You've got a hungry crowd gathering out there. Want me to help you get the meal out this morning?"

Suzie looked at his face, studied the ever-present, slightly crooked smile, and knew beyond a shadow of a doubt that she was a goner. She loved him. "I would like that very much," she whispered.

He gave her a quick peck on the lips. "Consider it done."

AN HOUR OR SO LATER, SUZIE SAID, "SURE IS QUICKER getting things cleaned up with you around."

Brad glanced up from his dishwashing to the kitchen island where Suzie bagged leftover muffins and croissants. "I bet. We always were a good team, you know."

She nodded, averting her gaze. "I think everyone ate a full breakfast this morning, so I shouldn't have to put out too much on the continental buffet for the stragglers." She popped another muffin into the bag. "Could be enough bread here to make a nice bread pudding tomorrow."

Brad flung excess water from his hands into the sink then dried them on a nearby towel. They did work together well but she was definitely avoiding the subject. Turning, he rested against the sink and crossed his arms across his chest, watching her.

Waiting her out was one thing. But she, too, had to participate in this game.

"We're good for each other, Suzie-Q."

"What do you think of the blueberry ones? Have you tasted them yet? It's a new recipe and I think I have it perfected for the cookbook, and—"

Brad stepped forward and reached for her hands. "Suzie, stop. Look at me."

Gradually, she stopped stuffing the bread in the bag and looked up. One look in her eyes told him loads. She was scared. Dammit! Why?

"What's wrong, sweetheart?"

She plopped on a bar stool behind the kitchen island, keeping her hands in his. "We are good together, Brad. I know that."

"Then what's wrong?"

She jumped up and jerked her hands away from his. "What's wrong? Can't you see? We don't have any of this worked out, we're both avoiding it, and...and, hell's bells mostly it's me because I..." She turned her back.

Shit. Don't clam up on me again.

Brad rounded the kitchen island. "Suzie, dammit, talk to me. I need to know what you are thinking, what you are feeling. This is driving me nuts. I can't go on much longer wondering what in the hell you want. Whether you are going to allow me into your life or not."

She whirled back. "Okay! All right. I don't want to be your sous chef!"

He stared at her, hands on hips. *What?* "Then why didn't you say that?"

Her shoulders fell and one hand went to her tummy, rubbing it. "I don't want to be your sous chef and I don't want to have anything to do with the hotel and I don't want to give up my bed and breakfast."

She went pale. All at once Brad noticed the dark circles under her eyes. This was wearing on her a lot more than he'd realized. "Suzie, it's okay. I know you are upset about the lodge. But do we have to let that come between us? And who said you'd have to give up the inn?"

"No one said it, Brad," she bit out. "But if you have this big monster hotel across the lake, who is going to want to stay here in my humble little house?"

"Lots of people! You will provide them an entirely different experience!"

She shook her head and then leaned against the kitchen island, rubbing her forehead. "Yeah, right."

"Are you okay?"

"Fine."

"You're sure?"

She jerked her chin up. "I'm fine, Brad."

"It's all just *fine*, Suzie, isn't it?" He paced sharply around the kitchen island and spun on his heel back to her. His voice rose. "The hotel is as important to me as your damn inn is to you. So get over it. It's going to happen."

Oh, that was likely not the best comeback.

"The *damn* inn?" She shot off her chair. "This damn inn is my life. It's all I have. I need it to survive!"

He grasped and held her upper arms. "Hold it. Is that all you need to survive? This old clapboard house on the lake? I sure was hoping you needed a helluva lot more than that, Suzie. I was hoping you needed me."

She opened her mouth to say something then evidently thought better of it. All of a sudden, like the wind being yanked out of her sails, she sank again onto a bar stool. He released her arms and cupped her chin in his hand. "Suzie, that's all I need to know. Do you want me in your life, or not? Do you want to be with me? Because I'm crazy in love with you and—"

She stopped him with a hand to his forearm. Immediately, her eyes grew misty. "Brad, I...yeah. Yes. I love you, but...."

The rapid-fire crescendo ring of Brad's cell phone suddenly split the air about the same time big fat tears rolled down Suzie's face. A deep-throated sob echoed across the kitchen.

He ignored the phone.

"Talk to me, Suzie. Let's get all of this out on the table."

"There is just...so much...to sort out!" she blubbered.

"We'll *do* it, sweetheart."

The ringing again cut through their argument.

She glanced away, sobbing. "Oh, hell, answer it!"

At a loss, he didn't know what to do. He'd never seen her in this kind of emotional state before and he wasn't handling it well. What was going on?

He punched the talk button on his phone and barked into it. "What!"

SUZIE TOOK THE MOMENT TO GATHER HER WITS. WHAT the hell *was* going on with her? Why was she crying like a whimpering idiot? This wasn't like her. She could usually handle this kind of stuff pretty easily. Why was she such a freaking mess?

"Sure," Brad said into the phone. "If they can get the heavy equipment in there next weekend, we can start the following Monday."

What? Suzie stood up and her stomach lurched. Abruptly, something more than sobbing confusion welled up in her. Anger.

She stepped closer to Brad the same time he disconnected his call.

"What's starting on Monday? Tell me."

Brad reached for her. "Suzie, look. It has to...."

She put her palms out. "You're tearing down the lodge."

He nodded. "Yes. Next Monday we'll start."

"That's barely a week away."

"True." He stared at her. "Let's talk about—"

She pushed back. "No, Brad. I don't want to hear it. This all makes me really, really sad and sick to my stomach. I don't know what to think, what to do...." Oh, God. She might throw up.

"Suzie, it has to happen sometime."

"Well, I don't want it to happen at all, Brad! Oh...."

"What's wrong?"

"I don't. I don't feel so well...."

"Suzie?"

Turning, she took a couple of steps toward her bedroom, faltered with her hand over her mouth, then raced toward her master bathroom.

Brad followed. "Suzie, sweetheart. Are you okay? What the hell is going on with you?"

She slammed the bathroom door shut before he could step across the threshold. She wanted to preserve at least some shred of dignity while she puked her guts out.

Chapter Fourteen

Suzie felt a lot more alive than she had a few days earlier. Convinced she had the flu, even though she believed she was sick at heart with all the stress, she stayed in bed two entire days while Brad graciously took over in the kitchen. Why he would do that after she'd been so difficult to deal with and they had argued so badly, she had no clue. Obviously, the man was nuts or something. Or he loved her. Maybe both.

He never gave up. She had to give it to him, he came in here with a plan and be damned if he'd stick to it.

Whether she liked it or not.

The smell of her signature cinnamon coffee blend brought her out of her bedroom and into the kitchen. The way Brad looked standing in her kitchen, wearing a white T-shirt and jeans, reading the morning paper over the center island with a cup of coffee to the side, made her want to melt into the floor in a lukewarm puddle. God, what a body. What a man. And what a scene to wake up to. One she wanted to preserve, forever, in her mind. Finding Brad in her kitchen looked a lot like home.

"Morning," she squeaked.

Brad's smile widened when he looked up. "Hi, sweetheart. How are you feeling?"

"Much better."

"Good. Coffee?"

"Please."

He moved to the coffee maker and poured her a cup. She settled onto a bar stool. "Here you go. A little cream and one spoon of sugar. Just how you like it."

She smiled. "Thank you."

They stayed silent for a few minutes while she sipped her coffee and he continued to read. All this time, everything she'd put him through, and he'd never faltered. Not once. He was so steadfast, so determined to have her in his life. Would he still be once he knew her secret?

"Brad?"

"Hm?"

"Can we go to the lodge sometime this week? Before they tear it down?"

He rose and looked at her. "If you want. Of course."

She nodded. "I do. I want to see it one last time. I've not been there in years, but I want to take one last walk through. For closure, I guess."

She'd told herself a million times that this was the right thing to do, so she was trying very hard to hold back the tears. She'd thought it all through while lying in bed the past couple of days. If she got through this, accepting that the lodge would be gone forever, then she could get through the next thing she had to tell him—that she couldn't give him a baby. Then after that, the chips would lay where they would.

Perhaps if she could give, he could too. Time would tell.

He moved around the bar toward her and took her into his arms. "I'll do whatever makes you happy," he whispered. "I want you to be happy."

Funny. That's exactly what she wanted, too. For him. She

wanted him to have his dream, somewhat, even if she couldn't give him everything. "I want us both to be happy."

Brad sighed and looked down into her eyes. "All I need is you, Suzie, and then I'm happy."

"Really, Brad?"

He nodded. "Of course."

"Are you sure? If I was the only thing you could have, would I be enough?"

He paused for a moment, studying her face. "Honey, I swear. You're enough." He bent to kiss the tip of her nose. "Are you sure you are feeling better?"

She nodded. "Yes. I am. Much better."

"I'm glad." He hesitated. "Suzie, I really hate to do this now, but I need to tell you something. I have to leave for a few days, and I want to make sure you are okay before I do."

A ripple of panic raced across Suzie's abdomen. "Leave?" The word squeaked out of her throat, and she didn't like that it sounded so weak. "For how long?"

"A couple of days. I need to run down to Atlanta. Some things to settle with my grandmother's estate. With my parents still stationed overseas, and my brother in Italy, I need to take care of it."

"Well, of course. I'm fine, Brad." But inside, she was already a mess. He'd popped into her life from out of nowhere and turned her world upside down. Now, he was leaving for only a few days and she suddenly felt so empty. She couldn't imagine him not being there.

"You're sure?"

She looked up into his face and grinned wide. "I'm sure, Brad. I'll miss you but I'm sure. You do what you have to do."

He pulled her close and wrapped his arms around her. "I'll be as quick as I can be. I'll miss you too."

She nodded against his chest. "When are you leaving?"

He pulled back and cradled her face in his hands. "In a couple of hours. I should get down there tonight. I have a meeting with the attorney in the morning."

Suzie stared at him. "Oh." So, he'd known about this for a while. Why was he just now telling her? She separated herself from him and picked up her coffee cup. She had been sick. She supposed he was waiting. "I'm going to finish this on the deck. I hope you'll come find me before you leave."

I HOPE YOU'LL COME FIND ME BEFORE YOU LEAVE.

The further away Brad drove from Harbor Falls and from Suzie, the more uneasy and anxious he grew about the entire situation. Why the hell *wouldn't* he come find her before he left? What was going on in that head of hers?

There was something about the rotation of the Harley's tires on the pavement that pulled his brain into a cycle of doubt as he played over the various scenarios of the past few days. He'd left her with a quick kiss on the deck and she had barely hugged him. Oh, she was pleasant and smiled but she wasn't herself. He didn't think she was mad, it was something else.

Something wasn't quite right.

She was emotional and that wasn't like her—at least not the Suzie he'd known eighteen months earlier. She hadn't felt well lately either, and even though she attributed it to the flu, that didn't entirely make sense. It wasn't flu season, although he supposed having flu-like symptoms wasn't impossible. Perhaps it was a virus of some sort.

But what if it was more—what if she was *really* sick. Worse than flu symptoms sick. Maybe there was something more serious going on. What wasn't she telling him?

She had been a bit evasive lately. Hadn't she?

He recalled the question she'd asked that still niggled. *If I was the only thing you could have, would I be enough?* The fact that she even had to ask worried him. But what she didn't say worried him even more. How could she question whether she was enough? Doesn't she realize just how much he loves her? Had he not made himself clear?

Maybe not. Maybe he'd been so damned focused on the lodge and everything that needed to happen to get the project moving, that he'd neglected her. And if that were true, he had to remedy that situation, and soon.

Very soon. The moment he set foot back inside Sweet Hart Inn he needed to set things straight with Suzie. Make sure she knew just how much he loved her, and how much he needed her. And that couldn't happen fast enough.

Of course, he could call her. They could talk tonight on the phone. But this conversation needed to be had in person.

There were things he needed to say, to make clear. And things he needed to hear from her. He wanted to look her in the eyes and understand how she was feeling and why. Suddenly, he felt there were too many unspoken conversations that needed to happen between them—from both sides of the coin. And of all the times to realize that, why now when he had to go away? Perhaps he had been evasive, as well. What was it that she was avoiding telling him?

He didn't know.

But as soon as he was back in Harbor Falls he would get to the bottom of it.

At that thought, Brad sped up and hurried to his apartment in Asheville. There, he traded his bike for his car and drove the remaining two hundred miles or so to Atlanta. He let no moss grow under his wheels either.

If he could take care of the remaining details of his grandmother's estate tomorrow, he could be back in Harbor Falls by the following evening. He had to make that happen.

Suzie worried him. His concern about her health was one thing but he was also worried about them as a couple. About their evolving relationship. About what she'd not been telling him, and that she didn't *know* that she was *enough*.

He couldn't lose her. He just couldn't.

To hell with the damn lodge. All he cared about was that Suzie was healthy and okay. That they were okay. He had to get back and make sure everything was all right—with her, and with them. And that couldn't happen soon enough.

The panic that had settled in his gut was not going to go away until he saw her again.

SUZIE GLANCED UP FROM THE BEIGNETS SHE WAS experimenting with—a possible new breakfast option—when a brisk knock came to her back door.

"Great," she said through her teeth. "I am so *not* in the mood for company."

She hadn't been in the mood for people for a couple of days now. Thank goodness there had been no guests. Since Brad left, she had pretty much holed herself up in her kitchen working on recipes for the cookbook. She wasn't even sure she had showered since he'd left.

Maybe if she just didn't answer the door....

The door latch jiggled and her cousin Grace peeked in the back glass, making eye contact.

"Busted." Suzie wiped her hands on a towel and headed for the door, pulling on a smile as she crossed the kitchen. "Grace! What in the world. I didn't even hear your car. How are you?"

Her cousin smiled. "I'm good. I popped in at the bakery this morning and Sydney told me you'd not been feeling well. Thought I'd drop by to check on you."

Suzie hugged her. "Oh, you're sweet, but you didn't need to do that. I'm okay." She headed back to the beignets.

Grace glanced about the kitchen. "I see you are baking. And baking."

"Hm?" Suzie measured out another cup of flour. "Oh, yes. I've been baking."

Settling onto a bar stool at the island, Grace replied, "I can definitely see that."

The tone of her voice made Suzie fix her gaze on her. "Why?"

"My God, Suzie. Look around you."

She did. Slowly, her gaze spanned the kitchen and shrugged. "So I've been trying new recipes."

"Yes, you have. I see bread and muffins and a beautiful cake over there complete with fondant and fancy roses, and pies and cookies and are those breakfast quesadillas over there?"

"Yes, made this morning. Try one if you like." Suzie put up her hand. "But you can stop now. I know where this is going."

"You're depressed. You always cook when you are depressed."

Suzie sighed. "No. I'm not depressed. I'm working through some things. Cooking helps."

"It's Brad, isn't it?"

"It's a lot of things, Grace, and I don't want to talk about it right now."

Grace exhaled a slow breath. "All right. Well, if baking helps, then have at it. Can I take a pie or something off your hands? Or deliver some goodies to the senior citizens center?"

Suzie grinned. "Please do! Lord knows I can't eat all of this stuff."

"All right. I will." But Grace stayed put, drumming her fingers on the island. Suzie waited for whatever was to come next. "Suzie, are you eating? I know you haven't been feeling well lately and you look a little puny..."

"Flu. I've had the flu or something but it seems to be getting better. I'm fine."

"And is Brad okay? I mean, he didn't get the flu or anything too, did he?"

"Far as I know Brad is fine. He's in Atlanta."

"Hm. And you haven't talked to him?"

"No. Not since he left day before yesterday but that's okay. I think we both needed a little space."

Suzie watched Grace's fingers drum again over the butcher block. "Hm," she repeated.

"Stop analyzing." Suzie quit working and pinned her gaze on Grace. "Look. I know you are here for a reason. Spill it."

Her cousin bit her lip and stared at Suzie for a moment, then she reached into her bag and pulled out a small square box wrapped in turquoise paper and tied up with a vibrant pink bow.

Suzie stared at the box and then lifted her gaze back to Grace. After a quick rinse of her hands and drying them with a towel, she reached for the box. "What is this?"

"For you."

"Why?"

"I'm delivering."

"For whom?"

"You'll just have to open it up and see, Suzie. That's how gifts work."

Suzie rolled her eyes but was a little bit intrigued. "Well, it is pretty."

"It is that. The paper is from my newest collection and my most favorite. See the shimmer when you turn it to the light? I love that embossed look it gets when you look at it just so."

Suzie smiled. "The box is just too pretty. I don't want to unwrap it."

"Oh but you must. The real prize is inside."

Eyeing her, Suzie said. "Well, all right, but I'm not tearing the paper and I'm keeping it and the ribbon."

Grace nodded and grinned. "I would do the same! Now quick, you have to look."

Suzie untied the fabric ribbon and set it aside. Next, she meticulously peeled back several pieces of tape, taking care not to tear the paper. Finally, she unfolded the paper away from the box and laid it on the counter.

"You know turquoise is my favorite color." She glanced up at Grace.

"I do know that. Why do you think I chose that particular color? Now open the darned thing!"

Suzie lifted the lid on the box. Inside, was a small piece white paper folded over. She lifted it up and caught a glimpse of gold underneath nestled in some white cotton. Unfolding the paper, she read the message aloud. "I miss you and can't wait to get home. In the meantime, please wear my heart next to yours."

In the box was a gold, heart-shaped locket. She sucked in a sharp breath and her heart leapt. Suzie looked to Grace. "From Brad?"

Grace nodded. "Isn't it romantic?"

Suzie touched the soft gold locket and wanted to cry. What a beautiful note and so very romantic. She missed him like crazy, even if she had thrown herself into baking and tried to tell herself she didn't. This was a sweet gesture, but... "But how? Why? I didn't think knew him that well."

Grace sat on a bar stool at the island. "Honey, I met Brad practically the second he hit town. Where do you think he got those chocolates he bought for you on the first day he was here?"

"Chocolates?"

Grace's eyes widened. "Did he not give you the chocolates?"

Slowly, Suzie shook her head. "No. When did he get them?"

Thinking, Grace replied. "It was before the festival, and a few days before the town meeting. So, a couple of weeks or more ago. Right?" She waved a hand in the air. "I lose track of time. I wonder why he didn't give them to you?"

A thought struck Suzie. "Unless they weren't for me." That panged her heart a little.

Standing, Grace said. "Oh, bull hockey. They were definitely for you. Now, where is his room. Let's go find them."

"Grace! We can't do that."

Grace arched a brow. "Don't you go in his room to make the bed and dust and things?"

"Well, I..."

"Can you help it where your eyes land? Did you see any chocolate boxes laying around? If not, then let's go dust."

So dust they did.

They entered Brad's room upstairs and Suzie glanced about. Brad didn't have a lot with him—just what he could stuff in the bag on his bike—so there were not many personal possessions lying around.

Grace jerked open the top drawer of a chest. "Here we are—" She lifted out a heart-shaped box of chocolates. "It's a vintage box but the chocolates, I assure you, are fresh. At least they were.... See? He even bought a card." She started to tug at the envelope.

"Grace! Don't do that!"

"But they are for you, I swear!"

Suzie rushed forward, took the box of chocolates out of her hand, and shoved it back into the drawer. "It's none of our business. He'll give them to me when he's ready. Now let's get out of here. I feel like I'm doing something wrong."

Grace rolled her eyes. "Good gracious, Suzie! The man is so in love with you. You're not doing anything wrong. That is, unless there is something I don't know."

"We're not going there so let's get out." Suzie ushered her from the room, down the stairs, and back into the kitchen. After a few minutes, she added, "Now, you just sit there and talk while I fry up these beignets. If you stick around a while, you can sample one or take a dozen with you."

Grace sat. "I can't stay an hour because I have to get back to the shop. But let's chat a bit."

Suzie rolled her eyes. "What *now*?"

"Brad."

Suzie poked at her dough and looked up. "Why? I just told you that subject is closed."

"No, you didn't. Not really."

"Well, I'll tell you now. I don't want to talk about Brad any longer. Remember? I'm baking and working through things."

"Are you working through his gift?"

Suzie glanced up. "What? Why?"

"You've not even said a word about that locket, Suzie. Because you refuse to admit that the chocolates are for you and that he probably stuck those in a drawer and forgot about them, or he was saving them for a special occasion. Because you're making yourself sick over this lodge thing. And because you refuse to admit that you could be happy, if you would just let yourself be happy."

Suzie let that last statement hang in the air for a moment. Her hands stilled on the dough and stared downward. "I want to be happy, Grace."

"You have never been a Debbie Downer. What's going on with you?"

"I know. I've been such an emotional wreck lately." She gave up on the dough and washed and dried her hands, then sat on a bar stool beside Grace. "I've been trying to use these couple of days while Brad is gone to get my head wrapped around everything but all I can seem to do is mope around because, A, he's gone, and B, when he comes back I need to tell him something, and, C, once I do that might change everything."

"And bake."

"Yes, and bake."

"Which is not a good sign."

"I know but there are worse things."

"So you need to tell him about not being able to get pregnant?"

Suzie stood. "Yeah. That. He wants a family."

Grace stood too and hugged her. "Suzie, that man wants you. He's gone to lengths to get here and convince you of that. And when he called me yesterday evening to help him pick out something for you and deliver, he was as homesick and heartsick as any man can be. And you barely looked at the locket."

Suzie's heart twisted. "I know. I miss him so much. It's like I'm almost afraid to let myself feel anything."

"Then just put the damn locket on and keep him close to your heart—the feels will come later, honey. You're sort of numb right now. But Suzie, whatever it is with you, make it right. That man is a keeper." Grace reached for the box and lifted out the locket. Stretching the chain, she said, "Turn around." And then she fixed the locked around Suzie's neck.

When Suzie turned around to face Grace, she reached for the heart, clasped it in her hand, and felt her tears stinging her eyes. "Thank you, Grace."

"You're welcome."

Both of them jumped when the back door opened again and Brad stepped over the threshold and into the kitchen. At that moment, Suzie couldn't contain her tears any longer.

"Brad," she whispered. "You're home."

He took one look at her tears and crossed the room to sweep her up into his arms. "My God, I've missed you," he said. "I needed to be home. With you."

She inhaled his scent and clutched the heart in her palm tighter. He smelled so good. She whispered back. "Welcome home. I love your heart. Thank you."

"I love *you*, sweetheart. More every day."

"And that," Grace said, heading for the back door, "is my cue to leave."

Suzie barely realized she was gone as Brad's mouth descended on hers.

From the Kitchen of Suzie Hart, Sweet Hart Inn

Blog Post, June 7: *A Place at My Table*

Sometimes the table feels too big.

Sometimes it feels too full.

Today, it feels *just right*.

The last few weeks have reminded me that no matter how perfectly I plan the place settings, life has a way of rearranging things. People leave. People return. People show up at your front door with their hair all windblown and a pie in one hand and your name in the other like they never really let go.

Harbor Falls is still as nosy and lovable as ever. But I've stopped worrying so much about what people are saying. Instead, I'm focusing on the way they show up—with casseroles and concern, with kindness and curiosity, and sometimes with a fork already in hand.

This week I made fried chicken brunch with homemade biscuits and gravy for guests who'd never seen a Blue Ridge sunrise before. One said it was like eating peace. I think that's what we all want: a little peace, served warm.

So, if you're reading this and need a place to land—or a biscuit to go with your broken heart—I'll set an extra place for you. There's always room at this table.

Today's Recipe: Buttermilk Biscuits with a Side of Hope

2 cups self-rising flour
1/2 tsp salt
1/2 cup cold butter, cubed
3/4 cup buttermilk

Cut butter into flour until crumbly. Add buttermilk, stir just until combined. Pat into 1" round, cut into biscuits. Bake at 450 for 12–14 minutes.

Serve warm, with butter, jam, or someone who sees you for exactly who you are.

All my best,
Suzie

Chapter Fifteen

On Sunday, they took the bike to the lodge. Brad and Suzie had mutually decided that for a few days they were spending time alone, talking and making plans for their future. It was much needed time spent together, away from the town, the lodge, and all of the talk that went with it. While they solidified their relationship, there was one issue off the table—the subject of the lodge. They tabled that until today, when they both knew that they would be facing the inevitable.

This was also the day Suzie knew she had to face her final demon with Brad. They'd had time to reconnect and she'd grown more confident in Brad's love for her—but now she had to tell him the truth.

Snuggled behind him on the bike, she loved the powerful feeling of him being in control as she held on tight. He felt so good as she pressed up against him. He was so strong. Solid. Her rock.

The wind in her face, blowing through her hair was refreshing after not feeling well and staying inside most of the week. They'd gone without helmets for the slow, lazy drive around the lake and up to the lodge. There was a hint of crispness in the air as they moved higher into the mountain, umbrellas of oak, pine and maple covering their trail.

Suzie cringed when they turned into the lodge property and saw the heavy equipment scattered about the lawn. Swallowing hard, she suppressed edgy emotion as Brad parked. She swung her leg over the bike and headed for the porch. Brad followed,

This was a good thing, she kept telling herself, to find closure today. To move on. To take a step forward in hers and Brad's relationship. It was all good.

Then why wouldn't that sinking feeling in her stomach go away?

Brad took her into his arms, facing her fully. "Thank you for doing this." Brushing a few stray hairs out of her face, he added, "This means a lot to me."

Smiling weakly, she nodded. "It means a lot to me, too." He started to turn away and she pulled him back. "Brad?"

"Yes?"

"I'm behind you. I want you to know that."

Grinning from ear to ear, he took her hand and they mounted the steps.

Suzie soaked in every detail, preserving it in her mind. She ran her fingertips along the silky and time-worn weathered log posts that made up the rail around the porch. She breathed in a lingering scent of pine and cedar and imagined decades of fingers, young and old, skimming the wood over time. The old timber, dark, rich and well-aged stood solid.

"I wonder if there is anything here we can preserve to use in the new hotel. Or at the inn?"

She looked at Brad, and he glanced about. "Not a bad idea. We'll have to check inside. Architectural salvage is a big deal these days."

"There used to be a magnificent stained-glass window on the second-floor landing."

He nodded. "It's still there. I already thought about that. I wondered if you could find a place for it in your house. Might have to retrofit, maybe upstairs, or in your bedroom, but...."

She smiled and put two fingers on his lips. "You do think about me, don't you?"

Placing his hands firmly on her hips he drew her closer and frowned a little. "I think of you all the time, sweetheart. I'm not sure why you think I wouldn't." He moved both hands to her face, threaded his fingers in her long hair, playfully tugging at the ends. He let them go and then cradled her face in his big palms. He looked longingly into her eyes and Suzie felt so loved, wanted. A stiff, warm breeze enveloped them both, his lips gently brushed across hers. Warmth and heady excitement welled up inside her as she returned Brad's kiss, softly mingling her mouth and tongue with his.

He broke away and she sighed. She did love this man.

They moved toward the side of the lodge. "I can't believe this thing is really falling apart," she whispered, glancing around the corner toward the lake, her gaze following line of the stone foundation. "It just looks so sturdy and well-built."

His arm draped around her, still holding her close, he replied, "I know. It does seem that way, does it?"

She turned to him. "Who told you the foundation was bad?"

He studied her for a moment. "The bank who took possession after the bankruptcy. They had it checked out."

That bankruptcy was over thirty years ago. And it's still standing. Suzie pulled away. "Let's go inside." She rushed back for the door. "Is it unlocked?"

"Should be."

She fumbled only momentarily with the large oak door, then pushed inward and hurried inside. She sensed Brad behind her. Suddenly, her heart beat a mile a minute. Maybe, just maybe this place could be saved? It looked so intact. Should she risk one last ditch effort to save it? Even at the expense of losing Brad? The thought niggled in the back of her brain but she pushed it away.

Brad loved her. She wouldn't lose him because of this. Would she?

The lobby was as she'd remembered. "Brad, look! It's still beautiful."

She ran from one thing to another. The huge reception desk. Massive. Solid. "Look at this wood. It's gorgeous!"

She twirled toward the large, floor-to-ceiling windows, partly sheathed with years old tapestry drapes. "What a wonderful view. The windows are still good." She ran her hand along the well-worn window casing. "They're not rotted or anything." She flew to the next one. "This one either."

She loped toward the stairway, looked longingly up, and ran her hand along the bottom baluster. Twisting back and grabbing Brad's hand, she pulled him toward the stair. "Let's go look at the window." Excited, she grinned at him.

"Slow down, girl." He raced to try to keep up with her. "How do you move so fast on those short legs of yours?"

She ignored him. Suzie could see the window as they grew closer. Sunbeams streaked through dirty painted glass, bouncing off dust motes floating a few feet off the floor. Abruptly, she stopped. "Oh my. It's beautiful."

Brad wrapped his arms around her from behind and nuzzled her ear. "It will look great on your landing, too."

Slowly, assuredly, she shook her head. "No," she breathed. "Not my landing. It's much better suited somewhere else."

In a flash she ran down the stairs, leaving Brad behind. She raced toward the French doors that separated the lobby from the dining room, fiddled with the latch, and the doors swung open with ease—like they had been opened like that every morning for the past thirty years. A vision of a time gone by flitted through her mind. Small and scattered square tables, white linens, crystal glasses, sparkling flatware.

Soft music in the background. The chatter of guests, all

dressed up for dinner. Servers hustling about. Wonderful aromas wafting in from the kitchen.

"Perfect," she whispered.

Her heart beat strong against her chest. She could feel its pulse in her ear. They could fix this. *They could!* She and Brad. *Together!* She could work here. Not in the new hotel, but here.

Would he listen?

The kitchen. She rushed across the door and pushed through the hinged doors that separated the dining area and the kitchen. Large. Open and airy. Old, but could be renovated. Functional. Spacious. She could envision a modern gas range or two and flat griddle against the west wall. Prep station over by the window.

Yes.

She didn't know if it was her hope or if it really was possible. How could he tear this down? How could they make this a reality?

She whirled back toward Brad, who was standing in the doorway. "We can do this," she said. "We can."

BRAD WATCHED SUZIE PING-PONG FROM ROOM TO ROOM, darting about like an excited little girl, and his stomach sank. Oh boy, bringing her up here was either a mistake or a blessing, and right now he wasn't sure which. Looking at the lodge through her child-like eyes, he was beginning to see something different about the old place.

That wasn't a good thing. Was it?

The thought did excite him a little.

No. He couldn't start thinking like that. He had a plan. And plans were already in motion. Saving the lodge wasn't part of the grand scheme of things. He couldn't switch gears now. This train was already moving down the tracks.

He found her in the old kitchen, her gaze taking in every nook and cranny as she scanned the room. She turned back quickly and looked straight into his eyes. "We can do this," she said softly. "We can."

But she didn't wait for him to respond. She rushed past him and across the dining room, where she fumbled with a lock on another set of French doors that led to the lakeside deck. These doors did not swing open as easily as the first, but creaked with age. Finally, they swung back to lay flat against the outside walls, opening up the dining area with a breeze and a flurry of dust. A breathtaking view of a sparkling lake peeking between low-hanging pine boughs gave way over the deck.

In a flash, Suzie was gone.

Brad stood still in the room and let her go. When the dust motes settled, he could see that the room was magnificent. He imagined another place, another time. The dining hall filled with people—laughing, eating, and enjoying themselves. Spending money.

Eating and spending money was a good thing.

Suddenly things seemed off kilter. Had she really come here for closure, or to convince him to change his mind? Was this her last-ditch effort to save the place?

Certainly, she hadn't deceived him with her ploy of having his back, just to get him up here to reconsider?

He shook his head and glanced at his feet. No. Suzie wouldn't do that.

But all of that was moot, really. It didn't matter. He could see why she loved this place. And on some levels, he agreed with her. The structure actually looked extremely sound—something that he had to check back on with the engineers—and it would be a shame to get rid of it and all of the history that went along with it. He would have to be a hard-pressed effort to make her see why she had to let it go, but he had to try. Right?

Coming up here *was* a mistake.

Within seconds, she burst through the French doors again. "Brad." Her breathing was labored. "Come out here. You have to see this." She motioned his way and Brad took a few reluctant steps forward. She grabbed his arm and pulled him onto the deck. "Look. We could put an outside eating area here. It's a fabulous view over the lake. A cozy canopy of trees and shade. I know you are going to love it. Maybe some umbrellas for summer."

Still grasping his hand, she tugged him further out on the deck. Brad took a few steps then halted.

She jerked again then glanced back. "Brad?"

He whooshed out a breath. "Suzie, stop. Just stop what you're doing. I know where you are going with all this and honestly, I get it, but I don't want to upset you any further. We can't keep the lodge. We can't do this, honey."

"But...."

God, he hated the look on her face. "Sweetheart, the lodge is going. We can't stop what's already in process."

"Haven't you been listening to me?" She thrust her arms out. "Look at all this. It's wonderful. The kitchen. Did you *see* the kitchen? I mean really look at it? It's doable." She pulled his hand again. "You cannot convince me this place is not solid as a rock. If you see the kitchen, you'll understand. We can renovate. It's perfect, and..." She sighed. "Don't you see? This we can do. We can. I can work here. I would be your sous chef *here*. I would *love* working here. We can do this, Brad!"

He let go of the longest breath. "Suzie, I've seen the kitchen. As old kitchens go, it's a fine one. Have you thought how much it would cost to bring that up to code? This whole place? It's got 1930s everything—wiring, plumbing, appliances, roof, foundation. It won't work. You have to give it up."

She shook her head. "No. I'm not going to give it up."

He chuckled. "What are you going to do? Chain yourself to a porch post come morning?"

Hands on hips, she glared at him. "Brad Matthews, don't you laugh at me. I just might." Then her face screwed up into some sort of crazy puzzle. Shit. Tears. "Don't you dare make fun of me or what I think is important. Do you understand? And yes, come tomorrow morning, don't be surprised to find me chained to that post out front and I'll dare you to send those bulldozers at me!"

The anger in her voice was one thing, but the red creeping up her neck to her face and the tears begging to spill from her eyes were another. Dammit all to hell. Was this woman worth this much trouble?

He exhaled long and hard. Unfortunately, yes. She was.

She broke away from him and jogged across the deck and around the corner, out of sight.

Holy shit. What the hell was he going to do with her?

He followed and found her at the opposite end. She stood gazing out over the lake, leaning over the thick wooden railing. The early afternoon sun tickled at the highlights of her strawberry blond hair falling in a cascade over her shoulders and hiding her face from view.

His gaze followed hers. Sweet Hart Inn sat quaint and peaceful across the way in a grove of trees. It really was a nice view from the deck off the old lodge. He looked around him, studying his surroundings. Large oaks hung heavy branches over the south end, making a natural awning. Pines and cedars flanked the old building to the north. As he stood still and closed his eyes, he noticed the quiet quality of life around him.

Waves gently lapped at the shore.

Leaves rustled.

Suddenly, the hustle and bustle of a big hotel and restaurant on the premises seemed grossly out of place here.

Could he make it work? As it was? Scrap his plans and take a different tack?

Then he heard her crying. *Ah, hell....*

"Suzie?" He took the few steps to reach her and placed his hand on her shoulder. "Sweetheart, let's settle down and talk about it."

She turned her tear-stained face toward him. "Why can't you leave it?" she cried. "Why can't you fix this!"

Fix it. How in the hell was he supposed to fix it? "It's too late, Suzie. The plans are already made. I've got men coming in the morning."

"Too late. Too late! Well, then maybe it's too late for everything. You could fix it if you wanted to. You don't want to."

The tears rolled again and she looked away. He turned her face back to him, longing to look into those incredible blue-green eyes and see happy tears, not sad ones. "Suzette, listen to me. Will you just listen to me please?"

She gave him a reluctant nod.

Taking a deep breath, he said, "Let's call a truce here, okay? Maybe I can put the project on hold. Temporarily. I'll get someone to look at the structure, at the foundation. I can't promise anything, but...."

A blank look broke across her face. "Really?"

With both thumbs he swiped tears from beneath her eyes. "Yes. Really. I'll make the calls as soon as we leave here."

"Thank you," she whispered. Suddenly her eyes squinted again, and she went on. "Brad, I know this is going to sound kind of random and out there, but there is something I need to tell you. It can't wait."

Her eyes closed for a second and she paused; he waited. "Okay."

Her weight shifted from one foot to another. "This is going to come totally out of the blue but I'm about to bust and I have to say this. I can't keep it to myself any longer."

Her tears spilled and Brad was concerned now more than ever. "Suzie, what in the world?"

"I can't have a baby. I mean, we can't have... Brad, about having a baby...."

Baby?

"I. Can't."

She stumbled a little and he caught her up and steadied her. "Honey, why are you talking about having a baby?"

"I can't have a baby. I... My eggs are rotten or dried up or something weird like that. I'm damaged goods, Brad. You're not getting the complete package with me. I'm...incomplete."

He stood there, stunned, looking at her. "What in the hell...?"

But before he had time to contemplate further, he watched her eyes flutter closed and she crumbled into a heap on the deck floor.

———

THE PAST HOUR OF BRAD'S LIFE WAS FILLED WITH frantic phone calls, an ambulance ride, juggling emergency room questions, and a very pissed off Suzie.

She lay on the gurney in the center of the small examining room of the ER while he sat off to the right. Her arm was thrown over her eyes and forehead. She hadn't looked at him for a while.

"You look cute in that little flowery gown," he offered.

"Oh, shut up. Brad Matthews, I can't believe you brought me here. I am fine."

He stood and went to her side, carefully lowered her arm to see her face—in case she decided to deck him—and gently laid it at her side. For good measure, he threaded his fingers with hers and caressed her knuckles.

He planted a small kiss on her forehead. "Sweetheart, you've been sick for days, vomiting and everything, and you passed out like a sack of potatoes falling to the floor in half a second flat. You scared the shit out of me."

"But I'm fine. It's just the flu. I've not eaten enough lately. And I hate hospitals."

"Well, it's almost over now."

She sat up. "You have no idea. They poke and they prod and they take blood and your temperature and make you pee in a cup and check your heart and your throat and your ears and then run this thing with icky goo all over you and...do you have any idea how much this little hospital bill will cost me?"

"Don't you have insurance?"

"Barely. I'm self-employed, remember? High deductible."

"I'll cover it then"

"No, you won't! I'll not let you do that for me. I can't have you...."

"What?"

"Pay for me like that. I'm an independent woman and I don't need anyone to...."

"What if we were married?"

That shut her up.

"Excuse me?"

"What if we were married?" he repeated. "Would you let me pay for you if we were married?"

"Well, I...uh... That's a moot point because we're not married, obviously."

Brad snickered. "True. But we could be."

Suzie glared for half a minute or so. "Is this a proposal, Mr. Matthews?"

"I believe it is, Ms. Hart."

Tears welled in her eyes again. Hell. Not more tears. "Well? What about the lodge? What about all that?"

Grinning inwardly, Brad had to hand it to her. "Are you really going to leverage the lodge against a marriage proposal?"

Suzie smirked and narrowed her gaze. "Damned straight. Do we have a deal?"

Standing, he turned away from her, pacing near the door. "I don't know, Suzie. That's a bit more than I was willing to negotiate for a marriage...."

A roll of bandages sailed by his head and hit the door. He turned back. "Damn, woman!"

"Be serious, Brad. This is important."

Moving to her side, he sat again and took her hand. "You were right, Suzie. I should have looked into renovation long ago. My ego wants me to always think bigger and better. You know, go big or go home. Your way is nice and quaint and more...us."

She sat up a little straighter. "Us. You mean that?"

"I do."

"You're not going to back out of it."

"What, the marriage?"

"No, silly man. The lodge thing. You won't change your mind, right, because if you change your mind, I'll take back my promise to marry you."

"Did you promise to marry me?"

"I...um."

"I need an answer, Suzette."

She chewed on her lip. "Brad, I need... I mean, you should know that... I need to tell you something that I was trying to tell you back at the lodge."

"Something about a baby? Yeah, I was going to ask you about that."

Exhaling, she said, "Brad, I can't get pregnant. I can't have children. And I know that is important to you and I should just put that on the line right now—since we seem to be making a deal on all of this. You need to know that I don't come with potential kids and family. So if that is part of your dream, part of what you think you are going to get with me—what's going to make you happy—I'm shooting you straight right now that it won't happen."

Brad stared into her misty eyes and felt the hurt in her heart dart straight to his. "Honey, that's a lot to take in, but you have to know that I want you first, over anything else."

"Over kids?"

He nodded. "Yes."

"Over the lodge and hotel and anything else on your plan list?"

"Yes, Suzie. Because without you, I have nothing else. No plan matters."

She burst into tears. "Then the answer to your question," she choked out between sobs, "is yes. I'll marry you."

Brad blew out one hell of a forceful breath. "Thank God!"

A brisk knock sounded at the door. They turned and a young male intern entered.

"Ms. Hart?" He glanced from Suzie to Brad and back again.

"Yes?"

He stepped to the opposite side of the gurney from Brad, grasped her hand, and looked down at her. "How are you feeling?"

"Better. This is all stupid. I'm not really sick. I had the flu over the weekend and I'm a little weak. It was warm outside, and the sun was beating down on me, and I hadn't eaten much in a few days and...."

"How is your nausea right now?" He gazed at the clipboard in front of him. All business, Brad thought. Don't they teach bedside manners any more in medical school?

"Well, almost non-existent. Just a little twinge once in a while, but it's okay."

"Manageable then?"

"Yes."

"Usually happens in the mornings?"

"Um...maybe. I don't really remember."

Finally, the man looked up and his face broke into a smile. "Good news, Ms. Hart. You are perfectly fine. Most of your tests came back normal. You're a very healthy woman."

Brad sat up and straightened his shoulders? "Most? What does that mean?"

The intern eyed Brad, then glanced at Suzie. "Husband?"

Suzie's gaze narrowed. "Potential fiancé."

"So I can talk in front of him?"

Brad stood. "Good Lord, Man. Yes, you can talk in front of me. What's going on that we need to know about?" He barked the words a little more loudly than he had intended.

The younger man stepped back and looked to Suzie. "We ran

the standard blood tests and also one for pregnancy. Ms. Hart, you are pregnant. That's all."

"That's *all*?"

Brad listened to those two words come out of Suzie's mouth but they sounded muffled and skewed, like she was speaking from a tunnel. Suddenly, it felt like the wind had been taken out of his sails. Brad clumsily backed into the chair behind him. Pregnant? He finally sat with a whoosh of breath.

His lips stretched into a smile so big he thought he might not be able to contain it.

The doctor turned toward the door. "My nurse will be in momentarily to give you instructions and a prescription for the nausea."

Brad watched Suzie's eyes grow wide. She bolted straight up. "Wait. *Wait!* Did you say, pregnant? I mean, you can't have said pregnant, did you?"

He turned and smiled. "You didn't know? I'm not surprised. You're just pregnant but everything looks fine. You were having a little morning sickness. Or maybe more than a little." The doctor turned to Brad. "Have you noticed any mood swings lately?"

Brad swallowed. Suzie glared at him. "Ah, maybe a little."

The doctor smiled. "Don't worry. It only lasts nine months. Usually." Then he left with a chuckle and the soft click of the door.

"I'm not sure what just happened here," Brad said. He looked at Suzie.

"I'm speechless."

Not trusting himself to stand, he pulled the chair closer and took Suzie's hand in both of his. Then on impulse, he reached up to caress her tummy. "Honey. Sweetheart. A baby." He marveled at the miracle of it all. Now he felt like crying.

Suzie still sat there with her mouth gaping open.

She was pregnant. It was real. He was going to have a family.

They were going to have a family. His plan, all of it, was coming true.

Suzie still looked awestruck.

"We're pregnant," he said to her.

She shook her head. "No, it's impossible, Brad. There has to be some mistake. I'm not pregnant. I can't be pregnant."

What in the world? "Suzie, you heard the man. You're pregnant. We're going to have a baby." Then he frowned. "It is we, right?"

She reached over to the supply cart and threw another bandage roll at him. "If I'm pregnant, Brad, you can be assured that it's *we*."

"Then why would you say it's impossible, because we didn't use protection. Hell, I thought you were on the pill. Didn't you tell me that months ago?"

"I know. I did. It's..." She slumped against the bed. "I lied. Brad, I didn't want to tell you. I never thought I could get pregnant. For years I never got pregnant with Cliff. I was told years ago that there something wrong with me and that I likely would never get pregnant, and since I couldn't give you the family you wanted I just worried that—"

Brad put up his hand. "Stop. None of that matters. Suzie, shut up and kiss me."

"What?"

"Come here." He pulled her closer and then kissed her lips. Within seconds, he was up on the gurney, spooning with her, holding her close and kissing her face.

"We're pregnant," he whispered. "It's real. You and me. Just like old times. Plus one."

"Yes, it appears so," she added softly. "And this baby needs a home with both parents who don't fight and are, well...married."

He nodded. "So, let's make it happen."

Chapter Sixteen

"I wish Shelley were here."

Suzie glanced up into her mother's eyes in the mirror. She'd been thinking about her sister all morning and couldn't get her out of her head. It made her sad that she'd chosen not to share this day with her. Of course, Suzie hadn't been able to share in Shelley's wedding either, but that was an entirely different set of circumstances.

Standing behind Suzie, her mother met her gaze in the reflection, fiddled with Suzie's veil, and frowned a little. "I do too, honey," Joan Hart said, "but it's not going to happen. Your father and I both tried talking to her with no success. I think the girl is so conflicted about what is the right and wrong thing to do that she just does nothing."

Suzie watched her mother lift the golden locket Brad had given her from the dresser and drape it around her neck. As Joan clasped it, Suzie's heart swelled a little and she fingered the heart and pinched it tight. Then she let it drop and settle between her breasts. She might just let it stay there forever.

"I know," she said, switching her thoughts back to her sister. "She wouldn't pick up my calls. I left voice and text messages. She had to have listened to and read them. I told her it was all okay. That we could work things out and that I just wanted her at my wedding. I do want us to get past this, Mom. I really do."

She turned into her mother's embrace. Joan hugged her daughter. "It's your wedding day, darling. We're not going to let this cloud the day. Today is the happiest day of your life, and even though Shelley is being stubborn and a bit foolish, there is nothing you can do about it right now. She's embarrassed and feels guilty about the entire ordeal. She will come around eventually and realize all she's missing. I think truth be told, she misses family. She has to face both her past, and her future, one day soon, and she knows that."

Pulling back, Suzie gazed into her mother's eyes. "I know. And I'm not going to be a sourpuss about it because I'm too happy!" She smiled and hugged her mother. "And nervous," she whispered.

"Nothing to be nervous about. You're getting a great guy."

"The best, Mom. Truly, Brad is just wonderful."

Joan stepped back, smiled, and took Suzie's hands and squeezed. "I'm so proud of you, honey. You've done great things with the inn, your agent found you the perfect publisher for your cookbook, and you've become a fine, upstanding member of this small community. And you know what? I know that Brad is going to be such an asset to Harbor Falls, too. You really make a nice couple."

"A team. We like thinking that way."

"I can see it all ready."

Suzie thought for a moment. "You know, Brad really will be good for the community, Mom. The plans he has for the lodge and the cabins... It's going to be good for us as a family, and for the town. I really am looking forward to the future. I love my life!"

"As you should." Joan glanced at her watch. "Well, dear, it's nearly time. That expensive limousine we ordered from Asheville should be here any minute. We need to get you up that mountain."

With one last hug for her mother, and a final look at herself in the mirror, Suzie sighed. She was getting married today and she was having a baby. Laying a soft hand on her small but growing baby bump, she smiled. Family. She and Brad were about to create a little family of their own, and an entire huge life together.

She gazed at her reflection and then fixed a stray hair or two in her upswept do, the veil and about seven thousand bobby pins holding the rest of her hair in place. "I'm ready."

Suzie turned and headed toward her bedroom door. Glancing at the grandfather clock, and taking in the fact that it was always ten minutes early, she knew her mother was right. Time to leave. In an hour the ceremony would be over, and she would become Suzie Hart-Matthews.

"I'm about ready to jump out of my skin," she whispered.

"I'll grab your train as you go down the porch steps," Joan said.

Suzie nodded and tried to tamp down the butterflies in her stomach.

BRAD STOOD ON THE BACK DECK OF THE LODGE overlooking the lake. The day was clear, the mountain air crisp, and his heart was beating wildly in his throat. He caught a glimpse of the black limo pulling out of Suzie's house through the trees and smiled.

It was happening. Everything he wanted would soon be his, and by God, he was going to take none of it for granted. He'd been handed several gifts over the past few months and he intended to make good use of them.

Harbor Falls would be home now and into the future. And he couldn't be happier.

It would take the limo about ten minutes to get around the lake and up the hill to the lodge. He waited another five minutes before meandering around the deck to the front. There, he glanced at Reverend Peters, from Suzie's church, and to his brother Scott, who had flown in the night before from Italy. His parents, who were stationed in Singapore, were not able to make it on such short notice. He took his place beside Scott on the wide lodge porch and looked out on the intimate gathering of close friends and family sitting in the chairs across from him. Suzie's father stood at the bottom of the steps waiting to give his daughter away, and her Maid of Honor, her cousin Sydney, stood opposite Mike Hart.

The music began. The limo nosed its way around a curve and into sight. Brad swallowed the lump in his throat and licked his suddenly dry lips. He was getting married today.

SUZIE'S BUTTERFLIES KICKED UP A NOTCH THE SECOND they rounded the curve and pulled up to the lodge. She glanced at her mother and blew out a breath. They had rehearsed this last night and she knew then that all would be fine—but now, this was for real.

Closing her eyes, she took a moment to just breathe and be, and center herself a little before stepping out into her future. Her window was cracked and she heard the soft tones of Bach's *Prelude in C* waft into the car with them. Then it stopped and there was a brief pause, and the *Arioso* began.

"That's my cue," Joan said, patting her on her knee. Leaning in, she kissed her daughter on her cheek. "I love you," she whispered. The door on her mother's side opened and one of her male cousins ushered Joan toward the lodge and up the steps. Suzie watched as her mother was seated on the deck landing and her father started toward the car.

At this point all thought ceased and Suzie simply moved on autopilot.

The processional music started. An usher opened the door again and her father reached out his hand. She got out of the car and stood, giving Mike Hart a quick peck on the cheek. The mist in his eyes didn't go unnoticed and his tears nearly made Suzie choke on her own pending mistiness.

Her father tucked her hand into his elbow and then turned and stood facing the lodge. Sydney slowly ascended the lodge steps in front of them.

The next few minutes were a blur as her father led her to her future husband and placed her hand in Brad's. She stood facing him and staring into his eyes as if they were the only two people in the world.

Reverend Peters spoke. They said their vows. And Suzie continued to get lost in the depths of Brad's eyes and his love for her.

As he slowly slipped the simple gold band on her finger, Suzie's tears glided over her eyelids and onto her cheeks. And as she placed Brad's wedding band on his finger, her heart soared.

"Mr. Matthews," Reverend Peters said, "You may now kiss your bride."

Brad smiled and tugged Suzie's hands. "I love you," he whispered, and drew closer.

"I love you with all of my heart," Suzie murmured back.

Then Brad kissed her with a scorching kiss that would be the talk of Harbor Falls for weeks to come.

Epilogue

"Well, he was a man with a plan. He knew what he wanted and damned if he didn't make it happen." Suzie smiled at her husband who in turn patted her growing tummy.

"You gotta have a plan, men, that's all I can say. You gotta have a plan."

The men chuckled and high-fived their agreement and the women batted away their Alpha male attitudes with a flit of their Southern belle eyelashes. They had gathered for an impromptu celebration—Suzie and Brad had married a month earlier and there was a baby on the way. If that wasn't enough to celebrate, the hotel renovation was on track, and the marketing plan for the launch of the renovated Falls Lake Lodge and Resort were taking off. Suzie and Brad had felt like entertaining so they invited over some old and new friends for an evening barbecue by the lake.

"So, until the doctor told you at the hospital, you really didn't know you were pregnant?" Nora Patterson picked at a brownie then held out something to her. She and Suzie had been strategizing some local promotional plans for her cookbook, which would release in the fall. It helped having a bookstore owner on her side! "Here, I brought a book for you from my bookstore. *Everything You Always Wanted to Know About Raising Kids in the 21st Century*. It is a bestseller."

Suzie took the book. "Thanks, Nora. You're a doll." She leaned over and hugged her. "No, I had no clue," she told her. "I was told by doctors years ago I would probably never be able to conceive. I had resolved myself to that fact—so yeah, I was shocked!"

Brad stood and hefted up his pants, broadened his shoulders. "Well, it only took me one time so...."

Suzie sat up in her chair and shot Brad a startled look. "Brad Matthews! Stop."

Everyone laughed.

Marnie poked her head out of the back screen door of the inn. "Suzie, where did you put the watermelon?"

"In the big fridge. But let one of the guys get it. It's a heavy sucker."

Marnie gave her a thumbs-up and then crooked her finger at Greg, who promptly rose to do his wife's bidding.

"Yeah, man with a plan," Suzie chuckled. "Brad, baby, pull that big ol' Adirondack over here for me please? I need to put my feet up."

"Yes, dear."

Everyone in the crowd chuckled.

Suzie felt full of life. The little munchkin growing inside her belly thrilled her to no end. The husband sitting to her right fulfilled her every dream. And the backyard with friends who came to celebrate their growing family, rounded out her simple life.

"How's the renovation coming, Brad?" James asked, sitting on the arm of another Adirondack chair, his arm draped around Eliza.

"Great! I was so amazed. What you told me that first day on the property was true. The old building was added to the federal historic registry a while back. Seemed the bank that owned it back in the day didn't want to put the money into the structure to remodel according to federal specs, so they claimed it was condemned and unworkable, the foundation falling apart. All totally untrue. The new architect I hired took one look at the place and said we were fools to tear down the landmark."

Suzie elbowed him. "I told you so."

Brad grinned. "Lesson learned. Have a plan but listen to the woman."

The crowd erupted in laughter again.

"It's solid though, and probably not as costly as I thought. It will take a year or so but will be worth it."

"At least the baby will be here before then. Oh Brad, the contractor came yesterday about the addition to the house. Forgot to tell you."

"You're building another room on the inn? A baby room?" Marnie joined the group and grabbed Suzie's hand to pull her up off the chair. "C'mon girl, we got plans to make. Show me where this new room is going to be, and then we'll talk about everything you need to put in it."

Shrugging, Suzie looked back at Brad and gave him a smile and a little finger wave good-bye.

Marnie tugged her along. "Eliza? Nora? Sydney? Y'all come too. This is a group project."

Brad chuckled. "Do they ever not do anything in a group?"

Greg slapped Brad on the back. "Rarely," he chortled. "Welcome to Harbor Falls, Mr. Matthews, and to the rest of your life."

With a soft whistle through his teeth, Brad replied. "No place else I want to be, man. All of my heart is right here."

From the Kitchen of Suzie Hart, Sweet Hart Inn

Blog post, November 19, One year later: *It's beginning to look a lot like...*

The holidays. I love them! Halloween flew by in a flash. Thanksgiving is just around the corner. And my favorite time of the year, Christmas, will be here before you know it.

So, I have a question for you, dear readers. What is your favorite holiday?

But I'm not going to let you off that easily. Tell me more. What is your favorite holiday recipe?

I want to hear from all of you so please comment below. I'm giving away some goodies over the next few weeks, so all comments count as an entry!

But let's leave all that fun and frivolity to the side for a moment. Holidays are more than food and gifts and parties. Holidays are for family first.

I am especially grateful this holiday season for all the wonderful things that have happened in my life this past couple of years. As you know, Sweet Hart Inn has been open now for nearly two years. I married the love of my life summer before last, and in

February we welcomed our first child, little Petey Matthews. Home, hearth, and family mean so much to me, and I look forward to spending this next holiday season with my husband and son and the rest of my extended family.

We are truly blessed and hope that you are too. There is little more that I want or need in life than to be with the ones I love. And I sincerely mean that about everyone in my family. One family member has had a tough time over the past months and could use your thoughts and prayers. I want her to know that no matter what, I still love her and I'm here for her. All she has to do is come home.

Happy Holidays to all! Don't forget to send me those favorite holiday recipes!

Love, Suzie

A Note from Maddie,

Friends,

I hope you enjoyed reading *All of My Heart*. Suzie and Brad's story is one of my favorites! And if you liked their story, just know that you will see more of them, and their friends and families, in the upcoming books in the Sweet Hart Inn series.

If you enjoyed this read, then please consider sharing with others. One of the best ways to tell others about the book is to leave a review at Goodreads, or at the bookstore where you purchased the book. You can also leave reviews at my website, maddiejamesbooks.com.

Ready for more Sweet Hart Inn? Read on for *Take My Heart!*

Will Suzie forgive her sister when she comes home?

If she comes home?

Take My Heart

Take My Heart

Maddie James
A Sweet Hart Inn Romance, Book 2

Take My Heart

A SWEET HART INN ROMANCE, BOOK 2

When Shelley Hart ran off and married her sister's fiancé, the whole town of Harbor Falls was in a twitter. A few years later, with her husband deceased and two little girls to take care of, Shelley realizes her only recourse is to go home.

The last thing Shelley Hart wants is to go home for the holidays. She left Harbor Falls years earlier and hasn't returned. Her leaving humiliated her entire family and caused friction with her older sister, Suzie. Who could blame Suzie for being upset? After all, Shelley ran off and married Suzie's fiancé, Cliff.

But everything has changed now—and going home is her only option.

Harbor Falls Police Officer Matt Branson values being alone, even during the holidays. Dubbed the town hermit, he prefers the solitude of his mountain cabin to socializing with friends—friends who say he still pines after the woman who got away. But the snowy day he pulls over an older model sedan speeding into Harbor Falls, things change. His gut slams against his backbone as a tearful woman rolls down the car window. His heart melts when she looks up into his eyes.

Shelley Hart is back in town—the woman who sent him into his cave in the first place.

Chapter One

"I can't believe I'm doing this."

Shelley Hart slammed down the trunk lid on her old Dodge Stratus and grimaced as the gas cap flew off and tumbled over the parking lot.

Darn thing. She stared as it rocked back and forth on the asphalt. The little door was sprung, and the cap never worked right after her tank got siphoned. The siphoning incident happened the first night she moved into her new apartment here in Dalton Springs, which occurred three months after the bank notified her they were taking the house, which took place six months after her husband had died.

Nine months. Long enough to have a baby.

No, thank you very much. One of hers was screaming from the backseat, already.

"Be there in a minute, sweet pea."

She glanced back at the apartment and frowned. She'd had high hopes she could make it on her own. Without Cliff. But no. Didn't seem to matter how far she tried to stretch the dollars, there were never enough. Her gaze lifted to the sky behind the complex. It was overcast and gray, tinged with a pink early evening sunset. A winter sky painted with cotton candy. The weatherman promised a white Christmas and the air smelled like snow.

The mountains rose in the distance, strong, sturdy, and secure.

"Harbor Falls is over there," she whispered. "Home...is over there."

Strong, sturdy, and secure. She supposed she needed that. She'd not had a strong shoulder to lean on since Cliff died—maybe it was time she leaned on family.

Her gaze played over the Blue Ridge Mountains. Only forty-two miles separated Dalton Springs from Harbor Falls—but a chasm of hurt and past indiscretions stood solidly in her way.

She swallowed hard and swiped at a tear with a gloved finger. Soon she'd have to swallow a whole lot more than spit. Pride. Yes, that was it. It had been nearly three years since she'd been home. The last thing her sister, Suzie, expected to see this Christmas was Shelley on her doorstep, homeless and penniless, with two little kids in tow—the ones she'd had with Suzie's fiancé, uh, *ex-fiancé.* Whatever....

Yes, she'd caused quite the small-town scandal. That disgrace even beat Polly Gruber running off with the preacher. Didn't seem to matter to anyone that she and Cliff were happy and loved each other. Oh, she knew the repercussions, running off with her sister's man. The whole town thought she was pond scum. Lower than pond scum, even.

But Suzie and Cliff were taking a break, officially, and Suzie had moved to Asheville for a while. And he was lonely.

Wasn't entirely her fault, was it?

One thing led to another and then—

Then they'd ran off and gotten married. Suzie found out later and all hell broke loose—in the family and in Harbor Falls. And then Cliff had to go and die and leave her in this mess. No insurance. No savings account. No family.

No matter. Home was where she was heading. Home to Harbor Falls, and for the holidays, no less. With no plans ever to return to Dalton Springs—Dalton Springs and Cliff were all in the past.

Sniffling, she wiped another tear before it froze to her lashes.

Home. Harbor Falls.

She was about to suck it up and head home to family, like it or not.

Taking three brisk steps forward, she bent, snatched the gas cap off the blacktop and twisted it back into place on the car. She rounded the vehicle and got in, not looking back.

Just forward.

"Come on, girls," she said. "Let's see if we can fix this mess."

A BRISK GUST OF WIND ROCKED THE VEHICLE. HARBOR Falls Police Officer, Matt Branson, turned up the heater and lowered the volume on the country music station on the radio. "Damn. Must be a helluva storm coming."

He pushed a few buttons to scan the stations, hoping to find something with a local weather report. Would be nice to know what he was in for tonight, sitting here on the side of the road waiting for unsuspecting speeders to dart by. Lucky for him, he was assigned the newest police cruiser the city of Harbor Falls, North Carolina owned. Nice vehicle, too. He did enjoy a perk now and then with his job. He liked to think it was because he was the only officer with a degree in law enforcement, but probably not. The other officers were homegrown and locally trained, but they were good ol' boys and did one helluva job.

Besides, it was Harbor Falls, right? The village force was small but reliable enough to handle anything that Harbor Falls threw at them. A domestic or two, a kid gone awry and of course, the speeders. Biggest trouble was the occasional tobacco smuggling, a few pot plants growing in the foothills, and once a homemade Meth lab run amok, but the county Sherriff's department and the regional ATF guys took over those, mostly. Harbor Falls was little more than a 21st century Mayberry, R.F.D.

He hoped he was a lot more than a modern-day Barney Fife.

He'd left town a year or so after high school—had pretty much fled with his head hanging and his heart on his sleeve, if he remembered it accurately—and in a few years had himself that degree from Eastern Kentucky University.

Damn proud of that, too. So was his Mama. Because of that degree, and the fact that he brought all that new-fangled knowledge back to his hometown of Harbor Falls, he was pretty much top dog cop in these parts. Well, not counting the Chief.

So here he was. Waiting.

Of course, it wasn't like he had a horde of family members at home. He probably wouldn't even see his Mama until tomorrow evening at the Methodist Church candlelight service, and his sisters were all due to arrive very late Christmas Eve night with a passel of his nieces and nephews. They wanted to be home in Harbor Falls on Christmas morning, much to the chagrin of their husbands.

Other than that, there was no one.

Frowning, he shifted in his seat, pushed that thought out of his head, and glanced out the window. Lucky for him, the east end wasn't the busy end of town. At least he wasn't walking the downtown beat sniffing out shoplifters. Lit up like a roman candle for about three weeks, the town of Harbor Falls eagerly welcomed the shoppers and they came in droves. All that marketing about Harbor Falls had paid off the past year or so. He had to admit it brought some mighty strange folk out of the hollers.

So, in a way, he was grateful not to be downtown. On the other hand, not a single car had ventured by in the last fifty-two minutes. The town council thought sitting out here was a wonderful idea. They needed revenue for the force, so they had passed a new ordinance lowering the speed limit in both directions. The guys on the west side were pulling them over right and left.

He could hear that on his radio. The action on the east, however, was, well, non-existent.

Bored, he watched as small ice crystals formed in little pellets on his windshield. He let them pile up on his wipers and then swished them away. That kept him busy for about three minutes. He breathed on the window next to him and drew funny pictures on the glass, then smeared them off with a leftover fast-food napkin, leaving behind ghostly images. He upped the temperature and turned on the defroster to keep the fog down.

Should a speeder happen to venture by, it might be good if he could see out his window.

Finally, he reached under the seat, pulled out a piece of wood, and dug deep into his pocket for his whittling knife. Not eager to get shavings and wood chips all over his new cruiser, he laid the napkin out on the seat beside him and started to whittle.

There. Perhaps this wasn't so bad after all. He could sit here until the snow piled up and whittle, if he had to. Putting knife to wood was the one thing that kept him company for hours on end when he was at home—in his cave, as his sisters called it. He loved that cabin he'd built up on the mountains, though. Cave or not, it was his, and he had learned to be okay with how his life was turning out up there.

So okay, his social life sucked. He refused to call himself a hermit, although when not at work, he spent most of his time at home. Living a solitary life had both its advantages and disadvantages. Carving wood helped him keep his sanity.

Just didn't do a damn thing for keeping his bed warm at night.

His knife hand stilled on the wood and his head jerked up. A vehicle raced in from the south, popping over the hill. He reached to swipe away the fog from the driver's side window that failed to dissipate. The dark blue sedan whizzed by, and he quickly stashed his knife and wood under the seat.

"Hot damn."

Tucked back in the lane of the old Casey place, he pulled out from his hidey-hole and turned on his lights and siren.

———

It wasn't like Harbor Falls was that far away from Dalton Springs, but in North Carolina, country roads aren't laid down in straight lines like they say a crow flies. Winding and narrow, the two-laner twisted through the foothills of the Blue Ridge Mountains. Mostly, Shelley took her time while the kids napped.

It was when she pulled into Village Grove that she made her mistake.

Even though the girls' tummies were full, she had not eaten herself since morning. Up early packing boxes, she'd scrambled a couple of eggs and then washed and packed her skillet. After that, eating hadn't been a priority. Figuring out what to do with the rest of her furniture filled her agenda that afternoon. Most had been sold earlier, but there were a few odds and end pieces she gave away. The cash would come in handy the next couple of weeks.

She'd sucked down caffeine in various forms all day. Hot, cold, it didn't matter. But no food.

As she cruised into Village Grove, a town larger than Dalton Springs, her stomach growled, and she was getting tired.

The golden arches loomed a couple of blocks ahead. Did she dare? Generally, the fast food place was the least expensive option.

A quick glance into the back seat and she knew her girls were still asleep. Katie, the oldest at nearly three, sat with her head cock-eyed and her neck crooked, her mouth agape and drooling. A thin shaft of fine baby-blonde hair was stuck to her face in her slobber. Fourteen-month-old Karly's right cheek was pressed hard up against the sidewall of her car seat, her one shock of blonde sticking straight up like a Mohawk. She clutched a beat-up Tickled-Pretty-Pink stuffed bear in her chubby little fingers.

Shelley looked back at the road, slowed, and pulled into the drive-through lane.

"Please let them sleep," she whispered, wanting a few minutes more of peace and quiet. Pulling slowly to the speaker, she rolled down her window.

A screech and a crackle met her. "Take your order?" the young man bellowed.

"Shit," she breathed and glanced back. Katie stirred. "A cheeseburger value meal," she said quietly, "and a large iced tea, please."

A scream went up from the back seat. Karly.

"Don! Don! Don!"

"Five-ninety-six, Ma'am. Please pull to the first window."

"Dammit," she hissed then smiled into the speaker. "Make that three of everything, please."

"Don! Don! Don!"

"Except the tea. Give me two juices instead."

"Yes, ma'am. Fifteen-seventy-two."

"Okay."

"Mom-meeee!" Katie shouted. "Karly woke me up! Oh! We're at 'Donald's! Can we play?"

"Slide! Slide!" Karly bounced in her seat.

"No, girls, we are not getting out."

Wails rose from the rear.

"Don! Don!"

Shelley sighed. "I have your food coming up. Hold on, girls."

She moved to the window and waited, pinching her nose while the girls chattered and bounced and squealed in the back seat. Karly still wanted to slide, and now Katie was yelling for her fries. In the end, she retrieved her meals from the window, pulled over and took the girls inside to eat. They did, barely, and then ran off to play in the huge play place while Shelley rubbed her temple and watched from a small table next to the multi-colored ball pit.

Luckily, the play place was nearly deserted. A quick glance

outside told her why. Snow pelted down at a nice clip now. People must be staying in. Or they were out shopping.

She was getting a damn headache. Should get on the road soon, she kept thinking. Then she remembered she had to stop and get diapers before she got to Harbor Falls. Ralph's was at the end of town. She'd stop there.

One more stop. One more time getting the girls out, and back in, the car. Buckling, securing, tucking, finding bears, having snacks within reach, making sure straps weren't too tight. Another shopping trip trying to avoid the "mommy I wants" and the "gimmee gimmees" while searching for diapers, and oh, yes, she also needed wipes.

Can't forget the wipes.

All in all, she calculated that stopping at Ralph's, coupled with the hour they would probably spend here at 'Dons,' her arrival back in Harbor Falls would be later than anticipated. Of course, no one was expecting her, so what difference did it make, anyway?

She rubbed her head more. Too damn tired. She really, really needed to get going.

And going she did. She rounded up the little boogers, made her trek through Ralph's and was headed into Harbor Falls from the east side of town when she popped over the hill near the old Casey farm. The snow was coming in sideways now, and she was glad to almost be at Suzie's, even though her stomach was in a knot. She had no clue how her sister would react at her arrival.

She sighed. It had already been a long day and now...

Lights flashed in her rearview mirror and a siren chirped behind her. The girls started crying again. She glanced up.

"*Dammit!* Dammit all to hell."

Tears immediately sprung into her eyes. This, she did not need. *What next?*

Chapter Two

"This was a mistake."

Icy and sharp, the snow slanted against him as Matt got out of his cruiser and headed toward the blue Dodge. It cut into his face and he tilted his chin into his chest to avoid it. The driver moved the car to the side of the narrow road, but he wondered about the sanity of pulling it over. Visibility was quickly becoming non-existent and he didn't relish being exposed and vulnerable should someone else pop over that hill.

They'd had a lot of snow lately. An unusual amount. It didn't seem to be letting up any, either.

Before he'd left the cruiser, he'd taken a moment to jot down the license plate number, noting the out-of-county plates. He didn't recognize the car and figured the person inside wasn't local. Somehow that comforted him, although he wasn't quite sure why. Perhaps he would feel less guilty giving a ticket to a stranger rather than someone he knew—especially during the holidays.

He glanced at his watch. His day was nearly up. "Short and quick," he told himself. "Then get home."

The windows on the car were tinted so it was difficult to see inside. That always made him wary. He approached slowly, came even with the front edge of the side door, and knocked on the driver's window.

The immediate sound of babies crying hit him as the window rolled down. He leaned forward. A woman was turned toward the back seat. He stepped closer to see the driver. A blond mane was all he could see. She faced the children as her frantic voice tried to quiet them.

"Be still. Hush, girls," she said. He thought he heard a sniff behind that plea.

"Ma'am." He leaned further and looked at the passenger seat. No one there. He relaxed inside but kept his stoic composure from an outward appearance.

He hoped.

The woman turned to look at him and, in a flurry of words and tears, blurted out, "Officer, I'm so sorry. The babies were crying and I have a headache and," *sniff, sniff,* "the snow is coming and I wanted to get to my sister's and," *sniff,* "I didn't realize I was going that fast and—oh, my—"

She stopped. Blinked. Looked up at him with those baby blues that he remembered oh, so well. The baby blues that sometimes still haunted his sleep.

Something punched him deep. His gut twisted and fell. His heart slammed against his chest. Straightening his shoulders and posture, he attempted to plaster the most stoic demeanor he could possibly muster on his face.

He wasn't sure he pulled it off.

The snow angled into her window and the swiped at the tears spilling onto her cheeks. A hand shielded her eyes from the stinging pellets. "Matt?"

He nodded with a single word. "Shelley."

That's right. Show no emotion.

"I...uh..."

He squared himself. "Been a while since you were in town, so guess you don't know the speed limit has changed. Might be a good idea for you to heed that."

With a puzzled look, she nodded. "Of course."

"Of course," he echoed. "Since you left out of here on a whim and a prayer, without a word to anyone, I figured you've probably not given anyone in Harbor Falls a single thought since then, let alone the speed limit."

"Matt, I—"

He cut her off. "I'm giving you a warning. Watch it." With that, he turned on his heel and headed back to his cruiser, his heart pounding more with each step he took. *Yes, watch it sister. You have a lot of nerve showing your face back in this town.*

No, he wasn't going there.

By the time he settled himself in the cruiser, the breath whooshed out of him in one fell swoop, fogging up his windshield.

"Dammit," he muttered and kicked up the defroster.

He waited for her to ease back onto the road before pulling out himself, then he followed her all the way through town. He sat, back rigid, fingers curled in a tight grip around the steering wheel, his chest taut as a drum.

His brain hummed. His heart ached.

She turned onto Lake Road. Seemed she was heading toward Sweet Hart Inn. He headed up the mountain.

He couldn't wait to get home. To his cave.

"Dammit, Shelley, why are you here?" He pounded the dashboard.

Everyone in Harbor Falls knew that Cliff had died, but...

His gut slammed against his backbone. Was Shelley home? Was his high school sweetheart back in town to stay? The woman who sent him into his cave in the first place?

He hoped with everything in him that it wasn't true. It was the holidays, right? Lots of people come home for the holidays. Even people who vanish from your life and never look back.

Hell, he hadn't realized how much his heart still hurt.

THERE WERE A MILLION THINGS SHE COULD FEEL RIGHT now, but Shelley pushed every one of them into some gray area of her brain. Matt was one. She could not deal with Matt Branson today. Not now.

The day had been too long. She was exhausted, emotional, and hungry again, not to mention frustrated with the crying babies in the back seat. Tired from fighting the snow and her emotions, she chose not to think any longer, just to do. So that is what she did.

She drove straight down Lake Road, turned into Suzie's drive, slanted her gaze at the sign that read, *Welcome to Sweet Hart Inn,* and prayed that she would be exactly that—welcomed.

She doubted it.

She knew the way even though she had never been to the house since Suzie had turned it into a bed and breakfast. Their Aunt Donna had lived there for all of Shelley's growing up years until she passed away—not long after she and Cliff had eloped and settled their lives into Dalton Springs. Shelley hadn't attended her aunt's funeral, either, and she felt a pang of guilt because of it. But things were as they were then, and there was nothing she could do about it now. What she *was* doing was what needed to be done— making amends, she hoped, with her sister and family—and that's all she could do.

Right now, at least. Any other past transgressions she'd deal with in time. Matt's face flashed into her mind's eye at that moment and just as quickly, she pushed the image away.

Not now.

The gray, snowy night matched her somber mood perfectly. The snow had stopped for a while. A couple of inches piled up around Suzie's front porch. She pulled alongside the house, and not bothering with anything but her purse and the girls, headed up the sidewalk. Karly was in her arms, her soft head resting on her shoulder. Katie toddled along beside her, holding her hand.

"Be careful of the ice, honey," she said to her oldest.

"Yes, Mommy."

Tears sprang to her eyes again at the sweet child. She loved her girls so much, and now that they had arrived at this decisive moment—as she navigated the steps up to Suzie's front porch with her most precious cargo—she wanted only one thing. She wanted Suzie to love her girls as much as she did.

Even if she didn't accept Shelley, maybe she'd accept her girls.

Too much to expect, probably.

With every emotion known to woman ready to cackle up and spill over inside of her, Shelley swallowed her pride and moved forward onto the porch. A cascade of greenery and lights arched over the front door. Beyond in the sidelights of the door, she could see someone milling about. Soft Christmas music met her ears and she could smell cookies baking.

Peanut butter with chocolate drops.

That notion made her smile. This was the Suzie she remembered.

If only...

The door swung abruptly open. "Shelley? Oh my God!"

Her sister stood there, framed by holly and twinkling lights, a questioning expression on her face. Her strawberry blond hair was piled high on her head. She had flour on her face and was wiping her hands on her apron. A little boy clung to her leg.

Tears poured. "Suzie," Shelley sobbed. "I'm so sorry. I am so, so sorry for everything. I am..."

Suzie grasped her sister and pulled her into the house, tears streaming down her face. "Come here, you," she whispered and kicked the door shut behind her. "Just come here."

Shelley sobbed on her sister's shoulder, and Suzie, always the gracious hostess, let her. She hugged her with several years' worth of longing, trapping the girls in their embrace.

"I've been so worried about you," Suzie whispered, pulling back to look into her face. She gently thumbed away tears from

Shelley's eyes and then turned to both girls, cupping first Karly's small face in her hands, and leaning down to do the same with Katie. "You are both so beautiful," she said softly.

Next, she grasped the little boy's hand that still clutched her leg. Shelley guessed he was a little younger than Karly.

Crouching, she said to the boy. "Petey, these are your cousins, Katie and Karly. Say hello?"

Petey turned his face into his mother's leg. Katie burrowed a little closer into her own mother.

Straightening then, Suzie looked long into Shelley's face and whispered, "Merry Christmas, Shelley. We have a lot of catching up to do but let's put one thing to rest right now. The past is the past. And I am so very glad that you're here."

Shelley sobbed, relief washing over her.

MATT DROVE ON AUTOPILOT UP THE MOUNTAIN AND past the old lodge, navigated the drifting snow on the narrow mountain road, and took his time getting to his isolated cabin. His escape. His refuge from the storm—and life.

Shelley was back, he was sure of it. As he'd thought over the situation of thirty minutes earlier, he realized that her car was packed up with things. A suitcase was jammed between the girl's two car seats. A couple of small boxes and bags were stowed in the passenger seat and floorboard. There was a grocery bag from Ralph's, too. He'd taken all of that in within a few seconds because that was what he was trained to do. Observe and record in his brain. Sometimes the details didn't jump back at him until he had removed himself from the situation and his brain had time to work over it.

The drive gave him more than enough time to analyze the situation.

He approached his cabin and pulled up close to the porch,

realizing that he was going to have to shovel himself out in the morning. He wasn't going to worry about that now. Shoveling came with the territory when you lived at a higher elevation and winter was here. Besides, he welcomed the physical exertion. Although snowstorms in the Blue Ridge Mountains were a part of life here, rarely did they get one that shut their world down for long lengths of time. But they did get them occasionally, and when they did, residents in and around Harbor Falls generally were prepared to hole up for a few days.

He hoped that wasn't the case with this storm. Just like he hoped that Shelley would land in Harbor Falls for the holidays and then leave to go back to Dalton Springs. That scenario was not likely, and he knew it.

Fiddling with the door lock, he twisted the knob and stepped inside. He shrugged out of his jacket and shoes, handing up the coat on a hook by the door and leaving his shows on a mat there as well. Glancing toward the fireplace, he decided to light a fire to take the chill off. The furnace was set to a low temperature while he was gone, but a fire was what he wanted and needed tonight.

A fire would chase the chill away from his bones and his heart. Hell, he hated that his heart had turned cold after all these years, but it had. There was a time he thought if he ever had the chance to win Shelley back, he would do it. But that time had long passed.

How many years was a man supposed to wait?

Chapter Three

Petey and Karly hit it off immediately. In no time, they were toddling about, circling the Christmas tree in the living room, and playing hide and seek in every nook and cranny downstairs. Katie poked at a homemade chicken potpie that Suzie had popped out of the freezer and baked for her.

"I'm sorry she's such a picky eater," Shelley said, sitting at the bar and scooping cookies off the sheet to cool on racks. "Always has been."

Katie looked up and smiled at her mother. "I picky."

Shelley grinned. "Yes, unfortunately, and you know it."

Suzie worked the cornbread stuffing with her hands, mixing up the ingredients. "No problem. Petey is as picky as they come too. Some days all he will eat are my chicken potpies and sweet pickles. Breakfast, lunch and dinner. That's why I keep them on hand."

"Good idea. I need to learn how to cook like you."

Suzie smiled. "You've been busy with babies. That will come later, if you want."

Shelley thought about that and smiled. What would her future bring? "I just don't know what I want to do with my life."

"That will come too." Reaching out, Suzie patted her hand. "Have you called Mama and Daddy yet?"

She shook her head. "No. I need a few more minutes." Suzie nodded and Shelley was relieved her sister didn't push it.

They talked for over an hour while Suzie managed to feed everyone and simultaneously do prep work for the meals she was catering tomorrow, on Christmas Eve. Brad was at the lodge for the employee Christmas party, and Suzie didn't expect him until late. That was nice because it gave them time to themselves. They'd discussed Suzie's marriage, the renovation of the lodge, the births of all the babies, and even Cliff's death.

"That had to be horrible," Suzie said, as they chatted about the shock of the accident. "I didn't realize cement mixers could do so much damage to a Honda."

"Anything running over you full-speed-ahead is going to be bad."

"At least he didn't know what hit him."

"True," Shelley replied, her gaze drifting. "If only he hadn't taken that detour and swerved for that dog."

"Freak accident."

"Yeah." *Pause.* Shelley pondered the freakishness of it all.

"Cliff always liked dogs," Suzie added.

"Yeah. It was a Bassett Hound."

Pause.

"How do you know?" Suzie picked at a piece of lint on a dishcloth.

"The truck driver said it in his statement. Said the dog lumbered off okay but poor Cliff got smashed like a people pancake." Shelley sighed. "Funny how people remember details like that."

Suzie giggled a little. "Sorry. It's just..."

Shelley grinned. "I know. It's okay. It is funny in an odd way."

"Makes sense though."

"What?"

"That he wouldn't want to hit the dog. Not the people pancake part."

Shelley nodded. "Oh. Sure." She was surprised and a little appalled at herself that she could even think this way about poor Cliff. Maybe humor was a way to deal.

A longer pause. Suzie looked straight into her eyes. "Shelley, you know we wanted to help you."

The mood shifted then, and she waited a moment to respond. "I know. I couldn't."

"You could have returned our calls. Mama and Daddy were so troubled."

That cut deeper than she anticipated. "I figured."

Suzie looked up from her mixing bowl. "Shelley, why? Why would you not let us help you through this? I know we were sort of joking around there a few minutes ago but this was a serious thing for you. Losing a husband is an awful, terrible thing. And it was so sudden." She bit her lip and stared ahead. "Besides, Cliff was, well...family. Sort of."

She'd thought her eyes were pretty much devoid of tears but at that, they stung again. "I assumed you all hated me."

Sighing, Suzie went to the sink and rinsed her hands, then stood at the bar and placed her palms on it. "Shelley, don't ever think anything stupid like that again."

She shrugged and stood. "Suzie! I stole your man! You went out of town to work at that job, so you could save money to open your own business, and I swooped in and stole him. He was lonely, and I was young and flirty, and before I knew it, we were in bed and I had fallen in love with him. Why would you not hate me?"

Suzie laughed. "Oh, believe me, I did." She moved around the bar, tugged out a stool, and sat. She pulled Shelley into a seat, too. "I hated you with a passion, but not because you stole Cliff. I hated you because you had something I wanted. A loving husband and a family. But all of that changed once Brad and Petey came into my life. Over the months, I realized I didn't hate you after all. In fact, you cleared the way for me to pursue the happiness I always wanted. Happiness that Cliff couldn't give me." She paused for a moment. "I can't imagine what it is like to lose a husband. Now that I have Brad..." she trailed off, thinking, "well, I felt for you, and wanted to help in some way, but you didn't respond. I didn't know what to do."

Shelley shook her head. "There was nothing you could do. I had to find my way out of this." She glanced off, and then added. "But Suzie, I can't do it. I wasn't making it in Dalton Springs on my own. I lost my house. The money wouldn't stretch. So, I needed..."

"You need to start over. Here. In Harbor Falls." Suzie reached for Shelley's hands. "You're home now, sweetie, and this time, you'd better let us help you."

Hesitant, Shelley grasped back. "I do need your help," she whispered. "Just for a while. I swear, once I get back on my feet I'll be fine, and I'll never be a burden to you again."

Suzie shook her head. "You're not a burden now."

"I hope not."

Suzie squeezed her hands. "You're not. We'll work out the details later. When Brad gets home, I'll have him fetch your things from your car and get you settled in upstairs. For now, it's Christmas and we are going to have the best one in years. Now, go call Mama and tell her you are here, or I will. I can't wait for tomorrow night."

Shelley couldn't either. It would be the first Christmas she would have with her family in years. Her Mama and Daddy had never even seen her girls.

A smile broke across Suzie's face, but Shelley also noticed her misty eyes. Suzie was on the verge of tears. "I can't either, Suzie. Thank you for everything. I'll go call them now."

LATER, AS SHELLEY LAY IN BED IN SUZIE'S GUEST ROOM, she thought about the numerous twists of fate life had dealt her. She refused to feel lonely and depressed any longer about all that, now that she was here. Now that she was home.

The hard part was history. She was going to make this work.

Shelley was tired but happy—and settling into this beautiful room provided her the comfort she needed right now. Suzie had called this the blue room, but really, it was mostly white with blue accents. All the furniture was white—the picture frames, the billowy sheers at the window and the plantation blinds underneath —all set against a backdrop of watercolor blue walls. The Irish quilt was navy and white, the sheets pale cobalt with starched cotton embroidered pillowcases, and a matching crocheted afghan tossed over an old over-stuffed chair. Blue Willow plates were on the wall and a blue-swirled glass ball hung from the curtain rod. The room had a beachy feel, which was a nice contrast in this mountain area.

The girls were asleep in the adjoining room—the turquoise room. Suzie always names her bedrooms after colors. Lucky for everyone, Suzie didn't take guests over the holidays. That meant she only had to share her bathroom with the girls, which was normal for them. Situated between the two rooms, it was also provided easy access to them. She could hear their cries and whimpers in the night.

So tired she could barely spit, she laid wide-awake looking up at the ceiling. Seemed it was difficult to turn off her brain and calm down her body. The worse part was over, though, apologizing to Suzie. Tomorrow she'd see her parents again, and she couldn't wait for them to see her girls. Her mother cried on the phone and wanted to rush right over, but Shelley convinced her that they were all tired and tomorrow would be better. Her dad finally talked some sense into her.

Her mama's last words on the phone had both pained and relieved her.

"I'll sleep better tonight than I have in years."

Nearly choking, Shelley quickly said her goodbye and hung up.

This was a beginning. A fresh start. She still had a long road ahead of her.

Turning onto her side, she closed her eyes. Just at the point of giving over to sleep, an image popped into her head.

An unsettling but nice image. Tall, broad shoulders, sandy-brown hair, eyes the color of a copper penny, and in uniform.

Matt.

Something clutched at her heart. He looked good. Damn good. No doubt, some young chic had snatched him up in no time with minutes to spare. She hoped so. He deserved someone. Someone who would be good to him.

She supposed she'd find out, eventually.

It was good seeing him though. He was her first love. Her first...everything.

Since you left out of here on a whim and a prayer, without a word to anyone, I figured you've probably not given Harbor Falls another thought.

He was wrong. She had thought of Harbor Falls, and of him, often.

But she'd dumped him. Obviously, he'd not forgotten about that. Odd how that notion bothered her.

Chapter Four

"**H**old onto you hats, folks, we're in for a heckuva snowstorm. What we saw yesterday was nothing compared to what's coming. This new front started rolling across Missouri and western Tennessee the past twenty-four hours, and the computers tell us it could be a doozey. So get those gifts wrapped and delivered and batten down the hatches. Santa, you may be in for a cold, snowy ride tonight. I hate to say the B word, but..."

Matt smashed his hand down on the clock radio beside his bed, halting the weatherman's prediction.

"Great..." he mumbled. "Blizzard."

He dozed again and five minutes later, *White Christmas* blared in his ear.

Smash!

The old clock radio slid off the oak bedside table. He glanced at it. Five minutes after six. Shit. Bing Crosby still crooned from the floor and then the DJ was back. "*Looks like we have a few hours, folks. Expect light snow to arrive around noon. We'll see six inches by dinnertime, and another two-to-three throughout the evening hours. Hey, we're not used to this folks, but look at the bright side—we'll*

*have a good ol' fashioned white Christmas this year. Get those sleds
ready, kids!"*

Groaning, Matt reached for the radio's cord and jerked it from
the wall.

"Wonderful." Sitting up, he rubbed his hands over his face. He
usually didn't work on Saturday but had taken a short shift for this
morning. With this weather though, he predicted he'd probably
get the call to work later, if needed.

Christmas Eve and a blizzard. Damn. With both of his sisters
driving down from Ohio, his mother would be worried-to-a-fritter
until they arrived. Not to mention he would likely spend his
evening helping people—who should know better than to drive on
winding mountain roads during a blizzard—get out of the ditch
they'd slid into.

"Bah humbug."

It's all right. He would find time with family and besides, he
was here to serve, protect, and help his community. It was his job
—it was who he was.

Rising, he stumbled to the shower, wondering why he was in
such a foul mood. Ah, yes, Shelley, combined with the effect of too
much bourbon last night. So why the hell was he even up?

Oh, yeah. He'd volunteered for the early shift so he could go
Christmas shopping later for his nieces and nephews. Nothing like
waiting until the last minute but he was a procrastinator when it
came to shopping, and he had to have gifts. Today.

Hot water rained down on his back and he reached up to
switch the nozzle on the showerhead to deliver a harsher stream on
his neck and shoulders.

"Oh. Yes..." he hissed.

Eyes closed, he tried to erase the vision of Shelley looking up at
him with those movie-princess eyes, summer sky blue, and all that
blond hair framing her face.

Tears.

Even stressed and upset, she was still beautiful.

"Dammit."

Worse part, she was clearly upset, and he had wanted to take her in his arms and smooth all the bad stuff away, whatever it was. Even after all this time, he'd been tempted, for a moment, to say, "How can I help? What can I do?" But he hadn't. Thank God. One touch to her face, one hint of her scent, one innocent and casual embrace could be his undoing.

No. He'd rescued many a damsel in distress in his day—was part of the job sometimes—but dammit if he'd risk rescuing her in any way shape or form. Shelley Hart was one woman who probably wouldn't welcome his rescuing her anyway. But he'd heard over the past few months that things weren't good for her and that did concern him. Still, he didn't want to get all White Knight and everything about her and think he could make her world right again.

That wouldn't happen.

Shelley made her choices long ago when she'd dumped him and ran straight into the arms of someone else.

Breathing deep, he let the water beat on his head and shoulders some more, hoping it would beat some sense into his thick skull at the same time. Then he stepped out the shower, dried off and dressed, and left the cabin to do whatever it was he needed to do today.

Work. And oh yeah, shopping. Right.

"I can't believe I forgot the baby wipes."

Slamming the door to her Dodge, Shelley muttered to herself and headed toward Ralph's. Only a ten-minute drive from Suzie's, the store parking lot looked fairly empty, and she hoped to sneak in and out with her purchase in record time. Since it was still early, she figured most people would be home in bed. Wrapping her jacket tight around her against the stiff breeze, she flipped up her furry hood and hustled toward the entrance. With any luck, she'd see no one who would recognize her and want to talk.

She didn't need that this morning. Once she realized she'd forgotten the wipes, and that the babies would be up soon, she rushed out of the house without washing her face or brushing her teeth. Bad choice, likely, but she did it. Even though she pulled on a pair of jeans, she still wore the t-shirt she'd slept in. No bra.

Not the way to introduce herself back into Harbor Falls, by any means.

"Okay," she mumbled, her breath steaming from her lips, "shop like a man. Get in, get out, get home." The automatic door to Ralph's swished open and she moved inside.

"Yes," she hissed. "Practically empty."

Some weird rendition of *Jingle Bells* played in the background.

She scurried along to the baby aisle. Glancing right and left, she let her hood slip down to her shoulders and scoped the aisle for her brand. There. Yes. She grabbed it, tucked it under one arm, and rounded the corner. She was outta here.

Then—

Coffee.

The heavenly smell of coffee hit her full force. Oh, could she use some caffeine. Definitely. The dark kind with extra octane. Looking to her left, she spied the self-serve counter and smiled. Ralph's was moving up. She didn't remember this coffee service before.

Hesitant for only a second, she looked about. Oh my God, was that Betty Jo still checking at the counter? How many years had she worked for Ralph? A hundred? Another glance back to the coffee. Yes, she would risk it.

Darting forward, she realized she may actually be salivating, longing for the taste of the warm and rich liquid on her tongue. "I swear I must be addicted," she muttered as she reached for the largest of the paper cups.

"Okay, so where is the yellow stuff?" She searched for the artificial sweeteners, quickly located them, tore off the tops of three packets and dumped the contents into her empty cup. Next, she poured the coffee on top, the aroma wafting toward her nostrils.

"Um." She closed her eyes, inhaled, and savored a moment of pleasure. "Come to mama..."

"Ahem. You going to stand there and breathe that, or drink it?"

Her eyes popped open. Shelley jerked. *Shit!* "Matt?"

"Yes. Mind scooting over so I can get some of that, too?"

Shelley looked where she was standing, right in front of the burners and the carafe. "Oh. Oh!" She backed up and searched for the lids. She rounded him and they switched places. In the process, she scooted her hood up a little higher to cover her face.

"I need a lid," she said, then edged away. "Ouch. And one of those cardboard protector thingies..." She fumbled with the plastic disk and couldn't get it on straight to save her.

"Here, let me."

Large hands reached in front of her. She tried not to look at him. After all, she was skuzzy. Hadn't washed her face...

She ran her tongue over her teeth.

He deftly attached the lid, slipped a cardboard sleeve on the cup, and handed it to her. "There you go. Complete with one of those cardboard protector thingies."

Shelley looked up into his face. He almost grinned. "Thanks," she said.

"You're welcome."

He didn't move. Just stood there. She stared at her cup. "Well, I should be going."

"Me, too."

Finally, she did look up. He'd not gone anywhere. *Move or say something, Shelley!*

"After you," he said.

She took a step toward the cashier, then halted. "Oh, Matt. Thanks for last night. I mean, you could have given me a ticket."

She swallowed and looked into his eyes, *really* looked into them, the first time in a long, long time. She had always thought his eyes were the most beautiful color of coppery brown...

He hesitated, looking like he wanted to say something, but couldn't find the right words. "You weren't going that much over the speed limit," he finally said.

She shrugged and held her coffee cup in both hands, clamping her left arm tight against the wipes still tucked into her left side. "Well, it was nice of you." She glanced at Betty Jo who was staring at them. "I should go."

She turned, slightly.

"At least one of us plays nice."

The tone of those words, as much as their implication, cut as deep as anything. She turned back. "Matt that was a long time ago."

"Three years, six months, seven days."

Shit. He hadn't... Had he? "What?"

"Three years, six months, seven days."

"Are you still mad at me?"

He squared himself, stance broad, as if ready for action. The look on his face said he meant business. "I'm mad as hell, Shelley. Why wouldn't I be?"

She had no clue. "I..." she glanced off. "I don't know what to say."

"Sorry, I think, is the appropriate word."

Looking at him again, she shook her head. "Somehow I think my saying sorry still won't cut it." She sat her coffee and the wipes down on the counter and reached for his forearm. "Matt..."

"It's a start." He jerked away, stepped back.

Surprised, she continued, "Matt, okay, I'm sorry. I know I hurt you. I hurt a lot of people and I'm sorry about all of that. I know..."

"You *know*? You don't know shit." He sat his coffee on the counter beside hers, although a little too hard. The bottom busted off the cup and hot coffee splattered everywhere. Both jumped, but he continued. "Hurt? Do you know the meaning of that word, Shelley? You made me the laughingstock of this entire damn town." His gaze narrowed and he leaned forward. "I don't ever, ever, want to see you again. Do you understand? So, if you are back in town for good, steer clear of me, you got that?"

Stunned, Shelley jerked back and stared into his face. "Sure. Got it. Perfectly clear."

Then he stomped off, leaving her standing there watching him walk away. She stood there until he left the store.

She guessed she just got from Matt what she had expected from her family. But could she blame him? She'd evidently hurt him bad—and obviously, he'd not gotten over it.

"Damn it."

She didn't move until Betty Jo came up with a mop.

"Shelley, dear, let me get this."

She stepped back and investigated Betty's facial expression. "Oh. Excuse me. I'm sorry Betty Jo. I didn't realize..."

No. She hadn't realized. No really. She'd been immersed in her own world and the concerns of others were second place. Truly, all this time, she had not known that Matt Branson hurt that badly when she broke it off with him—and ran off with Cliff.

"Takes time to heal," Betty Jo said, not looking up from her mopping.

"It was years ago."

"Yes," Betty answered, swiping the mop back and forth, "but small towns don't forget. Men don't forget. It's their ego."

Tears welled up in Shelley's eyes. "I guess not," she whispered.

Still looking at the door Matt had exited, she wondered if she would ever live down the actions of her past with the residents of this town. Especially, with Matt.

Somehow, it mattered. Now, it mattered.

"He's just hurt is all," Betty said.

Shelley finally looked at her. "I didn't know."

"You do now."

"He hates me."

Betty stopped her mopping and shook her head. "No, I don't think that's it, sweetie."

"But he said..."

"Men say a lot of things when they've been hurt bad." She patted her arm. "He'll come around."

Shelley wasn't so certain. "I don't know." Glancing at their feet, she noticed Betty Jo had everything cleaned up. "I'm sorry about this mess. Let me help." She grabbed some paper towels. "And then I'll pay for his coffee and stuff."

"Never mind about that." Betty took the towels out of her hands and picked up the baby wipes. "Let's check you out and get you back to the Inn. Two little girls I understand. I bet they are adorable."

Desperately trying to fight back tears, Shelley smiled and nodded, thankful for her kindness and change of subject. "Yes, and they are beautiful."

Betty Jo smiled. "Of course, they are!" She hooked her arm in Shelley's and led her toward the checkout counter.

"I need to get back before they wake up."

"Sure, honey." Betty Jo rounded the counter and scanned her purchases.

Wake up. Yeah. She supposed perhaps she was the one who needed the wakeup call this morning. Last night with Suzie had gone so well, she had hoped the rest of her reunion with Harbor Falls would be smooth sailing.

Apparently, that was not the case.

Families forgive. Old boyfriends do not.

Try as she might, the thought of that made her tears spill over. What was she going to do? No one in this town was going to let her forget the past. How could she move forward with the constant reminders all around her?

MATT SAT IN HIS CRUISER IN THE PARKING LOT AT Ralph's and let out a long and painful explosion of breath. His chest felt like it was going to detonate from pent-up anger and yes, hurt. He hadn't meant to unleash on Shelley like that but the sight of her had caught him totally off guard. He'd only wanted coffee, not an encounter with the one woman he was not yet ready to encounter. Again.

Two times in less than twenty-four hours. *Don't make this a habit, Branson.*

He still needed coffee.

Obviously, if Shelley was going to frequent Ralph's for morning coffee, he needed to change his habit. Drumming his fingers on the steering wheel, he stared at the front door of the grocery and within seconds, Shelley emerged. He watched her slowly make her way to the older model Dodge Stratus he'd pulled over last night, swipe at her face and get in the car, and then drive off toward Maple Street. Was she crying? That thought bothered him a little. He hadn't meant to make her cry. He followed the path of her vehicle until her brake lights came on at the courthouse square. She turned left. From there, she had a straight shot down Elm toward Lake Road, which would take her to Suzie's.

He assumed that was where she was heading. He stared down the road long after her brake lights were gone.

At any rate, he'd change his morning routine. After twisting the key to start the cruiser, he followed Shelley's path but made a turn off Elm onto North Main, then he parked in front of *Sugar High Bakery*, wondering if that was a bad idea too.

Shelley's cousin, Sydney, owned the *Sugar High*. Was this borrowing trouble too?

But she had coffee. And he needed coffee. Now.

Sucking in a deep breath, he exited his vehicle, crossed the sidewalk, and entered the bakery. The aroma of fresh baked goods and coffee overtook him. Good choice.

"Matt!"

He glanced to his right. Over by the window sat his colleague and fellow Harbor Falls police officer Chris Marks. Matt gave Chris a nod then glanced to the counter as he headed toward the table. Sydney caught his eye and said, "Black, right?"

"Yes, ma'am. And something sweet if you don't mind."

"That's the way we do it around here, sugar." Sydney winked and Matt smiled. "Good to see you out and about." Shelley's cousin had always been the friendly type and a straight shooter. There would be no games played here, he was certain. He wondered if Sydney knew Shelley was back in town.

Not his business to bring it up and he wouldn't.

He sat across from Chris. "Morning. What's up?"

Chris sat staring out the window. "Not a lot. Slow morning. I got patrol out on the east end in thirty minutes. Thought I'd stop in here for a few first."

Matt dipped his head in a quick nod. Sydney placed a steaming cup of black coffee in front of him and a gigantic glazed donut. "Here you go, Matt. Fresh out of the fryer. The glaze hasn't even hardened yet. Did you know Shelley was back in town?"

So, there it was. He glanced up into Sydney's face. "I did. And we're not going to talk about that."

Sydney screwed up her mouth. "I heard about it last night. Shelley's mom called my mom, and my mom called me. You know it was only a matter of time until she realized she needed family and all. And those two little girls, they need family too. I can't wait to see them. We are all going over there tonight."

Matt took a deep breath and exhaled. Sydney's sentences always seemed to flow together, and he wasn't sure how or if she took a breath while she was speaking—so he took a breath for her. "That's nice to hear. I hope you have a good time." He looked at Chris then, who was still staring out the window. Intent on changing the subject, he said, "What's got your attention, Marks?"

But Sydney went on. "Oh, that's Katie Long. The librarian. Chris sits here every morning watching her walk from the parking lot into the library wearing those tight, short skirts of hers and those three-inch stiletto heels."

Chris' brow furrowed as he turned to Sydney. "I do not."

"It's why you come here," Sydney countered.

"I come here for the coffee," said Chris.

Sydney placed both of her palms on the table and leaned forward. "As much as I would love to believe that, Chris Marks, I say bull hockey. You come here for the legs."

Matt grinned and watched Chris's face turn crimson. He glanced across the street. "Good looking librarian, huh? I haven't been to the library lately."

Chris frowned. "Well don't start now."

That's the last thing Matt needed, and he knew it. "Relax, Marks. I have no desire to tangle with the librarian. She's all yours to ogle."

"I'm not ogling."

Sydney stood and sighed. "Oh God, Chris. You are so ogling."

Matt laughed as Chris sputtered. "I... I..."

Then she turned to Matt. "Might do you a little good to ogle too, once in a while, Matt Branson. You're gonna dry up and get old before you know it and your life is going to pass you by."

Now it was Matt's turn to frown. "What the hell are you talking about?"

She leaned in again. "She's back. Make your move, Matt, before someone else in this town does. You'll kick your own ass from here to Asheville and back if you don't, and if she goes off and marries someone else again. Because you know it's going to happen eventually."

Matt swallowed and narrowed his gaze. "Don't go there, Sydney. I'm not ready."

"You better get ready."

He shook his head. "You don't understand."

Sydney shifted her weight to her left hip. "I understand perfectly. It was bad. Real bad. For a lot of us, but really bad for you and you've not gotten over it. Over her. But she's back. Make no mistake, she's vulnerable, and you don't need to rush in there like a house afire, but don't push her away before you and she even have a chance."

Matt stood and looked Sydney square in the eyes. "Stay out of this, Sydney."

"She's my cousin. And you are my friend. I'm in it."

"I'm asking you to stay out."

"All I'm saying, Matt, is that you might want to be a little nicer to her than you were this morning. She's had a rough time too."

This morning? "What the hell are you taking about, Syd?"

She shrugged. "News travels fast. Small town, you know? She was crying when she left Ralph's and feels like no one here is ever gonna give her a break again."

Shit. "Well people need to be cautious."

Sydney eyed him. "Sometimes people just need to throw caution to the wind, Matt Branson. Sometimes people just need to take their heart and run with it."

Chapter Five

"**I** was hoping you could help me out today, Shelley, if you don't mind. I know it's Christmas Eve, but, I could really use an extra pair of hands."

Suzie dumped a pan of piping hot potatoes into a huge colander in the sink. Steam rose and she turned her head to look at her sister. "The pies and cakes are on the shelves in the pantry, in boxes and ready to go. I have the name and order number on each. You'll see a little sticker on the top. The salads are in the fridge in the basement. We'll have to carry those up at the last minute. Same deal, sticker on top. The hot foods will be coming out in the next couple of hours. I have to do some shifty work here." She glanced up at the clock. "Great. It's just after noon now. Everything must be delivered by six and we're racing the snow. Oh, the list is on the bulletin board."

She pointed toward the wall above the built-in kitchen desk. "Matter of fact, could you go check that now and see what time we need to be at Clint Roberts' house? He called earlier this week and wanted to know if his delivery could be moved up. Poor man, eating alone on Christmas day." She peered at her sister. "And such a fine specimen. He really shouldn't be eating alone. Perhaps we should invite him over."

Shelley narrowed her gaze. "Clint Roberts? Stop. I know that look."

"What look?"

"That, *let's fix her up* look." Suzie had loved to try to find dates for her little sister all during high school. "I'm not ready, Suzie."

Suzie grimaced. "Oh, hell. Last thing on my mind."

Moving toward the list, Shelley looked for Clint's name. "Four o'clock."

Suzie hefted the colander of potatoes onto the counter and dumped them in a huge mixing bowl. "What?" She batted away steam again.

"Clint. He wants his meal delivered at four."

"Oh." Two huge sticks of butter went into the potatoes. "Wouldn't hurt for you to put yourself back out there though."

Frowning, Shelley replied, "Um, No. Maybe in another year or so." Suddenly she felt flushed, thinking about her encounter with Matt earlier this morning. With her reputation, there wasn't man in Harbor Falls who would touch her with a ten-foot pole.

"Well, Clint's not right for you anyway."

"Not sure anyone is right for me," she mumbled.

Suzie thoroughly salted and peppered the potatoes. "What about Matt?"

Shelley coughed. "Yeah right."

"Well, you two were very much in love in high school, and he's still holding a torch for you, I think."

She laughed aloud at that one. "Oh, I don't think so."

Reaching for the cream, Suzie stopped to look at her sister. "Why would you say that?"

She hesitated, and then decided to spill. "I've already seen Matt. Twice, in fact. He pulled me over for speeding last night on the way into town, but he let me off with a warning. Then, I ran into him again at Ralph's this morning when I went in to get the wipes. Believe me, he's not interested. In fact, he was darned blunt. I think his words were something like, 'if you are back to stay, steer clear of me.' Doesn't sound like torch-holding to me."

"Sounds exactly like it to me."

Vigorously, Shelley shook her head. "No. Believe me. He's not interested. He's mad as hell. So, I'll do as he said and leave him alone." She looked sharply at her sister. "And you will too! Do you hear me?"

Suzie turned to pour a cup of cream into the potatoes. "Of course. Whatever you say, sis."

After a pause, Suzie added. "But he looks good, doesn't he? Filled out in the past couple of years. Works out a lot, I think. And in the uniform..."

Shelley closed her eyes and immediately got a mental image. "Yes, dammit, he looks good." *Too good.* She shook herself and opened her eyes. "But that is neither here nor there. Matt Branson is no longer a part of my life, and he made it perfectly clear that he wants nothing to do with me. So, don't go getting any ideas."

Suzie turned toward her sister and grinned. "Noted. Now, who is on that list before Clint? This snow is coming down and we might need to move everyone up. Will you check?"

SOMETIMES PEOPLE JUST NEED TO TAKE THEIR HEART and run with it.

Matt knew what Sydney meant and he knew that for years he had been doing just the opposite. Oh, he'd been running all right —running away from his hurt, avoiding the subject of Shelley every chance he got, pushing away from a close relationship with any woman. But with all of that running, he'd left his heart out of it every single, damn time. Easier that way, he knew.

He didn't intend to risk the pain again.

He'd become a master at protecting his heart, not running

with it. In fact, the thought of throwing caution to the wind and going after Shelley just about made him nauseous. He'd not brought his heart out to play since the day she told him they were done—and he had no intention of bringing it out any time soon—with her or with any other woman.

He sighed, watching snowflakes drift over his windshield as he sat in the same place he sat last night when he'd pulled Shelley over. Thank God, his shift was over at noon today. He had things to do before the Christmas Eve family events tonight. He was ready to get those tasks done because the longer he sat there, the more he thought about Shelley. He had to admit, that the few minutes he had stood looking down at her last night had been a huge jolt to his heart. His ego. And messed with his head a little.

She was beautiful, even while crying. He'd always thought she was pretty and sexy, even when they were teenagers. It didn't matter if she was scuffed up and dirty playing softball in a field, or if she were dressed to the nines in a little black dress with pearls. He'd always liked her looks and any time he ever saw her, his heart lit up.

But it was more than the fact that she was a pretty girl. His heart just felt happy whenever she was around. He was happy.

Caught off guard last night, it had happened then too. His heart, for the first time in years, lit up at the sight of her. Her dewy eyes tugged at his heartstrings. Her lips were still pink and kissable, and how he had remembered kissing those lips for minutes on end when they were younger....

His heart hurt, dammit. His chest was tight. He hadn't felt anything in that spot for months. Nothing. Because he hadn't *let* his heart feel. He'd shut off the pain and yes, even the good feelings.

Dammit, Shelley! Don't do this to me. Don't make me feel.

But he *could* feel now, and the pain was real. He ached for her today just like he'd ached for her the day she'd left. He remembered how that felt like it was yesterday. She'd given him no real reason why she wanted to break up—just that she wanted to move on, and she felt like he should too. That they had grown up since high school and they had different goals. She'd never mentioned anyone else or wanting to be with anyone else.

It didn't make sense.

A week later it all came together. The news flew all over town like an out-of-control wildfire. Shelley Hart had run off and married her sister's fiancé—one week after he and Shelley had broken up.

It damned near killed him.

And Sydney wondered why he was cautious?

SHELLEY CROSSED HER ARMS AND LEANED INTO THE desk, searching the delivery list. "You want me to be the delivery girl?"

Nodding, Suzie pushed back a stray lock of hair with her forearm. Shelley went to her and clipped it back into place. "Thank you. That hair was bugging the tar out of me." She paused, reaching for the potato masher.

Shelley went on. "If you don't mind that the girls are here with you, I can deliver, run errands, whatever you need."

A huge sigh of relief escaped Suzie's lips. She tweaked her sister's cheek. "Thank God you came home. I can use some help. I'll let Brad deal with the kids."

About that time a squeal, a giggle, and a man's low chuckle came from the living room.

Suzie grinned. "I just love that." Then immediately, she frowned and reached for Shelley's hand. "Sorry, I didn't mean..."

Shelley stopped her. "It's fine. Really. I'm glad you have Brad. And the girls sure love him already. He's read them at least three stories this morning."

"He's really good with kids."

"They miss their dad." She glanced off.

Suzie went to her then and gave Shelley a hug. "Of course, they do honey. They will be adjusting to life without him for a long time. So will you."

"I know. Being here is helping though, Suzie. Thank you."

Suzie gave her another squeeze. Shelley pulled back, nodding toward the cackle of laughter from the living room. "They were calling him Uncle Bad a minute ago."

Laughing, Suzie went back to work on the hot spuds. "That fits." She looked at Shelley with a twinkle. "He is a bad, bad boy..."

"Suzie!"

"Well, it's true. And I love it." She mashed some more, slowed, paused, and looked back up at Shelley.

"What?" She wasn't sure she liked that look on her face.

"Shelley, I have more work than I can handle."

The buzzer went off on the oven. Shelley trotted over to turn it off then looked inside. "I think the cornbread stuffing is finished.

"Test it for me, huh?"

Glancing around, Shelley picked up a thin-blade knife and stuck it in the middle. Came out clean. Then she pushed the stuffing away from the side of the pan. Yes. It was done. "Ready here," she told her sister.

"Hm. Good."

Grabbing potholders, Shelley pulled the steaming pan of stuffing out of the oven and set it on a wooden cutting board on the counter. Once more, she pressed a finger into the dish to see if it would bounce back. Yes.

"It's done."

"Good."

"Shelley?"

"Hm?"

"I need help."

She turned to her sister. "I know. I'll do your deliveries today."

"No. No, that's not what I mean." She sat the masher down

on the counter and faced her sister. "I know you don't want handouts, and this is definitely not a handout. I've had more work in the past six months than I did in the first two years of my business. The inn is going strong. The second cookbook is in the can. It comes out in two months and the publisher wants me to do a book tour. I've nearly stopped doing my cooking classes because of the time factor, although I dearly love to do them. And the catering, sweet Jesus, the catering is my bread and butter right now since the inn is closed until February. I need your help."

Stunned, Shelley took a step back. "You want me to work for you?"

Suzie shook her head. "No, with me. Be my partner. You always loved to cook, and you're a natural. I can teach you the rest. With Petey now, and with Brad so busy at the lodge on top of everything else, I need you. Big time."

Shelley sat on a barstool. "I don't know what to say."

Suzie grinned. "Say yes. Please."

"Yes?"

"Well, that was enthusiastic."

"Yes!"

"Ack!" Suzie jumped up and down. Shelley sprung up too and they hugged, squealing. Suzie stopped and grasped her forearms. "Seriously, I don't think you will want for work. Sydney could also use some help in the bakery part-time. I told her I would mention it to you."

"Seriously?"

"Yep."

Some sort of seriously elated happy energy bubbled up inside Shelley. "That's fabulous!"

The pitter-patter of stockinged feet and little girl giggles joined them. "Mama!" Katie shrieked. "Uncle Bad got my toes!"

Shelley scooped her up. "Well, did he give them back? Let me see!" She grasped for one of Katie's feet.

A silly smile broke across the girl's face. "Bad didn't really take 'em. They still on my feets."

"What's all this?" Brad's voice boomed out.

Suzie grinned from ear to ear. "She said yes."

"Thank God." He reached for his wife and nuzzled her ear. "Maybe I can get my Suzie back at least part-time for a while." He kissed her cheek. "Did you tell her about the lodge?"

Shelley looked from Brad to Suzie. "What? What about the lodge?"

Suzie nudged him. "You tell her."

"All right." He looked into Shelley's eyes and even though she'd only met him the night before, she knew he was a sincere man and anticipated what he was about to say. She could see some seriousness in his thought. "The top floor of the lodge has a three-bedroom suite with two bathrooms. It is yours for as long as you need it. Rent free."

The breath whooshed out of her the second her butt hit the barstool. Her hands fluttered to her chest, stilling her heart. "Oh, no. Brad, I couldn't."

Brad leaned closer and placed his hands on her shoulders. "Yes, you can. We want you there with the girls. There's no kitchen, but you can use the hotel kitchen anytime you like. I know the head chef." He winked and stepped back. "Besides, when I cook, I cook plenty, and there will always be enough for you and the girls. Raid the refrigerator."

Almost giddy with excitement, Shelley was speechless. "I... Brad, Suzie, I don't know... this is too much. I don't think I can accept."

Suzie crossed her arms over her chest. "Hey, little sister. It's Christmas. Think of it as your gift. You gonna refuse your Christmas present?"

Again, Shelley glanced from her sister to Brad. "I, uh... I don't know what to say..."

"Say yes," they chimed simultaneously.

"All right. Yes! But this is only temporary until I can get my own place. I want you to know that I realize that." Her gaze bounced between Brad and Suzie.

They nodded. "Of course," Suzie said.

Shelley exhaled and whispered, "Thank you."

An hour later, Shelley slammed the trunk lid down on her Dodge and rechecked the packages in the back seat. She and Suzie worked the afternoon away putting food into plastic containers, stuffing dinners inside insulated sleeves, and gathering cold dishes from the basement. It was nearly three o'clock, another two inches of snow was on the ground, and she needed to get moving. Fortunately, all her deliveries were in town, except for the one errand she needed to run for Brad. She'd offered to pick up the lodge deposit for the day in exchange for him watching the girls this afternoon.

If she didn't get to the bank before five, Brad warned, they could make a night deposit. But she did need to get to the lodge before his assistant manager left for a three-day holiday, and before the roads in the mountain got too bad.

Feeling good about her day and her decision to come back home, she waved to the porch where Suzie, Petey, and the girls stood in the doorway, then headed out. Smiling, she marveled how yesterday her life was in turmoil. Today, it had done a complete three-sixty. Her heart warmed at the prospect. As she drew closer to the bend in Lake Road that would take her to the lodge, she wavered. If she made her deliveries in town first, then she could stop by the lodge on the way back home.

But then she'd have to go back into Harbor Falls to make the deposit.

Turning right would take her to the lodge. She *could* get the deposit, then backtrack to run all her errands and deliveries in town. But it was early. Would Brad's manager have the deposit ready yet?

Left would take her into Harbor Falls. She glanced at her watch and the sky.

There was plenty of time. People were waiting on their meals. She glanced at the delivery schedule Suzie had typed out for her and knew she had to keep to that schedule. She glanced at the roads. They had been brined the night before and the town snowplow had just gone by. The sky was blue, and nothing was coming down right now.

She turned left and headed downtown.

Chapter Six

"I shouldn't have stayed so long in Asheville."

Learning forward in his seat, Matt stared ahead and realized his were the only wheels breaking through the several inches of snow on the road in front of him. Even if someone had come before him, the rate at which the snow was falling covered everything very quickly. They sure weren't used to snow like this here, and he worried about drivers not knowing how to handle this kind of weather.

The sun had set as he approached Falls Mountain on the southern side. Wet and heavy, the white stuff was piling up. A quick glance to the trees showed weighty branches thick with snow. At least there was no ice. Yet.

"Hope the power holds out," he muttered. "I've got too much to do tonight."

Thankful for his four-wheel drive, he leaned into the steering wheel and concentrated on driving. Soon though, he was mentally ticking off the tasks to do before he could finally relax and get some sleep. He was no Santa, to be sure, but it seemed this night, he might be up all night long. With the back of his Jeep full of presents, he had a couple of hours to get home, wrap some, put together others, and get them all back in the Jeep before heading into Harbor Falls for the midnight candlelight ceremony. If he was lucky, he'd find time for a shower.

He'd tried all day to get his mind off Shelley and his stupid reaction to her at the store. He supposed he'd apologize, eventually, but he didn't want to. He'd put up this stout wall of protection about him for years. He didn't talk about it to anyone, and if someone was insane enough to bring it up, he set them straight right away. The subject of Shelley was off limits. He dealt with it in his own way.

Yeah, by hiding out, you bastard. Is that really dealing?

"Shut up," he said aloud. Chastising himself wasn't going to do any good, either.

Thing was, he didn't know if he wanted to come to terms with the hurt Shelley dealt him. It had dulled, of course, but no one—not one woman he'd encountered since then—had been able to replace her.

That's what scared the hell out of him. He was a strong man, physically, but if he let himself succumb to Shelley, would he survive if she dumped him again? If it somehow didn't work out?

He honestly didn't know.

But no time to dwell on that tonight. He took another hard look at the road before him.

His two older sisters were supposed to be home in time for church. The roads all over were getting icy and slick. That worried him. Could take them longer than expected. It was tradition that if humanly possible, the four of them—his two siblings and his mama—would spend Christmas Eve together at the service. They'd done it since they were kids and their daddy were alive. They'd miss him as always, although he'd been gone for a while.

Once the ceremony was over and the kids were all tucked into bed at his mama's, he'd unload the Jeep, put some things under the tree and hide others, then hightail it back home for a few hours rest. He knew that his oldest nephew, Brian, nearly ten now, would be calling and waking him way before daylight.

Those plans might have to change. Would he be able to make it back up the mountain to his place after the service?

Hell, it was likely he might not make it back down to the service. Maybe he should turn around and go back to his mother's while he could.

Squinting, he peered through the windshield and increased the rate of swipes his wipers were making. "Seems worse up here," he muttered and frowned while turning onto Lake Road, determined to move forward. His home sat a few miles past old Fall's Lodge and off a dirt road further up. Suited him fine. The more difficult it was to get there, the harder for someone to make the effort.

For good measure, he turned on the radio to the local station. Having spent his afternoon in Asheville, he'd not paid a lot of attention to what was happening in the foothills.

"*Three more inches in the last hour, folks, so we're up to seven here in downtown Harbor Falls and it's just six-thirty. I've heard it's worse in higher country. This stuff is coming down fast, furious, and wet. Forecast says we're not finished yet. Stay in, stay warm, and stay off the roads.*"

"Great." Matt glanced to his cell phone. No calls. He frowned, picked up his radio, patched into the station, and asked for the Chief.

He waited, turned his lights on low beam, and slowed.

The snow shifted into a sleeting mass of ice that blanketed his windshield all too quickly. As he followed the road, now significantly narrowed because of the snow, he began to think that his plans, so thoroughly laid out in his head, were likely to change.

"Matthews?" The crackle met him from the radio.

"Yeah, Chief. Need me down there? Just checking in."

"Didn't want to bother you son, during your time off."

"Yeah but looks bad up here. I'm heading up Lake Road toward home. How is it there?"

"For the most part, fine, power is on, no accidents, people keeping of the streets, but..." The thing crackled and sputtered some more. "are you... lodge?... didn't get... frantic."

"You're breaking up. What?" He crept along, his gaze fixed ahead of him.

"Are you near the lodge?"

"Yes."

"Good. Matthews... sister didn't... home."

What the hell was he saying? Matthews. Suzie?

Matthew's *sister*. Shelley?

"What?" Squinting, his gaze caught and held onto a flash up ahead. Lights.

Something garbled came back.

"Come again, Chief."

"Shelley... missing. Might be... lodge. Didn't make it there."

Lights. Deeper trenches in the snow heading off the edge of the road.

Shelley?

"You hear me Matthews?"

Shit!

A cold iron fist clutched at his chest and squeezed his heart. The lights. The beam. Casting not at him, but straight up into the trees. He braked as easily as he could without sliding off the road. To his right, he could see down over the embankment.

A small car had slid off the road and practically climbed a tall cedar down the hill. If it weren't for the lights, he would have passed it by.

"Gotta go."

Please, Lord, no....

SHELLEY SAT WITH HER HEAD AGAINST THE STEERING wheel, gripping the thing like her last minute on earth depended on it, and panted out breath after breath after breath. Adrenaline shot through her, throbbing in her veins. Crying, she attempted to control her errant breathing and tried really, really hard not to panic.

She wasn't going to be successful on that last part.

Her heart pounded, and fear of what to do next raced through her entire body. Oh God! It all happened so fast, the curve, her tire slipped off the pavement—she couldn't even tell where the freakin' pavement was!—and she'd tipped, slid, and rolled once.

Flipped! She'd flipped the car!

"I don't know what to do," she whimpered. At least she was now upright. "I don't know what to do!"

She was in a tree. A freakin' tree! But thank God, it stopped her from going further down the mountain.

Stupid, stupid, *stupid!* She should have picked up Brad's deposit earlier. She didn't think about the roads being worse at the higher elevation.

Stupid!

She huffed out one huge breath that thoroughly steamed her windshield. "Okay," she whimpered. "Am I hurt?"

No. She didn't think so. Her chest ached from where the seat belt grabbed her and something hit her in the head—maybe her purse?—when she'd rolled.

She glanced to her right. Cell phone. "Where is my..." She leaned to her right.

The car shifted in the tree and she screamed. "Oh, God!" Panic raced through her. "Oh, God!"

Thoughts of her girls ran through her head and she teared again and sobbed. "I want to see my babies!"

Something knocked against her window and she screamed.

"Shelley!"

Someone was out there! "Yes!" she screamed and frantically reached for the button to roll down the window. "It won't work! I can't get the window down!"

The voice came again from outside. "Stay calm. Sit still. The windows won't work when the engine is off. Hold on."

The voice. "Okay," she said and slumped into her seat. "Calm, he said. Stay calm."

He shouted again. "I'm trying to see how stable the car is before I try to open the door. Sit still, okay?"

Matt. It was his voice. "Matt?" she screamed. "That you?"

Pause.

"Yeah. Just hold on."

She blew a long, slow breath out of her puffed cheeks. Of all people... "Hold on," she whispered. "God, please let him not be so mad at me that he lets me slip on down this mountain..."

Closing her eyes, she tried to breathe evenly, to still her panicky heart. She prayed this would all be over soon.

She heard the latch on the door and risked a glimpse to her left. Slowly the door opened, and framed there in the moonlight, sleet slanting over his face, was Matt. He'd never looked so damn good to her in all her life.

Leaning in, he reached across her—his face way too close to hers—and pushed the latch on her seat belt. She got a whiff of Old Spice. Funny how that scent made tingles shoot through her. He'd been the youngest man she had ever known to wear Old Spice back in high school. She realized she still liked it.

Funny she should think of that now.

He lingered. Looked into her face.

Their gazes caught and every past remembrance of them together shot through her with sudden awareness. At that moment, she realized how much she did not want him to hate her.

"I think your belt is jammed."

She sniffled and a tear fell. "Please cut the damn thing off and get me out of here."

"I don't have anything to cut it. Have to go back to the jeep."

She grabbed his arm. "No! No, please don't leave me, Matt. Please."

"Shelley, this car could slide down the mountain at any moment. We have to get you out."

"I know. I know! But Matt, please don't leave me. I'm begging you. Please don't leave me alone. I can't bear the thought of it."

MATT THOUGHT ABOUT THE IRONY OF THAT. HE DIDN'T want to leave her. Never, ever wanted to leave her all those years ago. It was she who had left, and he who was left alone.

"I won't," he told her. He knew that should the car shift and start to slide again, he'd be there right alongside her. No way would he leave her alone—no matter what happened in their past. "Okay, let's try something."

Her tears were nearly his undoing, and once again, he was sucked into the overpowering feeling of wanting to protect her. Hell, at this point, he only wanted to save her, get her out of this car. He'd deal with any other emotions later.

Go into cop mode, he told himself. Serve. Protect.

He tried hard not to put any more pressure on the car than he had to, so he didn't lean too heavily into her. The vehicle was rather precariously perched, and he couldn't quite tell what was holding it up, so he didn't want to take any chances and linger.

"Your coat is bulky and you're small. Let me pull the shoulder strap from around you and see if you can take your coat off. Then maybe that will give us enough room to slip you out of the lap belt."

She nodded. "Okay."

He pulled the shoulder belt back and she started peeling out of her coat.

"You're going to be cold."

"I don't care. I'd rather be cold than dead."

He stifled a grin.

"We'll get it back on soon as possible."

She wiggled out of it and he tossed it on the passenger seat.

"Now, I'll hold the lap belt and you..."

The car did a crazy shift to the right. Shelley clutched at his neck about the same time he grabbed her and tried to jerk her up and out. Somehow, in the commotion, the belt gave way, and Brad tumbled out of the car with Shelley landing on top of him.

With a crack and weird buffered scrape of metal against wood, the car tipped to the right and rolled downward.

Shelley buried her face in his chest and let out a huge sob. He wrapped his arms around her and held her tight

"I have you. Don't worry. You're okay."

He heard and felt her crying against his chest. "Thank you," she squeaked out. "For not letting me die." She shook in his arms and he wasn't sure if it was from the cold, or shock.

Matt titled her face and cradled her cheeks in his hands. "I would never let you die, Shelley. My God." He wrapped his arms around her tighter then and held her close. "Let's get out of here," he said after a moment, "You're freezing."

Chapter Seven

Shelley welcomed the warmth as Matt wrapped her in his coat and half dragged, half carried her through slush and driving snow up the incline to the Jeep. When they reached his vehicle, he tucked her into the passenger seat, got in on his side, and turned the heater on full blast. She listened as Matt radioed back to the police station and asked the Chief to call Suzie and tell her that Shelley was fine, and that he'd radio again later. After a moment, the chill left her, and she stopped shivering. Somewhat relieved that her family would no longer be worried, she was still bothered by whether the girls knew what had happened. She hoped Suzie had kept that from them. Suddenly, she missed those two chubby faces terribly.

They rode in silence while they climbed in elevation. For a short while, she didn't think about where they were going until they passed the lodge and pulled off the main road—what she could see of the main road anywhere. She wasn't even sure if they were on a road any longer.

"Where are we going?"

Matt didn't respond but concentrated on this driving.

"Matt?"

He finally spoke. "Your seatbelt latched?"

"Yes."

"Good. The road is getting worse."

She stared ahead and burrowed into his lined suede jacket. It smelled like him and she breathed deep. It was a comfort. "We're not going back to Harbor Falls. Are we?" She angled her gaze his way. He stared straight ahead, peering down the road. She noticed that even without his coat, he showed no outward appearance of being cold. In fact, he showed no outward appearance of anything, emotion included.

"No," he finally answered.

"Then where?"

"Can't go back down, the roads are too bad. No way to turn the Jeep around safely."

"I asked you where, not why."

He didn't respond.

It was Christmas Eve and she was going to be away from her children. Tears stung her eyes. Tomorrow would be Christmas morning. And here she was, stuck in God-knows-where with her moody ex-boyfriend.

A sob caught in her throat. Dammit, she would not let him see her cry anymore. Every time he had seen her the past day or so, she was crying. At least she was alive. That should be consolation enough, and there would be many more Christmas Eves with her children.

She should count her lucky stars.

She should thank *him*. Had she?

"Matt, Th—"

The vehicle lurched to the right, and then back to the left. She didn't finish her words and grasped at the door handle. He turned the Jeep and she looked in front of them. A security light shone through the falling snow and rested on a small cabin nestled in some pines not far away. The building was barely visible.

Uncertain about this turn of events, Shelley looked at him, and finally he met her gaze with a look of determination.

"Matt, where are you taking me?"

He didn't blink an eye. "Home," he said, "Where I should have taken you years ago."

Something both physical and emotional hit her in the gut right then. It almost took her breath away.

***

THE SECOND THOSE WORDS WERE OUT OF HIS MOUTH, Matt regretted them. His gaze locked with Shelley's eyes and he watched as a flurry of emotion swept through them. They misted slightly and her lips parted. She shook her head a little from side to side.

Her words were soft spoken, hushed. "Matt, I... I don't know what to say. What do you mean?"

Matt watched Shelley's chest rise and fall, her breathing a little unsteady. He broke the connection and glanced to her hands, knit into a knot on her lap. He was an idiot. The words shouldn't have come out of his mouth like that, but they were the words in his head. Sometimes he needed a brain check. Now was one of those times. He studied her face again. This time she was searching his eyes for answers.

"Matt?"

He reached for her hands, clasped them quickly, and then released them. In the same moment, he physically straightened himself as much as possible to provide some distance. "I shouldn't have said that. Just forgot it."

She grasped his shirtsleeve. "No Matt. Tell me."

The emotion raking through him with the tug of her fingers and her seeking eyes was nearly his undoing. He wanted to haul her up close and kiss her with all the pent-up hormonal passion of the teenage boy he was when he first kissed her. He wanted to sink himself into her core and make her his again. He wanted to carry her over the threshold of his cabin and never let her go. Ever.

But he wouldn't.

He reached for the placket of his jacket and pulled it tight snugly around her. "We need to get inside. Hold this tight and pull it up around your neck and head. I'll come around and help you to the porch and up the steps."

He avoided looking into her eyes until the very last second, and then he did. Her feathered lashes fluttered and framed her doe-eyed stare into his face.

She whispered, "Matt, I'm so confused."

Her breath was soft against his cheek. Nodding, he replied, "That makes two of us, sweetheart."

THEY MADE IT INTO THE CABIN BY HOLDING ONTO EACH other and tripping their way through the growing drifts. Soon, they were inside. Shelley stood in the entry, slithered out of his coat, and held it protectively in front of her. Matt tramped his feet on a rug, pulled off his boots and set them by the door, then moved to the fireplace across the room. He bent to stoke the fire burning there.

In awe, Shelley glanced about.

Not huge by any means, the cabin was warm and cozy, with a clear-cut male influence. The stone fireplace was the focal point, looming large and masculine beneath exposed rough-hewn beams. The walls were bare wood. It looked to be a true log cabin. A dark brown leather couch with a couple of heavy afghans draped over it sat facing the fireplace. Oversized armchairs balanced each side.

She spanned the larger room and noticed an open kitchen to the left, complete with a small breakfast nook tucked back into the corner. It appeared well equipped with all the necessary appliances, and well kept. To the right was a half-closed wooden door to another room. His bedroom?

She was sure she would never find that out.

His statement earlier still rang in his ears. *Home. Where I should have taken you years ago.* What the hell did that mean? He didn't have this cabin all those years ago.

No. He built one here for himself. And a fine one.

Without her.

She didn't want to think about it.

Well, yes, maybe she did. They were young and idealistic years ago. Just out of high school and talking of a future home together. They had even sketched out the plans for a cabin in the woods, with kids and puppies and....

It was what she wanted then. He wasn't ready for that responsibility yet. They were too young and they both were looking at colleges. But they liked the dream and talked of it often.

Suddenly she knew why that ache landed deep in her tummy a moment ago. Reality. He had built their cabin, even though she had dumped him.

Why?

Her gut clutched. She knew exactly why. *Don't think about that right now, Shelley. Not yet.*

So, while he fiddled with the fire she concentrated on the room about her. Yes, that was safe. Furniture, fireplace, things on the wall. What drew her in was the essence of wood. Not only the beams and the walls, but also the intricately detailed carvings that sat about the room. Her gaze landed on first one item, then another. A small black bear cub lay on its back on an end table. An eagle perched majestically on the mantle. A mother deer and twin fawns quietly grazed on a shelf. A carved picture of the mountains, with layers of dimension and depth, hung on the wall next to the fireplace. A set of wooden bowls on the counter graced a lake scene.

"Oh, my," she whispered.

Matt looked up and her gaze fell to meet his. He stood and ran his hands down his thighs. Finally, he moved toward her. "Here, let me take the coat. Slip out of your shoes, okay?"

She nodded and did what he asked, not quite sure why she was so taken aback with Matt's home. She remembered when they were kids he used to whittle all the time. One time he made her a small heart and put it on a chain. In fact, she still kept it in her jewelry box.

His gaze met hers as he reached for the coat.

"Matt, did you do all this?"

He pursed his lips and glanced about. "Yes."

"All of it?"

His gaze circled the interior of the cabin. "Yes. I had help with the cabin, of course, but some of the wooden furniture and all of the carvings are mine." He looked back to her.

"Matt, it's all...breathtaking." She reached for the bear cub. "May I?" He nodded and she lifted it closer to her face. "You are very talented."

Slipping the coat over a barstool, he glanced off and perused his cabin, then back to her. "I had time on my hands." He shoved his hands in his pockets. "Bought a little patch of land before Brad Matthews bought the lodge property."

Finally, Shelley found her feet and moved further into the room. She knew she should be thinking more pertinent things, rather than how Matt had occupied his time for the past few years —like how in the world they managed not to argue thus far, and when they would be able to get back down the mountain—but for some odd reason, she was spellbound, and in awe of Matt's work.

She turned toward him and caught him staring at her. "Matt, I..."

A muffled crack sounded from somewhere outside, then a lengthy scrape against the side of the cabin. The lights flickered and

Shelley kept her gaze on his face. He looked away but she still watched as the lights came back on, briefly flickered again, and finally, thrust them into darkness.

Chapter Eight

Matt swore under his breath but was secretly glad the lights went out. With Shelley standing there in his cabin, his heart pounded, and he wasn't quite sure how he would get through the evening. Now, perhaps, in the dark, he might be able to survive a little better.

Although he really did not want to lose power, the cover of darkness felt safe. He knew the fireplace would keep them warm and he had enough food and water to sustain them until this storm passed. He had a backup generator but didn't relish the idea of traipsing out back to the shed in this storm to kick it into action. If he had to, he would, but for the moment, he preferred staying put.

"Stay still," he told Shelley and started toward her. "I think we can see well enough with the fire. Maybe it will come back on in a minute." He doubted it, sure that a low-hanging branch weighted down too heavy with snow, had ripped the power line from the side of the house. Easy enough fix, but not tonight. He'd see to it tomorrow but knowing that tomorrow was Christmas day, and given the conditions of the mountain road, getting a power truck up here seemed unlikely.

Matt grasped her elbow. "Let's sit by the fire." He wanted to say, *We need to talk,* but didn't.

He led her there and settled her on the raised hearth.

"This feels good," she said. "Maybe the heat will dry my jeans."

Dammit, he hadn't noticed that her clothes were wet. Glancing down at himself, he was in the same boat. "Hell, I'm sorry. I wasn't thinking. Let me see if I can find us something dry to put on."

He left her by the fire and trekked off to his bedroom. Thoughts flew through his head like a house afire. One glance back as he entered his bedroom door and his heart began a slow thrum. He left the door open so partial light from the fire would give some illumination in the darkened room.

Shelley was here in his cabin. Not his plan, yet it had happened, and he had to deal with it. But how?

He found his chest of drawers in the low light and fumbled through a couple of drawers. Hell, he had nothing small enough to fit her, did he?

Finally, he brought up a smaller pair of jogging pants and an old high school sweatshirt. Smiling, he wondered if she'd remember it. He quickly changed himself, grabbed the clothes for her, and stopped abruptly at his bedroom door to observe her silhouette against the fire.

The flame flickered over her blond tresses, setting off a fiery halo around her head. She threaded her fingers through her hair, fluffing to dry the length. His breath caught in his throat.

He knew at that moment that he still loved her. Had never stopped.

Hell, he'd always known he'd loved her but had kept his heart locked and safe while she was gone. He hadn't let his emotions rest on that fact for any length of time over the years. He'd been working on "getting over her" as he'd been told to do by his guy friends, and an occasional date, and his family.

But he'd never, truly, been able to get over her. She'd lingered in the back of his heart. No one ever come close to touching that part of his heart and he'd guarded it and kept it safe—just in case she ever did come back into his life.

And now here she was. Back. In the place they'd dreamed about for their future. Where he'd dreamed she might someday come back to.

But could he trust her?

Could he trust himself?

He wasn't so damned sure he could guard his heart now that she was here.

Had only he'd been ready to be a husband, to give her what she wanted and needed all those years ago—a home, family, children, the goddamned picket fence and all that—then maybe she wouldn't have run off into some other man's willing and able arms. Some guy who was what she thought she wanted at the time.

But no, he hadn't been ready then, couldn't handle those responsibilities. They were too young. He wasn't ready to take on what his father had at a young age and had died trying to keep intact. They'd grown up poor and his father worked his fingers to the bone to support them. Without a college degree, he'd labored hard. Even at nineteen, Matt knew he'd be damned if he would do the same thing for his future family. His path was different. He would go to college, get the degree, and provide for his future family without struggling.

Back then, he'd desperately wanted to give Shelley everything. She was the only woman he wanted.

But she couldn't wait... And he wouldn't change his plans.

Suddenly, he realized there was nothing he could do about the past, but he damn well could make some alterations to his future. Their future. If he could only let go of the hurt, the lack of trust.

Physically, he was a strong man. Could his heart be strong enough to risk the emotion again?

"SEE IF THESE WILL WORK. I'M SURE THEY ARE MUCH TOO big but at least you'll be dry and warm."

His soft voice came to her on a whisper. Shelley's gaze drifted up to meet his. He thrust something toward, her but she didn't see what. Clothes perhaps? All she could see was the fire reflecting in his deep brown eyes looking down at her.

Warm, inviting, lonely.

She'd been such a fool. Young and naive. And for the few minutes he was gone, she had stared into the fireplace and realized just that.

She didn't regret marrying Cliff and she loved her girls to no end. But she did regret all the pain and hurt she'd caused so many people.

Swallowing hard over a growing lump in throat, she rose and stepped closer to Matt. Gathering up the clothes he held out to her, she clutched them to her chest but never let her stare waver from his. She peered deeper.

"I know I've said this once, but I'm going to say it again. I'm so sorry, Matt," she whispered. "For everything."

Something broke in his expression and she waited while his gaze played over her face, searching, probing. It landed on her lips, and then lifted to catch her stare again.

An overwhelming desire to rush forward, lift her face to his and kiss him came over her. She tamped it back. No, she could not do that. He was angry with her. Hated her. She was stuck with him here and who knew what his reaction might—

He reached out and skimmed his fingertips along her cheek and jawline, and a burst of pleasure sped through her, confusing her even more.

"Matt..." she squeaked out.

In one swift moment, he grasped the clothing from her hands, tossed them away, and hauled her up against him. His mouth came down hard on hers and she gasped at the sensation. Firm and determined, he kissed her thoroughly, his hands at her back holding her against his chest, his lips playing over hers, his tongue searching for more.

The unleashed passion boiling up in her was like an answer to a long-awaited prayer—an urgent yearning suppressed and set free. It was like a piece of her heart had been put back in her chest—a piece that she didn't know was missing until that very moment. Heat welled up until she thought her chest would burst.

She was kissing Matt. *Matt!* Not her high school boyfriend, but Matt, the man. The one she'd left behind. And unless she was mistaken, he was hungry for more.

But... But what could this lead to? Where could it go?

Those thoughts dissipated as his mouth left her lips and trailed lazily down her neck in a sensual rhythm. A deep sigh escaped his lips. She melted against him.

"Let's get you out of these wet clothes." His voice was deep and raspy against the crook of her neck and shoulder.

Shelley pulled back and searched his face. She wondered if he could read her question. Should they?

With a forefinger on her lips, he shook his head. "Don't...talk. Let's..."

This time she was the one who sprung forward and met his lips in a sensual embrace. No words. No thoughts. Only lips communicating with lips, bodies speaking to bodies.

They tumbled to the floor in front of the fireplace, landing on a plush rug. Matt shoved the coffee table out of the way and pulled an afghan down from the sofa. She lay on her back, looking up at him as he cradled her close and stared into her eyes.

The fire made the ambience perfect. Soft flickers of flame wrapped them in a sultry glow. Perfect, *perfect...*

But it couldn't be perfect, could it?

That second came and went as he reached for the placket of her shirt and unbuttoned in a lazy, southerly direction. His fingertips grazed the tender skin of her breasts, along her tummy, all the way down. His gaze never left hers.

She shivered at his touch and the fire within gathered to meet the one raging beside her in the hearth.

She wanted him. After all this time. And he...he wanted her, too?

Yes. He did.

Matt pushed the shirt off her shoulders, and she lifted slightly while he removed and tossed it aside. The heat from the fireplace warmed her but as soon as he placed his palm over one of her breasts and kneaded, she knew that fire was insignificant compared to the one burning deep in her belly.

The next seconds were filled with a frenetic tangle of limbs and peeling off damp clothing, searching for and taking care of a condom, frenzied breaths, and frantic kisses.

"Your skin is so cold, Shelley. Come here," he rasped, and covered her body with his. "Let me warm you up."

She nodded against his lips, fused with hers.

Their bodies came together, and Shelley knew that the skin-to-skin contact they shared had never felt so good. Scorching against her, his body covered hers and she opened for him. She relished in the feel of his length, the caress against her folds, and realized that this coming together of their bodies for the first time in years was far superior to simple skin-to-skin contact. She ached for him and eagerly took him. His body rocked into hers and they melded together despite the years of anguish and hurt.

From that moment on, any doubt, any question, any insane thought that she shouldn't be exactly where she was at this moment in time, vanished.

WITH A DEEP INHALE, MATT BREATHED IN SHELLEY'S scent as he sank into her. Dizzy with the sensation, he settled his face against her hair and stilled for only a second as he reveled in the feel of being inside her again. His thoughts didn't linger except for one.

This was right. Yes. This was right...

He thrust deeper as she whimpered and urged him on, her legs wrapped around him, her fingertips grazing his back.

He wanted to savor, linger, slowly bring her to climax, and then spill himself inside her. His body took over, however, and did the opposite. As did hers. She gasped and clenched her thighs around him as he moved in and out. He growled in her ear. He couldn't stop pumping. Filling her. Feeling her velvet insides pulling him deeper. Wouldn't stop. No. This beautiful thing that was them, together, moved him in ways that took him from the past to the present and back again.

"Oh...oh, Matt...."

His whispered name on her lips was nearly his undoing.

Hold on. Hold on...

She trembled and gasped in short pants, digging her fingernails into his back, her legs clamping him to her, while she shuddered beneath him. The sounds, her whimpers of satisfaction, gratified him. He'd always loved giving her pleasure. Simultaneously, he groaned his eruptive release and pushed one last time into her, her quaking body settling around him like a caress.

Melting into her, he wasn't quite sure where he ended, and she began.

Chapter Nine

Shelley blinked herself awake and stared into a smoldering fire. The embers were red and glowing, pulsating against the semi-darkness of the room—much like her body thrummed in the night each time Matt made hot and steamy love to her. The first time they came together was fast and unrestrained. The second was slow and deliberate, making up for years of neglect.

Now, as morning closed in, the room was chilly and the fire dying. She hoped that was not a metaphor for things to come. Few words were said while they made love and Shelley knew that today, the dialogue they had avoided during the night would have to happen.

Matt spooned her from behind as they faced the fireplace. He'd wrapped her in a cocoon made of his body and the afghan after their last, exhausting love-making session. His breathing was even, with deep easy breaths, warm against her neck. His arm lay heavy across her shoulder and chest, holding her close.

It would be easy to get lost in this. Waking up with him every morning. Feeling safe and secure and protected, here in this cabin.

No. It was a fantasy. Couldn't happen.

Could it?

Sighing, she squeezed her eyes tight. No, she was vulnerable. It was too soon. He really didn't want her. They had succumbed to... Something physical. Need. Want. A reaction from the accident. Right?

This wasn't real. This couldn't last.

Could it?

Shivering, she pulled the afghan up closer to her chin, unsure if it was an effort to keep warm, or ward off negative thoughts that tempted to invade her momentary bliss.

"COLD?"

Awake for several minutes, Matt avoided stirring, not wanting to wake her. Dammit, that wasn't the truth. It was more primal than that. He didn't want to move, to break contact with her body. Having Shelley nestled up against him was like a balm to his aching heart, a salve for his soul.

He didn't want her to leave. He didn't know how to ask her to stay. Or if he should.

"No, not really," she said quietly.

With his eyes closed, he tightened his hold on her and pictured them together in his mind's eye. What would it be like, to wake up like this when they were old and gray? "I'll get up in a minute and stoke the fire back to life," he mumbled.

He'd rather stoke her fire, but now, as daylight teased through the windows, he didn't feel as confident about that as he did in the dark of night.

"Take your time," she whispered. "I'm warm enough."

Again, she sighed deeply, and he wondered what that meant. He'd like to think it was a sigh of contentment, although not convinced that it was. "Me, too."

Quiet settled around them, interrupted only with an intermittent crackle and hiss from the fireplace.

"Has the snow stopped?" She sounded tentative, uncertain.

"Not sure."

Sitting up on an elbow, he glanced at the kitchen window and then back to Shelley. The afghan fell to her waist and his gaze trailed over the curve of her naked back. He debated massaging her shoulders and trailing his fingers over her satin skin until she gave in and let him take her again, but he didn't act on it. She didn't turn toward him either, instead continuing to stare into the fire.

Awkward.

Instead, he settled behind her. His palm lay loose over her chest and he was certain he felt the subtle beating of her heart. "I think the snow has stopped. I'll check on the road conditions in a minute."

He felt the nod of her head. She said nothing.

"Are you okay?" He whispered, not certain how to begin the conversation he knew needed to be had.

She didn't immediately answer, still looking intently ahead. After a moment, she turned in his arms toward him. A ray of morning light slanted in the window across her face. She looked dewy and soft, her eyes a bit misty, her face lined with worry.

"I don't know how I am."

Matt traced the outline of her face with his forefinger, and then crooked it under her chin. She trembled as he stroked her tender skin with a light touch of his thumb while searching her face. "Guess we're in a weird place, huh?"

"Sort of. You hate me, Matt. I—."

He put a finger on her lips and huffed out a breath. "Shelley, if I hated you I couldn't have made love to you last night like I did. Like *we* did."

Her eyes shut tight. Tiny crinkles shot out from the corners.

"Matt..." she sucked in a breath and exhaled, "I don't know... We..."

"Shelley, look at me."

She did, her blue eyes questioning.

"I don't hate you."

"You told me to stay away from you."

"That was yesterday. I was mad."

"You've been mad at me for a long time. I hurt you. Bad."

He paused, careful with his next words. She was right. The hurt, even though for a while last night had lessened, still hadn't gone away. He didn't want to lie, and he didn't want to sugarcoat. "Yes. I've been mad at you for a long time. You did hurt me."

"That doesn't go away overnight."

"No. No, you're right."

"But you could still make love to me?"

"I... Shelley, yes."

She stared at him. "How can you turn it off and on like that?" Her voice rose.

"Shelley, you were finally here, in my house. So many things were going through my head... I wanted—"

"You wanted sex."

Stunned, he pulled back. "No, it wasn't like that. I wanted you."

Her head shook and he wasn't sure she heard anything he said. Not really.

"I didn't think," she began. "I... I didn't think, Matt. I let you, us.... I didn't think of the consequences. And now..."

Shit. What was she saying? "And now what?"

She pushed away and drew the afghan up to her chest. "Maybe... Oh, Matt. Maybe this was a mistake. I just don't know..."

Dammit! How in hell could he let himself get sucked in again? He sat up, tossing the afghan off him and fully onto her. Standing now, he found his sweatpants and stepped into them. "Never mind, Shelley. I get it. You just woke up with the realization you had 'oh shit' sex."

"What?"

He raked his fingers through his hair and paced. "You know, 'oh shit' sex. You wake up, realize you're in bed with someone, and you're not sure why you did it, and you think, 'oh shit, what the hell have I done?'"

Shelley sat straight up. "Matt, that's not what I was thinking! I would never think that about you. It's just that we are starting over. It's very soon, and... Oh hell."

He waved her off. "Never mind. I get it."

Her eyes widened. "Get what?"

He needed a change of venue and fast. Shit. They were snowbound. Were they still? What were the roads like? His brain spun with confusion. Could he get out of here? Didn't matter. He needed out of the house, now, away from Shelley. To think.

To put up that guard around his heart again, perhaps.

A quick glimpse to the hearth told him they were low on firewood. "I'm going to get wood. While I'm out, I'll check on the weather and radio down to Harbor Falls to see about the roads."

With a brisk turn toward him, she wrapped the afghan around her and stood. "Do you think we can get out of here today?"

The look on her face held a sense of urgency.

"In that much of a hurry to leave?"

Her brows knit and she glanced toward the door. "No, Matt. I—"

He stomped away, then halted and spun around, and her words cut off. Laughing aloud, he interrupted. "Of course, you are in a hurry to leave. That's what you're good at, Shelley. Leaving. Why should I expect anything different?" His stare bit into her eyes. "Don't worry. I'll get you off this goddamned mountain. I wouldn't want you to stick around for too long and get, well, attached or anything."

Immediately, her eyes welled up and she lifted her chin in defiance. He knew that gesture well. She used to do it when they were kids and he'd pissed her off. Dammit, but he didn't want or need to see it again because it has always melted his resistance like butter on a corn cob.

He'd hurt her. Hadn't meant to.

Maybe it was better this way. If she hated him, it would easier all the way around.

"It's Christmas morning, Matt," she bit out. "I was thinking about my girls."

He deflated. Feeling like heel, he swiped at his sweatshirt and picked it up. With the same motion, he tucked his heart back deep in his chest, safe and secure. Why the hell had it let it out? This was impossible, and the sooner they both realized it, the better off they'd both be.

"Of course. Your girls."

"They are important to me. Matt, they are all I have."

Of course.

Dammit. His brain swirled with uncertainty. With emotion he couldn't pin down. Fear. Trust, or the lack of it. Worry. Love?

He clenched and unclenched his fists, trying to gain some semblance of control. "Of course, Shelley. I'm sorry. I understand that you need to get to your girls. They want their mother, too, on Christmas morning. I get it."

"Okay..." She bit her lip. "Matt, this is all a mess and we need to talk about it. All of it."

He nodded. "Yes. But not now. Let's get you back to your family, and honestly, I need to see if I can get to mine. Looks like we both have obligations."

After a moment, she agreed. "Okay, Matt. Okay."

Somehow, he didn't think it was okay. Dammit, he wasn't good at this relationship thing. Not good at all. He'd screwed them up years ago with his lofty dreams and goals. What made him think he wouldn't screw it up again? He jerked the sweatshirt over his head while she watched. Her gaze trailed his every move. He really didn't want to look at her, wrapped up in his afghan, naked underneath....

Couldn't. His resolve might crumble.

Striding toward where his coat and boots rested, he donned them with a brief backward glance.

"I'll be back in a few minutes. Make yourself at home."

Immediately, he regretted those words. *Hom*e. This cabin would never be a home for Shelley. There was too much bad history between them. He doubted either of them had the energy or the inclination to turn all the negatives around.

He knew he didn't.

Yanking open the cabin door, he stepped out onto his snow-drifted stoop and looked at his Jeep. "Dammit all to hell." He'd have to dig out but dig out he would. No way could he spend one more night alone in this cabin with Shelley. He was too confused, too...something.

The door slammed shut behind him.

Staring at the large wood door, Shelley stood by the fireplace unmoving, sniffing away tears as she contemplated the symbolism of that slamming door. It stood solid and unmoving between them, like the chasm of hurt and betrayal she was darned certain would never go away.

It was all her fault. All of it.

She had caused the pain for Matt and everyone else she loved when she stupidly made the one decision that would haunt her for the rest of her life

Possibly, that one decision was going to take away one of the best things that could have happened to her.

Matt.

It was over. No hopes and dreams here, so she might as well get used to it.

With a cleansing exhale, she played a lazy gaze over the room, landing on each carving Matt had done, taking in the loving care he put into each detail. She perused the rough-hewn beams, and her search lingered on the precise layering of chinks between the cedar logs. Closing her eyes, she imagined Matt up here working on this cabin in his spare time—nights, weekends, any time he could muster. That was the way he was.

Determined. Goal-oriented.

Again, she sniffled, but even with her eyes closed, she couldn't stop the tears.

She'd screwed up.

But the past was the past. She had to move forward and let Matt go. And if he knew what was good for him, he needed to let her go, too.

She opened her eyes. Yes. That was exactly what had to happen.

Turning, she glimpsed at her clothes scattered near the hearth and prayed they were dry. As she reached for them, her gaze landed on the plush rug, the coffee table pushed askew, the indentation where they had lain in the night—all evidence of their lovemaking.

A pang settled in her tummy.

She dismissed it. Another memory. It meant nothing.

"Liar," she whispered, swiping away a lingering tear. "It means everything."

But she would not dwell on it. There was no hope. She wasn't worthy of Matt. He was a good guy and he was confused as much as she, and she wanted the best for him.

That wouldn't happen with her. She was not the best thing for him.

Snatching up her clothes, she tossed the afghan aside.

"Get dressed and be ready to leave as soon as he gets back." That was her only defense. Get the hell out. Yes, Matt nailed her with that earlier. She was good at leaving.

So be it.

Chapter Ten

The silence in the Jeep split the cool climate between them like a razor-sharp icicle hanging from a rooftop. Although unspoken words hung in the air, neither of them dared break the silence. Matt supposed they'd each come to the same conclusion.

Give it up. This wasn't going anywhere.

When he had returned to the cabin earlier, he found her dressed and ready to leave, sitting on the hearth and staring at the dying embers.

Appropriate.

Ready to go.

Saying nothing, he changed into dry clothing. Once dressed, he motioned toward the door and led her to his vehicle. The hardest part was getting out of his short dirt road. After that, the Jeep plowed through the six inches or so of snow on the mountain road with cautious ease, the morning sun already having melted some of it. He was thankful this side of the mountain faced east.

He sensed a change in Shelley the moment he stepped inside the door. There was something final about that sensation. He didn't question but accepted.

It was over. Finally. Maybe now he could move on.

That was the way it remained as they drove the five miles or so back toward Lake Road. They passed the lodge and the place where Shelley's car slid off the road. With a peripheral glance, he saw her look down the mountain. Her chest lifted and lowered with a deep sigh.

"Thank you for saving me," she whispered, still looking out the window.

He wanted to say many things then, like, *How could I not save you? I love you*, but he didn't. "You're welcome," he responded, his stare fixed on the road.

That was their only exchange until they turned into Suzie's drive. Shelley sat up straighter as she watched the front door of her sister's house. She scooted a little closer to the edge of her seat, as far as the seatbelt would allow, and clutched at the door handle.

Eager to get the hell out of here.

He stopped the Jeep, and everything froze. Finally, he turned and found her peering back at him, her eyes glazed with tears.

"I know you will probably never forgive me, Matt," she said softly, "but I am truly sorry. You have to forget about it, and me, and move on."

Well, there it was, the final blow. Confirmation that there was not a snowball's chance in hell that they would ever come to terms.

He held her stare for way too long and her tears spilled over. At once, he softened toward her a little. Giving her a quick nod, he hoped she understood what that meant because he didn't want to have to say it out loud.

He would forget. He would let it go. Let her go.

The lifting of the door handle latch broke the silence and Shelley turned away. In an instant, she was out of the truck, picking her way through the snow, and toward the house.

Make sure she gets inside and then leave.

In truth, he wanted to linger, catch the morning rays glinting off her hair, take in her determined step across the porch, wait and see if perhaps she might give him a backward glance.

She didn't.

Suzie opened the door and within a half-second, Shelley was whisked inside.

He exhaled, steaming up his windshield.

Abruptly, the front door opened again,

and his heart picked up a cadence. Suzie took a step out onto the porch and waved. A thank you, he was certain. Huffing out one last cleansing breath, an attempt to still his racing heart, he waved back and put the Jeep into reverse.

"Put it to rest, Branson. It's over."

It was time to get to his own family. Where he belonged.

Where his heart was safe.

"ME! ME! IT'S MY TURN UNCLE BAD!"

Shelley watched Karly jump up and down in front of her uncle and beg for his hands. He grasped both of her tiny palms in his while she climbed flat-footed up his legs and thighs and turned a flip, grinning all the while.

"Again! Again!"

Brad tossed a look of feigned despair at Shelley. "Your kids are wearing me out!"

"He loves every minute of it," Suzie said from her right. "It's good practice for him to manage multiple kids."

"Oh?" Shelley wondered what that last part meant. "Are you indicating anything, Suzie?"

She watched her sister toss her husband a quick smile, then back to her. "No indication of anything, dear sister. We're just *practicing*."

Shelley sniggered. "I'll just let that stay right there."

"Good idea." Suzie turned back to her work.

All three children—Katie, Karly and Petey—giggled and bounced on the floor, amidst wads of Christmas wrapping paper and scattered toys, in front of him. "More!" Petey said.

Shelley watched as Brad scooped his son into his arms and sank into an overstuffed chair behind him, propping his legs on an ottoman. "I'm pooped."

The girls started to climb.

"Katie. Karly. Come here. Uncle Bad is tired." Shelley motioned for her girls and they came running. She gathered them onto her lap.

Suzie leaned closer and whispered. "And we definitely do not want to wear Uncle Bad out, he needs to save some of that energy for me."

Shelley looked into her sister's eyes and caught the twinkle. She laughed aloud.

Grinning, Suzie hugged her. "Well, that was nice. That's the first laugh I've heard from you all day.

Glancing off with a frown, Suzie chided herself. She thought she had hidden her sadness pretty darn well. Seeing her parents earlier made her temporarily forget about Matt and the previous night. She was lost in the moment of hugging and crying and apologizing—seemed she was always apologizing lately—and focused only on the events happening right in front of her. She thought she'd pulled it off.

Obviously, her sister could see through her ploy.

"Oh, I beg to differ," she replied. "I'm pretty sure I laughed earlier when the kids were opening their presents and Petey got tangled in the ribbon. And what about when Daddy slurped up that banana pudding and it spurted on his shirt? I'm sure I laughed then."

Suzie shook her head. "No. You smiled a little. But no laughter."

She waved her off. "Ridiculous." She thought for a moment. "What about when Brad brought the puppy in for the girls? I know I laughed watching the kids all-a-tumble on the floor with the pup. That was pretty funny when the pup took off with Petey's sock."

Again, Suzie shook her head. "No, you barely smiled then."

Smirking, Shelley exhaled hard. "Well, all right. Maybe not."

Chaos ensued. The girls rolled off her lap and wrestled with the puppy again on the floor. Petey climbed all over his dad trying to avoid getting tickled. Joan Hart, their mother, scurried about picking up stray ribbon and wrapping paper. Her father fiddled with the stereo, attempting to find a radio station with Christmas music that fit his taste. He was tired of *Rock Around the Christmas Tree.*

"What happened, Shelley? Up at Matt's cabin?"

Surprised that she would ask—or even sense that she should ask—Shelley looked away. She didn't want to meet Suzie's stare, and felt every iota of its intensity on her face. "Nothing. Nothing that I want to talk about right now, anyway."

Suzie remained quiet and pressed her hand into her sister's palm.

"I just want to sit here and enjoy my family," Shelley whispered.

Suzie squeezed. "Yeah," she said, "Look at us. We're pretty darned good-looking to be so dysfunctional, aren't we?"

Shelley bit her lip and looked at her sister. Both women burst out laughing. She laughed so hard she hoped no one noticed her tears.

ACROSS TOWN, MATT STOOD IN HIS MOTHER'S KITCHEN drying dishes while his two sisters took a smoke out on the deck, and his nieces and nephews played with their toys in the den. He hated that both of his siblings smoked, but at least they didn't do it in front of the kids.

His mother handed him the turkey platter and said, "I hear Shelley is back in town."

He took the platter but didn't say a word, only gave a half-nod. Silence drifted between them for a moment.

Then his mother added, "The last thing I want for you is to hurt again, Matthew."

He could agree with that statement. His mother dipped a pan into the dishwater and silently washed the dish for a few long seconds. Matt set the platter on the counter.

Turning, his mother stopped the washing motions and rested her hands on the edge of the sink. "Yes, the last thing I want for you is more hurt, but I also want to you to face this situation, Matthew. You either need to get on with your life without Shelley, or you need to go after her."

Little do you know, Mom....

"Do you know what I mean?"

"I know exactly what you mean."

"Then what will you do?" Her eyes searched his as only a mother's could. He could see the love and caring in them, and he knew she only wanted what was best for him.

"I already did that, Mom, and it didn't work out."

She took the dishtowel from him and dried her hands. "What are you talking about?"

Crossing his arms over his chest, he leaned a hip into the counter. "I went after her again. Last night. Shelley got stranded up by the lodge and I took her home with me for the night. I dropped her off at Suzie's before I came here."

A hint of a smile broke across her face. "And?"

He inhaled deep and let the breath out slower. "It didn't work. I went after her and she told me to let it go, Mom. So that's what I'm doing."

His mother's smile morphed into pursed lips. "Not exactly what I wanted to hear. I'm disappointed in her. I thought perhaps..."

Matt stepped closer. "It's not Shelley, mom. It's me. I gave it a shot, it didn't work. I'm fine now, or I will be. I needed this to happen so I could get past everything. Past her. Don't worry about me, okay? I'm fine."

He hugged her then and she hugged him back. "I love you son and want you to be happy."

He nodded. "I promise. I'm happy. Or I will be soon."

She broke away to investigate his face, cupped his cheek in a palm, and smiled. "I know you will be. I had high hopes—back then and now. I've never seen another young couple like the two of you, so much in love. I was sure that love of yours could stand the tests of time and that eventually, even after everything, you would get back together."

"I had hoped that too, Mom. It's just not the reality."

"You still love her, Matthew. I can still see it in your eyes when you talk about her."

He sighed. "Mom, I'll never stop loving her. I just have to figure out how to love her and live without her."

She clasped him close again and hugged him tight, like only a concerned mother could.

Chapter Eleven

Thankful for the busy day, Shelley sat on the edge of her bed some hours later and blew out a heavy sigh. For a variety of reasons, she'd fought tears all day. The children were beautiful and funny, so full of life. She mourned the fact that Cliff would never see them grow up and become young women.

So grateful that her parents were forgiving and loving people, she'd choked back tears more than once just looking at them, watching them enjoy her children. When her father came close to tearing up himself, she'd almost lost it, but held on. And Suzie—her compassionate sister Suzie who loved her unconditionally and should probably hate her—was always there with open, loving arms. She owed her so much and didn't deserve the kindness her sister had shown her.

There truly was nothing better than family. At least her family. Of course, Harbor Falls had built a tradition on family, which was why coming home was both hard, and wonderful, all at once.

Shelley wondered what Matt was doing today with his family.

He had filtered in and out of her thoughts most of the day but by dinnertime, she had mastered pushing him out of her head.

Well, not really. She'd only told herself that. Pretending was a skill she had acquired over the past few years.

Now, in the quiet of the evening, the cacophony of Christmas laid to rest and her children tucked into bed, her mind longed to still itself—to empty of the chaos of the holidays and her homecoming and finally relax.

But when her mind did turn off, he was there.

Matt was in her head. She could taste him on her lips. Feel him in the palms of her hands.

He was tucked firmly in her heart.

Twisting toward the bed pillows, she tugged at the quilt and slipped between the cool sheets. The pillowcase was crisp and sweet smelling, and she wanted to bury herself in the comfort. Just twenty-four hours earlier, she'd lain on her same side, looking into a rolling fire, with Matt spooning her back. Now, she lay alone, looking into the small night lamp on her bedside table, and finally, the tears flowed.

She wasn't sure if they were tears of joy, loss, or relief. Perhaps they were simply a manifest of the release she needed to allow herself.

A soft, quick knock sounded on her door and without waiting for a response, Suzie slipped inside.

"Suzie?" Shelley pushed up on an elbow and knew Suzie could see her tear-stained face. No use to hide it now.

Her big sister approached, and Shelley sat fully up. Suzie sat and embraced her, circling her close. Shelley continued to cry.

"Did Matt hurt you?" Suzie asked. "I mean, not physically. Matt isn't that kind. But with words?"

She shook her head. "No, of course not."

"Was he angry?"

"Not too much. Some."

"Hm." Suzie stroked her hair and Shelley kept her face buried on her sister's shoulder.

After a moment, she whispered, "We made love, Suzie. Um, maybe I should say we had sex. I don't think there was any love."

"Shit."

"Yeah."

"You're sure?"

Shelley glanced up. "I'm pretty sure I know about having sex."

"No, I mean, are you sure there was no love in it?"

She couldn't reply to that out loud, but internally, she knew. Yes, there was love in it, at least from her perspective. She'd never stopped loving Matt. Not really.

He obviously didn't feel the same.

Pulling back, Suzie cupped Shelley's face in her hands and tilted it to look straight into her eyes. "Give yourself time. Give him time. Shelley, he's been miserable for years. Hard to turn misery off on a dime."

"No, Suzie." Shelley blinked away tears and shook her head. "It's too late. I told him to forget me and move on. There is too much hurt. Frankly, I'm not worth it. I'm the last person he needs. I'm so screwed up."

Suzie pursed her lips. "You are *not* screwed up. You are emotional. You are confused. You gave into sex when maybe you should have waited but you're not screwed up. And dammit, you *are* worthy."

"Suzie..."

"I don't want to hear any more about that. You hear me? Stop beating yourself up." She stood. "Now, get some sleep. Tomorrow, we play. Shopping first, and then going to pig out on all those leftovers. Then we get to work. Next week is full and I'm relying on your help. Got it? So get yourself a good night's sleep."

Was this her sister's way of keeping her busy so she wouldn't think about Matt? Confused a little at her sister's turn, she said, "Sure, Suzie. It's just...."

Suzie headed for the door, talking over her shoulder. "I mean it, Shell. You don't have *time* to pine away about Matt so snap out of it. We've got work to do."

That was it.

Suzie paused for a second, and then left the room, closing the door behind her. Sighing, Shelley flicked off the bedside light and fell back onto the pillows.

"Snap out of it. Sure. I'll just do that."

Dark blanketed her and she was surprised to realize that her tears were gone, and she didn't feel like crying any more. That was good. At once, her door opened again, a triangle of light pushing through while Suzie poked her head inside the room.

"One question," she said.

"Okay."

"Was it good?"

No hesitation. "It was wonderful."

"Then that's all I need to know." Click.

The door closed and the dark was back. *Thank God.*

MATT COULD HAVE SPENT THE NIGHT WITH HIS MOTHER, sisters, and the kids, but opted to head back up the mountain. According to the road crews, the mountain road was passable, but he still had to be cautious. He took his time, letting his mind drift a little about the past twenty-four hours or so, even though he had to pay close attention to his driving.

He'd become comfortable with his self-pity. That was a fact. The comfort lay in the fact that it was safe. He shook his head at the thought. What had he become? He'd been a bit of a risk-taker in his youth and now it seemed that a woman had turned him into a man who lived in a safety net.

Not that safety wasn't a bad thing. Hell, he was a cop. He was supposed to be all about safety—keeping the town's residents safe, making sure drivers followed the rules, teaching street safety to kids at the elementary school.

Naw, that wasn't what he was talking about. He was living the safe life. Not putting himself out there anymore with women to keep himself safe emotionally. And yeah, he was wallowing in his self-pity and pining after a woman who had set him free—not just last night, but years ago.

Shelley *had* set him free and instead of dealing with it and trying to move forward, he'd stuck himself somewhere at the crossroads of pity and longing—longing for something, or someone, he was never going to have again.

No more.

His mother was right. He deserved to be happy.

His resolve remained high the last few miles to this cabin but once inside the doors of his home, he was immediately taken with the lingering scent of Shelley and the remnants of their night spent together in front of the fire—blankets scattered, ottoman pushed back, the clothes of his she wore in a heap by the sofa.

Empty. The place where he'd carved out his safe existence suddenly felt empty without her—even after one night.

He rounded the furniture and sat on the ottoman, staring at the place where they had made love. His heart raced, recalling how he'd felt. How she felt in his arms. How perfectly happy he had been with her for that one, beautiful, night.

Propping his elbows on his knees, he raked his fingers through his hair, his head hanging. Dammit. He loved her still. How was he going to do this? Do what he told his mother?

How as he going to figure out how to live without her, while still loving her with all his heart?

Chapter Twelve

"**O**kay, so here is the deal. I've dropped the kids off at Mama and Daddy's so you, my dear sister, are coming to the lodge with Brad and me. It is, after all, New Year's Eve."

Shelley looked up from the book she was reading and took in her sister's stern expression. "I thought I was babysitting."

"No. Change of plans."

"But I wanted to babysit."

Suzie stood hands on hips, her stance broad, her barely five-foot-three frame erect, her look determined. They'd been through this no less than a dozen times already. Brad was hosting a big New Year's Eve bash at the lodge, the first one in a couple of decades or more. With the renovation finished, he had invited the entire town for a New Year's celebration.

Suzie wanted Shelley to go.

Shelley wanted none of it.

Babysitting was her excuse.

"You've worked your fingers to the bone all week trying to forget about Matt. You've brooded long enough. You're going to get out and party tonight."

She fiddled with a page of the book. "I'm not brooding. I've already told you. I'm not going."

"You're a stubborn little minx."

She returned to her reading. "No more stubborn than you. Besides, now that I'm not babysitting, I can finish this book."

Plopping beside her on the couch, Suzie grasped the book and pushed it into Shelley's lap. "You can read anytime. It's New Year's Eve. That only comes once a year. Come on, sis. Let your hair down."

Snorting, she shifted on the couch. "I don't need to let my hair down. My hair is fine. My life is fine. I want to stay here and read." She snatched up her book and turned a page. "Besides, as soon as tomorrow is over, I need to start moving the kids and me into the lodge, so I should probably pack a few things. And plan. Since I don't have a car now, I need to figure that out too. I just have stuff to do, Suzie, so I'll stay here."

Suzie huffed. "You can't stay cooped up here forever. You've got to get back into the Harbor Falls social life sooner or later."

"I choose later." She didn't look up. "Besides, I've only been here a week. Give me a break. I don't need to start the new year with back-stabbing whispers about me being the town slut."

"You're not the town slut. I'm pretty sure Candy Crane has that title all tied up. Besides, it's a party! It will put a smile on that sourpuss face of yours."

Not liking that last comment, she glared at her sister. "I do not have a sourpuss face."

"You do."

"Not."

"Do."

"Not! Crap. I'm not arguing with you!"

"I bought a dress today. I think you should try it on."

Nice twist, sis. "No. Me and my sourpuss face are having a night in. I'm looking forward to popcorn. Maybe a bubble bath. Mind if I use your tub?"

Rising, Suzie looked down at her. "You can be so damn difficult."

Smiling into her book, Shelley replied, "I know. I like to get my way."

"All right. You've got it." Heading toward the kitchen, she called over her shoulder. "I'm going to leave the dress on my bed, in case you change your mind after you take that bubble bath."

Shelley listened for her fading footsteps.

"Not freakin' likely," she muttered, her nose stuck further in her book.

MATT STEPPED ONTO HIS MOTHER'S PORCH AND twisted the door handle to let himself in. "Mom? I'm here," he called into the room. "You ready?"

She called out from the back of the house. "Almost. Be right there."

He paused at the entry and looked at himself in the antique hall tree mirror. Adjusting his tie, he loosened it a bit, pulling it away from his neck. "Damn tie," he muttered. "I would only do this for you, you know."

"What?" His mother stepped beside him.

"I said I would only do this for you. I still can't believe you talked me into it." She looked stunning standing there beside him. "By the way, you look beautiful. Papa was a lucky man."

She smiled at his reflection and straightened his tie. "You're looking pretty spiffy yourself. And you're right, your Papa *was* a lucky man."

Grinning into the mirror, he caught the sparkle in her eye.

"Do you good to get out, Matthew. Holed up there in that cave of yours," she said. "You need to come out and play once in a while."

He snorted. "I'm not a social butterfly like my sisters. You know that. But I'm working on it."

Shrugging, she smiled again. "Ah, but you don't have to be the social bug. Just be you. That's good enough."

She grasped his shoulders and turned him to face her. "Matthew Branson, I'm going to say something that I never thought I would say. Son, you need a woman."

Heat flushed his cheeks and neck. "Mom, don't go there."

She narrowed her gaze. "Matthew, what is it you want in life? You worry the hell out of me."

He never meant to worry her. Never had. He loved her with everything that was in him. "All I ever wanted was what you and Papa had. A home, a family..."

"A wife."

"Yes."

"Shelley?"

He paused. "Once upon a time."

Squinting at him, she went on. "You won't find a wife, or make amends with Shelley, moping around in that cabin of yours."

He studied his shoes. "No, ma'am, I suppose I won't." Having a conversation about Shelley was the last thing he wanted to do tonight. "But let's get things clear, making amends with Shelley is never going to happen. So, give me time on finding someone new. I can't just turn off loving her like that."

Crooking her finger under his chin, she lifted his face. "Son," she began softly, "and you're never going to. Let the past go. Make her yours. Before it's too late."

Staring into his mother's eyes, he sensed the unspoken words. She'd lost her love, his Papa, way too early.

"There are no guarantees, ever. All you have is today. Don't waste it."

He swallowed hard, knowing it was already too late, but he nodded and smiled at his mom. "I'll work on it," was all he said, knowing it was a lame promise.

"Do that," she told him. "A lot of time has already gone by. Don't dismiss the time you do have. You won't regret it."

WITH BUBBLES UP TO HER EARS, SHELLEY SANK INTO Suzie's whirlpool tub, leaned back with her book, and toed the lever to turn off the water. Letting loose of a long sigh, she delighted in the hot water and the steady beat of the jets against her tired muscles. They'd had a long week and had worked hard. In a couple of days, she would move into the lodge with the girls, so more work was headed her way. Tonight, now that she was off kid duty, all she wanted was to relax.

She soaked until the water grew tepid, the bubbles gone, and the book finished. The bathroom was chilly, so she dried quickly and wrapped herself in a thick towel. The inn had the best towels, Suzie didn't skimp on that. Rarely did she skimp on anything. The soft terry felt good against her skin. Hurrying through Suzie's bedroom toward her own, she stopped abruptly at the bed and stared at the simple black dress that lay across it.

Chapter Thirteen

The lodge was full of people, and well, people weren't his thing. Of course. Matt slipped out a French door leading out onto the deck and braved the winter cold. The deck was cleared of snow, thankfully, so he didn't have to worry about slipping. The lake sat like a giant jewel beyond the lodge, moonlight flickering off its icy depths. He moved to the rail, peered out into the night, and exhaled.

"Sometimes crowds get to me, too."

Matt looked to his left while Brad Matthews stepped closer. "Yeah. I'm not much for parties." Then thinking better of that statement, he added, "But as far as parties go, this is a great one. My mother is having a wonderful time."

Brad chuckled. "I love to entertain but I've been prepping for this for days. I needed a break." He glanced to the lake. "Man, I am so glad I didn't tear this place down."

Matt agreed. "Me, too. I sure was sweating it with my cabin a mile up the road. I'm glad you left it as is."

"Well, if it hadn't been for Suzie's stubbornness, it probably wouldn't have happened."

"Must run in the family."

"Stubbornness?"

"Um. Yeah."

"I hear that goes two ways."

Matt's gaze landed on Brad's face and he wondered what he meant. Well, of course, Shelley had probably talked with Suzie, and Suzie had discussed with her husband. There was no time to ponder that notion, however, when the French door cracked open again behind them and the commotion inside spilled out onto the deck.

A sequined Suzie squeezed through the door.

"There you are!" She sidled up next to Brad and smiled. "Hi, Matt. It's so good to see you here." She turned her attention to her husband. "Honey, a couple of heat cans under the serving dishes have gone out and I can't find any more. Where do you keep them? Oh, and we are out of pâté. You know how Claire Harper loves her pâté..."

Rolling his eyes, Brad patted her arm. "I'll take care of it," then turning to Matt, he added, "See you later man, glad you're here. Hey, there could be a poker game later tonight if you want to stick around."

Matt nodded and Brad was gone.

Suzie faced him. "It *is* good to see you, Matt. It's been a while and I wish we could see each other more often. I sort of miss the old days when... Oh!" Reaching to her waist, she pulled a cell phone from her skirt waistband. "On vibration. Just a sec. Could be the kids." She swiped at the phone and he waited while she said things like "um-huh," and "yes, of course," and "you're sure?" and then finally, "see you in a few." She ended the call, slipped the phone back in her waistband, exhaled long, bit her lip and then squared her gaze on him.

"Matt Branson, I need your help. I know you are here for the party and I hate to take you way from it but... Oh, Lord, I really need some help."

Concerned now, he wondered if this was a police matter. "What is it, Suzie? Is there trouble?"

Her brow knit and she paused. "Not sure. Yes, maybe. Yes. There is trouble. At my house. Someone is sneaking around outside. Strange noises too, Shelley said, and..."

Panic raced to his throat, constricting his breath. *No.*

"I'm just not exactly sure what kind of trouble there could be, but Shelley said the lights were flickering and she wondered if the man outside had—"

Matt grasped her forearms. "No problem. I'm on my way." He turned away from Suzie and jerked open the French door to the dining area. "Tell Shelley I'm coming. Tell my mother I..." he shouted over his shoulder. "Just tell her I'm going after what I need to go after."

"Shelley?"

"Yes!"

"Go Matt go!"

THE DRESS FIT LIKE A GLOVE. SLEEK AND BLACK, THE length hit above the knee, the plunging neckline showed a comfortable amount of cleavage, the three-quarter length sleeves skimmed her forearms.

Shelley turned and looked at herself in the mirror from all angles. Suzie was right. The dress was perfect. Too bad she didn't have the guts to wear it out in the light of day.

Or to a New Year's Eve bash.

After her bath, she couldn't resist trying it on. She found it difficult to stop at just wearing the dress, though. She donned pantyhose and found a pair of Suzie's black pumps. Getting into the dress-up thing, she rummaged through her sister's jewelry and found a very nice pearl necklace with matching earrings. Oh, and a nice diamond tennis bracelet.

"Might as well put on a little makeup," she mused, stepping back from the mirror.

In fifteen minutes, she was dressed, fluffed, decked out, spit-shined, and polished.

"All dressed up and nowhere to go."

Staring at herself, she wondered... Did she dare? Before she could back out, she picked up her phone and called her sister.

"Talk me out of this," she said, "I think I want to come to the party."

"Um-huh."

"Can you come get me?"

"Yes, of course," Suzie replied.

"Okay." Her heart skipped a beat. Would she really do this?

"You're sure?"

"Yes."

"See you in a few."

They hung up. Shelley bit her lip and stared at her reflection. "Shit. I'm going to a party."

***

HIS HEART POUNDING, MATT SPUN HIS TIRES AS HE rounded the corner and sped into Suzie's driveway. Running the Jeep almost up to the doorstep, he haphazardly parked the vehicle, left it running, and jogged up the sidewalk and onto the porch. Repeatedly, he jammed the heel of his hand on the doorbell.

"Answer the door, Shelley. Answer the door."

Impatient, he shifted from one foot to another. It wasn't until the door jerked open that he realized the lights were on in the house.

"I'm coming! Geez, Suze." Shelley's voice trailed off as the door swung fully open. Her jaw dropped. "M-Matt?"

He pushed his way inside. "Close the door. Tell me what you saw."

She wrinkled her brow. "What?"

"You called. Suzie said you saw someone messing around the house. Where was he? In the front or back by the lake? What did you see?" He knew his voice was frantic. Why was she standing there so calm? And why was she so dressed up?

"Matt, I didn't see anyone messing around. I called Suzie to come and take me to the lodge."

Realization hit him. He stepped back, distancing himself from Shelley. "What?"

"I didn't call Suzie about a man, Matt. I called her to come pick me up."

"Hell fire." Raking his fingers through his hair, he paced away and then turned back toward her. He couldn't do anything but stare. "Shit. And goddamn, you look so, freaking, hot. I mean, beautiful." Finally, he sat with a thud on the sofa, his elbows on his knees, his head in his hands, staring at the floor. "Shit."

Shelley stepped toward him. "Matt, calm down. I'm okay. This is..."

"This is a set-up," he told her, looking up into her face. *Dammit.*

"I don't understand."

"You called. I was there standing by Suzie. She said there was trouble here at the house, someone messing around, and that... Hell, never mind. You get it, right?"

Shelley huffed out a breath and rolled her eyes. "Oh my God. My sister! Matt Branson, if you think I had anything to do with this, you're wrong. My sister has been playing matchmaker. I did *not* call to have you come get me."

Neither of them said anything. Matt washed his hands over his face and stared at the floor again. After a moment, Shelley moved to the couch and sat down beside him.

He looked at her. "I thought my heart was going to jump out of my chest I was so worried about you."

Shelley nodded. "I could tell you were upset."

"Dammit, Shelley, I'm a mess. I thought you were in trouble."

Sighing, she touched his hand. "Thank you for caring, Matt."

"I never stopped caring, Shelley.

She smiled. "We're a pair, aren't we?" She stared straight ahead into the Christmas tree lights.

"Yeah." He lowered his hands. He studied her profile. The twinkle of the Christmas lights reflected against her soft skin.

"Matt," she whispered, "I lied."

His heart rate kicked up a notch. "About what?"

She faced him. "I don't want you to forget me. I don't want you to move on. I don't want to let you go. I want... a chance." Her gaze fell to her lap and she fiddled with the hem of the dress.

"Shelley..."

She shook her head. "No, please don't stop me. Let me say this while I can. I know I hurt you. I know you don't like me very much. And I know there is this big chunk of history that we have to get over. But I can't get you out of my head, and I can't ever forget how much I loved you once upon a time. Beyond that, I ache every minute of the day knowing that I hurt you so damn much and that you are still hurting." She took a deep breath and exhaled. It was then he noticed the tear trailing down her cheek. "The thing is, I don't know what I can do to make it better. I've apologized. You still hate me. I don't know how to fix this."

Closing his eyes, Matt swallowed and gathered his wits about him. His mother's words rang in his ears. "I don't hate you," he whispered. Turning, he placed his hands on both her shoulders and turned her to face him. "I know how to fix it."

Her eyes brimmed with tears. "How?"

"I need to let the past go."

"I need to think there could be a future."

He slipped the tear away with his forefinger. "Just love me. The rest will come."

"I've never stopped loving you, Matt."

Grasping a tendril of her hair, he twisted it around his forefinger and pulled her closer. As his lips moved in to capture hers, he whispered, "I have loved you every day of my life, Shelley Hart. Every. Single. Day."

He kissed her. She tasted like home—like a million years of wandering, finally settling in the place of his dreams. Pulling away, he peered into her eyes.

"We need time."

She nodded. "And lots of talk."

His gaze dropped to her lips. "And kissing?"

Leaning forward, she lightly touched hers to his again. "Yes. Kissing may help." Her gaze played over his face. "And making love?"

He growled and nuzzled her neck.

"Matt, more than anything, I want us to try again. I'll do anything..."

Wrapping her up in his arms, he held her close. "All you have to do is love me," he breathed, "and let me take you home."

Home. Where he should have taken her all those years ago.

"That's easy," she whispered back. "Home is the only place I want to be."

A Note from Maddie

Friends,

Did you enjoy reading *Take My Heart*?

I have to admit two things: the first, I cried when I wrote the scene where Shelley showed up on Suzie's porch, and second, my heart literally pounded when Matt and Shelley finally got back together. Happy endings abound!

If you enjoyed reading Shelley and Matt's story, then please consider sharing with others. One of the best ways to tell others about the book is to leave a review at Goodreads, or at the bookstore where you purchased the book. You can also leave reviews at my website, maddiejamesbooks.com.

Match My Heart

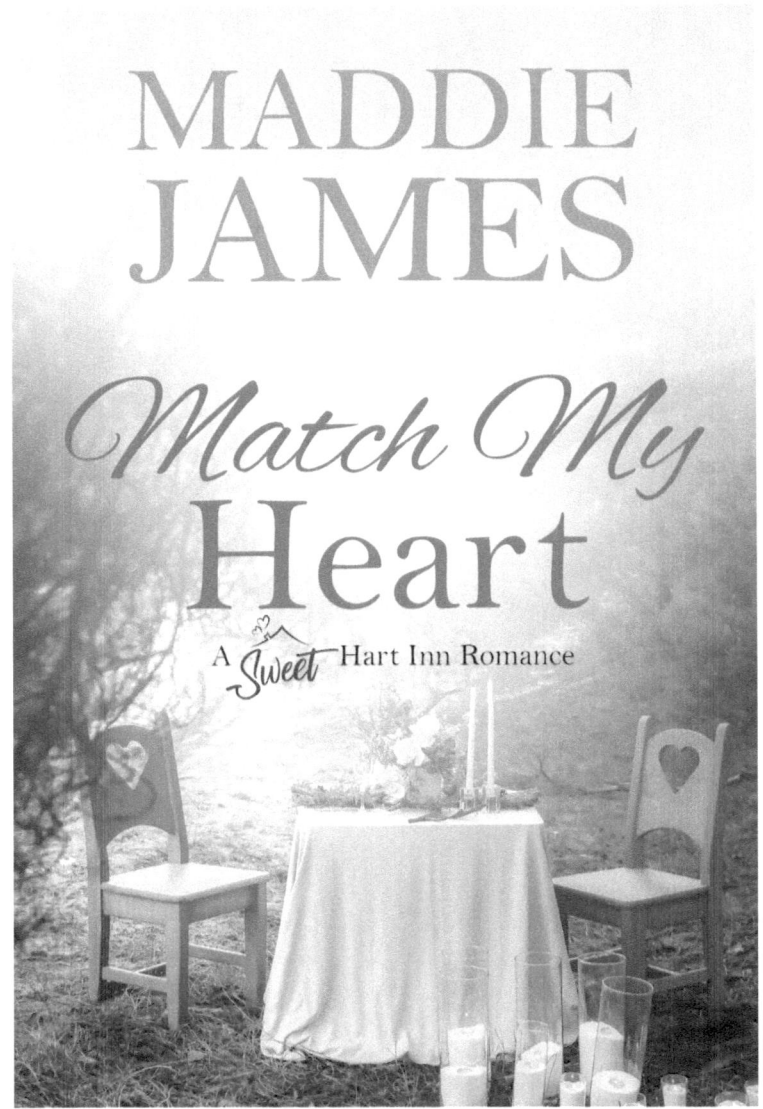

MADDIE JAMES

Match My Heart

A *Sweet* Hart Inn Romance

Match My Heart Sample

Chapter One

The sushi looked fabulous.

Suzie Hart-Matthews glanced up at the smiling Japanese girl behind the counter rolling rice, spicy tuna and seaweed, and shrugged. "Who would have thought that Ralph's Grocery would ever hire a sushi girl?"

The young woman smiled back and said, "See what you want? I make more."

Shaking her head, Suzie returned, "Oh no. You've quite a selection here." She reminded herself to tell her husband, Brad, about her new discovery. The two of them being chefs, they were always interested in the new food offerings in their small town of Harbor Falls.

Somehow, though, she couldn't imagine sushi on the menu at Falls Lodge, Brad's business. Nor could she imagine it at Sweet Hart Inn. Even though breakfast was the norm at her inn, occasionally she hosted dinner parties or events. Sushi on the menu in this Blue Ridge mountain town seemed, well, a little out of place. Yet, intriguing.

She picked up a pretty salmon roll—it looked and smelled fresh—and slipped it into her grocery cart.

A deep voice came from behind her. "What do you think of my sushi bar, Suzie?"

Suzie turned to face Ralph Myers, owner of the grocery. Rumor had it he bought out his business partner and was going independent. Recently, he'd been trying a lot of new twists to get Harbor Falls residents to buy their groceries local rather than driving to one of the big box stores in the next county. Keeping business local was of prime concern to the residents and small business owners here.

Hence, the sushi attempt.

Glancing at the display again, she said, "The sushi looks great, Ralph. But whatever possessed you?"

He cut her off with a wave of both hands and leaned her way. "Did you meet my new sushi chef? I stole her from a restaurant in Charlotte, temporarily, to see how it works out. Just the thing Harbor Falls needs." Then he proudly stepped back and crossed both arms over his chest while nodding. "We're uptown now."

How can you doubt a man who is so pleased with himself? "I hope it works out, Ralph." She glanced toward the meat counter. "Now, tell me about your beef sale. I need a couple of nice juicy ribeyes."

He led her to the counter and proceeded to tell Bart Shackler behind it to get her a couple of extra-thick cuts, the best he had.

"Now, Ralph," she batted her eyes, "y'all don't have to give me special treatment."

He bowed and swept a hand in front him. "Ma'am, yes I do. If I keep you buying from me, Ms. Famous Cookbook Author, I can claim you as my own customer. See?" He pointed to the wall beside of the meat case.

Suzie cast her gaze on the wall there. "Well, knock me over with a noodle. Ralph, what in the world have you done?"

A huge poster graced the wall. On it was a picture of her—the same photograph on her just-released cookbook, *Best of Sweet Hart Inn*—with a tag line that read, *Harbor Falls' Celebrity Chef, Suzie Hart, Shops at Ralph's!*

"Oh my! Ralph, you shouldn't have done that!" She was embarrassed to say the least, but not one bit surprised that Ralph would try to capitalize on her recent success. At least he got her name right on the poster. She had chosen to stay Suzie Hart professionally, in her cookbook world. Still, she was homegrown Harbor Falls and while she was flattered, it made her uncomfortable. But she guessed it was fine with her—as long as that was as far as it went.

Ralph leaned and winked. "Hope you don't mind, Suzie. I'll give you ten percent off your order if you let me keep it up. I'd like to put an ad in the paper, too."

Now that made her a mite uncomfortable. She smiled sweetly. "Ralph Myers, I've shopped your store all my life and I have no intention of shopping anywhere else. I'm honored to have my poster up in your store and you can keep your ten percent, because," she reached out and grasped his hand and leaned forward herself, "that's the way we do things here in Harbor Falls." She smiled and then added, "Oh, but before you put that in the paper, we will need to get permission from the publisher to use that photo." She bit her lip and gave him a frown. "Sorry to say sometimes these things take time. Let me work on that, okay?"

Ralph's smile turned frown-like as well. "I didn't think of that. Do you mind taking care of it?"

She didn't. Suzie also knew that the likelihood they would agree would be zero-to-none. Her publisher was mighty hands-on and picky with publicity so this could truly take a while—or not happen at all. She didn't mind the national publicity she'd recently enjoyed for her cookbook, but the local hype was a little embarrassing. In Harbor Falls, she just wanted to be Suzie, detached of the celebrity persona.

He covered her hand with his and nodded—in gratitude, she

suspected. Then he left her and headed toward the front of the store, tossing a hand up at another customer coming down the aisle.

Sighing, Suzie looked back at the poster. "Oh boy," she said under her breath. "Brad will get a kick out of this." She pulled out her cell phone and snapped a quick picture of the poster.

Movement to her right caught her attention as someone else stepped up to the meat counter. Mary Lou Picketts stood staring at the wall, too. *Oh dear, what will the rest of Harbor Falls think of this?* Again, she was a tad embarrassed.

She followed Mary Lou's gape, however, and realized that she wasn't exactly looking at the Suzie poster, but that something else had caught the young woman's eye.

A different kind of sigh exited Mary Lou's lips. Suzie watched as the young woman gazed up at another poster of a man, lean, dark and gritty, standing with a guitar slung over his shoulder. Suzie studied her side profile as Mary Lou took in the full-color and full-body likeness of Nash Rhodes, Nashville's newest up-and-coming country music star.

Adoration. That was the look on Mary Lou's face.

No, that wasn't it.

Adolescent crush-like puppy love?

Good God no. Mary Lou had to be close to thirty and was way past the adolescent crush phase of her life. The look was something else. Like staring at something just out of reach. Perhaps lost and given up on.

Longing?

Love?

Suzie shook her head. Of course not. No one falls in love with a celebrity icon. Oh, they may *think* they are in love, but how could they truly be? You cannot fall in love with someone by reading their fanzines, watching them on CMT, scouring the Internet for tidbits of information, and going to their concerts.

Longing. Maybe it was more like longing.

Suzie thought about that. Mary Lou lived a quiet and perhaps slightly isolated life here in Harbor Falls. Suzie had known her since grade school, even though Mary Lou was a few years younger. Still, everyone knew everyone in Harbor Falls, pretty much. Mary Lou was the type of girl who never really had a best girlfriend and kept to herself most of the time. Suzie seemed to remember that she did go off to college—but she wasn't quite certain what Mary Lou had done with her life since then. She'd heard she worked from home, but at what, Suzie didn't know.

Mary Lou heaved another sigh. Suzie watched her chest rise, her breasts lift, and then fall in a half-defeated motion. She felt a little sorry for her and wasn't quite sure why.

Suzie took a few steps and leaned Mary Lou's way. "Hard to believe he's going to be in Harbor Falls next weekend, isn't it?" The poster advertised the benefit concert to raise money for the children's wing of the hospital. Nash was the star attraction but there was a local act opening Nash's performance. Suzie's husband, Brad, who was on the hospital board, had a big hand in bringing Nash to their small town, so she had some personal scoop on the musician and his appearance.

The young woman swung her way and jumped back a little. "Oh! Suzie. I didn't know anyone was there!"

Smiling, Suzie reached out to grasp her elbow. "No problem, honey. Didn't mean to startle you. Thought I'd say hello. Came in to pick up some meat."

Mary Lou rotated her gaze back toward the poster. "Yeah. Meat. A hunk of it."

"Mary Lou!" Suzie chuckled.

Her hands fluttered to her neck. "Oh! Did I say that out loud?"

"Sure enough did, sweetie." Suzie stepped up beside her and they stood and ogled the poster together. "I do have to agree that the man is definitely one prime choice of—"

"Beefsteak?"

The women rolled their gazes toward the meat case and Bart who was holding out Suzie's ribeyes.

"Ahem. Yes. Thanks, Bart."

"No problem, dear." A sly grin broke his lips and he retreated.

Suzie grabbed her steaks and gave Mary Lou a smile as she turned to set them in her cart. Mary Lou waved as she headed in a brisk walk toward the bakery.

But Suzie couldn't stop thinking about the look on Mary Lou's face and how discontented that sigh sounded earlier that came from her lips.

Still watching, Suzie took stock. Her clothes were rather baggy, but underneath, her frame was small with rounded hips moving beneath the jogging pants. Mary Lou turned and Suzie caught site of a rounded contour in the chest area.

Mary Lou Picketts was hiding a rack under those old baggy clothes!

Moving to her face, devoid of make-up, Suzie took stock of a smooth, peaches and cream complexion hiding behind a mousy brown ponytail caught high on her head, which hung down to frame part of her face.

An interesting notion was growing in Suzie's heart and gut. She glanced once more at the poster of Nash Rhodes, and then back to Mary Lou. Nash *was* doing that big benefit concert at the lodge, and her husband Brad *was* hosting the thing.

Did she dare?

Yes. Consider it a gift to humanity. Besides, she had managed to hook her sister Shelley, and her high school boyfriend, Matt Branson, back up again, hadn't she? That was a rematch made in Heaven. Maybe she could work a little matchmaking magic on Mary Lou.

Lord knows, the girl could stand a break.

Determined, she gripped the cart handle and ventured forth.

"Mary Lou? Wait!"

Several hours later, Suzie stood in her kitchen facing her husband. Obviously, he was not drinking the Kool-Aid she was handing him.

"No. Absolutely not," he told her.

"It's just dinner, Brad. It's the least we can do. Besides, it would probably be the one high point in Mary Lou's life. Can't we make a dream come true?"

"As much as I would like to, Suzie, it's impossible." Her husband stared at her. No, glared was more like it.

"Relax, Brad." She stepped forward and smoothed her hands over his muscled chest. "This will not be a problem, I promise you. It's just a quiet dinner here at the inn. No muss no fuss. Please?"

"Out of the question. Nash's people have spelled out exactly what he will, and what he cannot do, while he is in town."

Suzie picked at a piece of lint on his shoulder. "Oh pooh. The boy needs a home cooked meal occasionally, right? He's country through and through and we're just small town. He'd probably welcome it. Why don't you reach out and see if you can make it happen. After all," she sidled in closer and slipped her hands around his waist, "you can be very convincing."

"As can you." He frowned. "This is above and beyond the call of husbandly duties, Suzette."

With a wicked smile, she slipped a couple of fingers under his belt. "I'll repay you later by going above and beyond the call of wifely duties, husband."

Brad groaned and grasped her about the waist.

She continued, "All you need to do is wrangle him away from the lodge for a couple of hours, either before or after the show, and I'll do the rest."

Brad stopped her hands at his waistband by placing his big paws over hers. Those dark eyes of his, always so mesmerizing, peered down. "Not happening. I have no control over his agenda once he gets here. He'll be sequestered away in his bus most of the time, whisked in for the concert, and then back out again. It's a benefit, one that wasn't on their books and they aren't making any money on this—Nash Rhodes is not going to be lingering in Harbor Falls long and I'm not asking for special favors. Especially for some lovelorn wallflower."

Suzie dropped her hands and frowned. "Mary Lou is a very pretty girl under all that hair and fabric. She just lacks confidence and needs a little coaching."

"Whatever. Still, I can't do this."

"He's not staying at the lodge?"

"No. He's parking his bus behind it and staying there."

"Crap. That was my Plan B." She batted her eyes again. Thinking. "Could you get him here a day early, perhaps? Some sort of pre-concert event?"

He grasped her face in his hands. "You persistent little minx. No. The way his manager talks, he's practically on 24/7 call."

"But I bet you could arrange it. Give him the presidential suite and all the amenities you can muster. I'll bake and have a ton of goodies there. I hear he has a sweet tooth. I can't work magic in that trailer of his. I need to get him out of it."

"My dear wife... I love you to pieces, but I am having no part of what you are planning. The man is the current young gun of Nashville. Their shooting star. They've got him booked so tight he doesn't have time to call his mother without being scheduled."

Leaning up on her tiptoes, Suzie smiled and kissed her husband's salty lips, not to be discouraged so easily. "I'm counting on you, Brad Matthews," she whispered. "Did I tell you about the pink furry handcuffs I bought in Asheville the other day? And that strawberry flavored massage gel?"

The groan came from deeper in his chest this time.

"Now go call and see what you can do."

Learn more about *Match My Heart* on my website, or purchase at your favorite bookstore.

More Sweet Heart Inn

Cozy up at the inn where the heart of the Blue Ridge beats strongest...

Welcome to Sweet Hart Inn, a charming bed and breakfast nestled along the peaceful shores of Falls Lake, at the foot of Falls Mountain. At the center of it all is chef and innkeeper Suzie Hart, whose kitchen is always warm, and whose heart is always open. Together with her husband Brad, Suzie serves up matchmaking advice and comfort food, along with second chances, and a generous helping of happily ever after.

The Sweet Hart Inn Books

All of My Heart
Take My Heart
Match My Heart
Tame My Heart
The Dating Game
Miss Matched Hearts
The Husband List
Chase My Heart
No Sweeter Match
One More Kiss

The Falls Mountain Books

Welcome to Falls Mountain, and the quaint town of Harbor Falls.

Tucked deep into the Blue Ridge Mountains, bricked streets, lakeside views, and charming local shops set the scene for small town romance.

In this standalone-but-interconnected series, you'll meet bakers, bookstore owners, chocolatiers, school teachers, and more —all trying to run their businesses, chase their dreams, and keep their hearts in check. But in Harbor Falls, love has a habit of showing up unannounced...

From second chances to secret babies to grumpy-sunshine pairings, each book brings a satisfying happily-ever-after and a cast of characters you'll want to visit again and again.

Falls Mountain Romance is a companion series to the Sweet Hart Inn Romance books by Maddie James.

Dance into My Heart
The Christmas Nanny
The Heartbreaker
Star Crossed

Not This Christmas
Convince My Heart

I hope you'll check out these books, and my other series, on my
website at:
www.maddiejamesbooks.com

About Maddie James

Romance with a pulse—small towns, big love, and a dash of drama.

Maddie James writes small-town romance with heart, heat, and the occasional haunting. Her stories range from sweet to spicy, suspenseful to supernatural—happily-ever-afters guaranteed! From stand-alone love stories to binge-worthy series, Maddie delivers love next door, some cowboy kisses, an occasional hint of danger, and just enough drama to keep things interesting.

Get all the drama delivered to your inbox when you sign-on to Maddie's VIP reader list!

Free books, sneak peaks, bonus content, giveaways, and more...

Learn more: maddiejamesbooks.com/pages/newsletter